ORIGINS OF RAGE

ELLA GRAFF

Fllaouent Books

Buffalo, New York

Author: Ella Graff
Editor: Jennifer Thomas–Hayes
Contributing Editor: Bill Hayes
Cover Art and Design: OriginalSyn
Body Design: Jennifer Thomas–Hayes

ISBN: 979-8-9874867-0-2 Softcover, English
ISBN: 979-8-9874867-1-9 eBook
Library of Congress Control Number: 2023906913

First Edition
Published in the United States of America
Printed in the United States of America

This book is dedicated to all of you, the believers.
To the friends who never gave up even though it seemed
to take forever to complete Origins of Rage.

For you, we worked tirelessly to give you a book
that not only brings dreams to reality
but is a gift that, when read,
will hopefully provide you hours of enjoyment
and maybe something to take away: Friendship.

ORIGINS OF
RAGE

PROLOGUE

THE ANGER BEGINS AS A STRUMMING *in her ears. Soon, the beat takes over her body. It's as though a thousand different drums are playing solo performances of fury inside her head.*

As the pounding continues, the thumping increases to a decibel no human can overcome and her rage grows. The force of it is so strong, it assaults her body with a potency that takes all of her will to withstand. Feeling her innermost parts pummeled, she stumbles back to catch her breath.

An angry red haze blurs her vision, and she feels her control slipping. She vowed never again to give this kind of power to anything or anyone; but here, she's left no choice.

She no longer feels like a part of herself. She's standing outside her body, watching someone else lose all resolve. And she somehow knows pain will come next. Her heart feels wrenched from her body, rendering her like a doll, disassembled and broken. The scream that emanates from deep inside her is like an animal cry of suffering and hatred.

She lunges.

Allowing the rage to rule her mind and body, she loses all perception of time.

When the onslaught finally stops, she feels as though she's waking from a nightmare. She looks at her surroundings. The home she so lovingly decorated has been destroyed and she's utterly spent. She inhales in deep gulping gasps.

What could have been only a few minutes has felt like hours.

As her senses fill with the rotten stink of death, she looks down at the blood dripping from the knife in her shaking hands.

"Oh god, what have I done?" echoes the single thought.

And then all she can hear is the pounding of her heart and the drip, drip, drip of blood from her knife to the floor.

Finally, everything goes black. All that remains is the thrumming of a heart that's been broken into a million pieces.

CHAPTER 1

2:00 A.M.

It's starting again—another dream of murder and bloodshed.

I lie very still, trying to control my labored breathing. My heart beats so rapidly, I fear it will burst out of my chest and run for its life. I wonder if it's my own heart pounding in my ears or that of the killer in my dream.

This one had a lot of blood—I can almost smell the copper scent of it in my room. I look down and thank whoever it is that listens to prayers that my hands are not covered with it. I was almost sure they would be.

This dream was not so different from others I've had over the years, in that someone is going to die unless I can decipher the pictures being fed to me. At this stage in life, I have almost no one left to lose. But someone out there does. I know how they will feel when they get the news. I know the pain that will steal their breath. I know how they will continue to suffer, long after the first sting of loss has dissipated.

What's odd about *this* dream, though, is that I felt a fleeting twinge of sympathy for the killer. And that is certainly a disturbing twist. I've never felt sympathy for the murderers-to-be in my nightmares. If anything, I've feared that while searching for them, I will somehow become their next target.

Beads of sweat trickle down my back although my window is open and it's a cool spring evening—or morning, maybe. I'm not sure. Either way, I know there will be no more sleep for me now.

Every time the dreams start, I wonder if I'll ever have a full night's sleep again. Then I think how selfish I'm being, as the victim in the dream will end up a lot worse off than I am if I don't act. Their sleep will be the sleep of forever. So, as usual, I decide I'm okay with no sleep at all until this is solved.

I get out of bed and take a few notes while I satiate my system with coffee. Coffee is the only thing that sustains me when the dreams are at their worst.

I really need to be on my game to solve the dream puzzle before something happens in real life, and the lack of sleep takes a toll on my mind and body. And since I generally don't have a timeframe for when a dream will become reality, I need to move forward with maximum urgency on both counts.

Fully caffeinated, I go into my spare room, which I've set up as a painting room. Although I'm a sweaty mess, I don't bother showering, since the reality is I'm just going to get paint all over myself and no one is going to see me or smell me anyway.

The painting room is the only room in the house with enough light for my purpose. I had larger windows and extra light fixtures installed for that reason. It's on the same floor as my bedroom so that if I need to do an emergency painting in the middle of the night, I can just run in.

I also keep all my supplies at the ready in case of a murder-painting crisis. Who does that, anyway?

Oh, yeah—I do.

You'll notice I make fun of myself. That's because if I don't laugh I'll just cry, which won't be a help to anyone. I need to stay on task.

I pick up a paintbrush and as I bring the dream into my mind, my hand takes over. I close my eyes and feel myself making large strokes. I try to put myself back into the dream so that I can remember the smallest of details. I've found that the details are often the most important. That's why I hate it when people say "don't sweat the small stuff." Whose idea was that? Anyway, I'm getting off track.

By closing my eyes, I've found that I can concentrate on the vision before me. Sometimes I can bring it back as clearly as when I was asleep.

The first image I see is of the killer's hand. That will be the focal point of this first of many drawings.

I should probably clarify something: I'm calling this person "the killer," but in truth, they haven't killed anyone yet—or at least haven't committed the murder in my vision. What I see is their *intention* to kill. In this dream, though, it felt more like a compulsion—or even a fear—than a plan, per se. This is new to me.

My dreams are vivid in a beat-around-the-bush kind of way. I feel what the would-be killer feels and I see bits and pieces of the murder they're planning. I can see the killer's face only if he or she happens to envision themselves looking into a mirror. As you can imagine, this is a rarity.

But it did happen once.

In this latest dream, I felt the strongest sense of rage I've ever experienced. So overpowering, it seemed to blind the killer's vision so she could not see or comprehend what she was doing. Which means that I couldn't see it, either.

I mainly saw her hand holding the knife.

I bring the hand back into my mind's eye. I see it as pale, slim, and elegant with graceful elongated fingers. I wouldn't call it dainty, though. It appears strong and has short unpainted fingernails.

An idea springs to mind that it's the hand of a pianist. I used to play as a child but lost the taste for it as I grew older. My music teacher always told me I had the hands of a virtuoso, but she was wrong: I have the hands of a murder-dreaming artist. Who knew? Anyway, maybe the woman I dreamed about *is* an accomplished piano or organ player.

I'm nowhere near the answer to that yet.

Just once, I wish I would dream the whole murder up front and see the murderer, so that I could just paint or draw the picture in full, take it to the police and say "Here's the killer and here's what they're planning," and be done with it.

Better yet, I could add, "And here's where he or she lives." Oh hell, if I knew that, I wouldn't even have to paint anything. I could just go to the police and give them the info to find the killer.

But that's not the way it works. I see bits and pieces throughout what usually amounts to several weeks of nightmarish, sleepless hell. I draw those pieces until I can get a somewhat clear picture of what's going to happen, and then I try to stop it.

In retrospect, if I saw the whole murder up front and center, my life would be much less interesting. I hate murder, of course, but I'm good at solving puzzles and pulling all the pieces together.

Occasionally when I'm painting, I lose myself to the process. I go a little crazy. That's why I get paint all over myself. So, I wonder: If I lose myself painting the dreams, does that mean the killer loses him- or herself while imagining the crime? I have no experience in psychology and I've certainly never murdered anyone, but it seems like a solid theory.

I've seen plenty of doctors concerning my "gift"—since over the years, authorities tried to prove me insane many times. But once the bodies started piling up and the blood had been shed, they were forced to believe.

When I'm done painting, I look at the piece. It's just the hand with the knife. Right now I'm simply painting the outline in black and using the white of the canvas as the inner part of the hand. The blood splotches look odd, so I add red to the painting. I decide it's finished, at least as far as this dream has taken me, and I feel pretty proud.

Where did these skills come from? I wonder, not for the first time. The dreams, my artistic ability…my parents never had these talents. But, then, they weren't my true blood family. They were family in every way that matters and I loved them and have never felt the need to search for my biological parents. But… does someone else out there have the same abilities I have? Does someone else out there dream of murder?

Because I have to wonder, *Why me?* Who in the universe said "Hey, Melanie Morris, you have been chosen to be a major freak"?

That's pretty much how I've been the majority of my life. No one has ever looked at me and said "Melanie is so cool." I don't know why I even have these thoughts. If someone did say that, I'm sure I'd die of embarrassment anyway.

So a freak is what I am and what I always will be.

I'm hopeful that someday someone will like that about me. Not for the dreaming-about-murders part, but for who I am deep down inside. I know I'm a good person; so I wonder why all the bad seems to happen to me. Is it a side-effect of the gift? Do I just have to deal with it? I have too many questions and no time for reflection.

I clean up my area and wash my hands. So far, I feel positive, considering this is just the opening dream in this particular doomed drama.

As I look back over the painting, the sense of sympathy washes over me again. I know that this woman wants to kill someone, but I don't feel afraid. I'm usually fairly terrified once the dreams start. As though one day a killer I dream about is going to learn about me and I'm going to be in deep trouble.

I straighten up the room, cover the piece, and then close the door on the dream for today. I always close the door. My dreams are my private reality and no one sees them without my say-so. And I need some separation from the dreams. They'll take over quickly enough.

CHAPTER 2

AFTER LEAVING THE STUDIO, the first thing I do is change my bedding. For some reason, every time I dream I sweat like a hormonal teenage girl. It's disgusting to say the least.

Good thing I'm a loner. Who would want to sleep with a sweaty murder-dreaming virgin who doesn't know how to be a woman?

I don't even know what I am anymore. But I should probably stop making myself sound like a crazy person who talks to herself. I'm not crazy—though sometimes I wish others would try dreaming about murders and see what their lives turn out to be. Okay, done ranting!

As I shower, my mind wanders to the first painting of a dream I ever did.

And what it led to.

EIGHT YEARS AGO

I was seventeen years old.

I remember the dream so clearly. At first, I didn't understand it to be anything more than just a horrible nightmare. I'd had violent nighttime visions before—in fact, throughout my childhood— but this was the first time I'd felt the urge to document what I'd seen. The urge was so strong, I couldn't ignore it.

My art teacher at school had praised my talent for painting, so I asked her what supplies she recommended and got to work.

I hid the first painting in the deep recesses of my closet, out of fear. Fear that anyone who saw it would think I'd lost my mind *and* fear that it somehow meant more than even I was willing to believe.

The dream recurred over a period of several weeks.

In the first dream, my mother was in some sort of parking lot and couldn't get her car to start. In the next one, someone came to her car window and asked if she needed help. Though I couldn't see the person, I knew it was a man.

It took a few more dreams for me to realize that the reason I couldn't see the man was that somehow I *was* the man. And I felt consumed with evil intentions.

I woke up sweaty and terrified.

The next night, I saw more. My mom rolled down her window, and through the eyes of the killer, I saw him reach in and give her some sort of injection. I saw my mother look down at her arm and then back up, her eyes filled with horror as she realized her fate. I felt the killer's satisfaction at achieving a conquest.

Each dream brought a clearer picture to my mind and to my canvas. I was more frightened than I'd ever been.

Especially as I watched the killer do something strange: He reached into the car and, with gloves on, positioned my mom's hands on her steering wheel. Then he shut the door and went back to his own car, parked right next to my mom's, and from there, he coldly watched my mom die of asphyxiation, apparently from the substance he gave her.

Her face and body were unable to move the entire time, but the look in her eyes will haunt me for the rest of my life.

When the deed was done, the killer drove his car out to the country to an old house—white, with peeling paint and green shutters. Out front was a mailbox standing on a plain wooden post. On top of the roof, an old rooster weathervane squeaked loudly as it spun around and around in the wind.

The property was surrounded by a picket fence that, like the house, was far from well cared for. The wood was rotting, and some posts were lying on the ground as if to say: "I'm done holding up these rickety old slats."

With each dream, my fear that my mother would be murdered grew. People commented on the dark circles under my eyes from lack of sleep. It was a harsh look for a seventeen-year-old girl.

Finally, I had a dream in which the killer smiled at himself in the rearview mirror as he drove away. I will never forget my first look at the face of the man who I was now sure would kill my mother.

But there was no one to tell. When I woke up from that disturbing image, my mother was safe and sound in her bed.

Why was I seeing all of this? What was I supposed to do? I wanted to grab my mom and beg her to stay home. But I was given no timeframe for when this might happen. Plus, I knew she would just think I was crazy—just as she had when all my "violent nighttime visions" had begun as a child. She took me to a therapist back then, but at this age I might get locked away forever.

Of course, knowing what I know now, I wouldn't have let that stop me. I would've been willing to be put away for the rest of *my* life if it would have saved *hers*.

As THE DREAMS CONTINUED, I was able to study the killer's reflection. I started on a new canvas.

His long, straight hair was greasy and stringy, and as black as I'd ever seen. His face was splotched with dirt, as if he had not showered in a long time, and it was disfigured—perhaps burnt. He looked like a depraved Phantom of the Opera. The eyebrow on the damaged side looked like it had been cut into a square.

When he smiled, I saw that his crooked teeth were extremely yellow, almost green. His mouth was pulled down in a frown on the damaged side, while the other side turned up in an evil smirk. It was as if he knew on some level he was being watched, which I supposed wasn't impossible. After all, if I was seeing things others wouldn't find possible, why couldn't someone else—like this malicious killer—see them too?

I also took great pains painting the house and the other details of the crime. I prayed it wasn't important, but in my heart, I knew it was.

A few mornings later, I awoke with a start. My mom had gone out shopping the evening before and, exhausted from my nightmares, I'd fallen asleep on the couch waiting for her return.

She never came home.

I was frantic. I had to accept what the dream was. Knowing I had seen this man's face and had done nothing to alert her, I was awash in guilt.

But maybe I could still help her.

I'D TAKE MY PAINTINGS to the police. I gathered them by the back door before realizing in a panic I had no way to get there.

The small key holder by the door caught my eye. I grabbed a set of keys and went out and opened the garage door.

There sat the red 1964 Volkswagen Beetle. My father had harbored a great love for old cars and had found this one shortly before he died. We'd kept it after he was gone because his love for this car became mine.

But I was terrified to get behind the wheel.

The transmission was manual, and though my dad had shown me how to work the stick shift, letting me drive in parking lots and the occasional side street, I hadn't touched it since his death. It was too painful.

I didn't even have a license. In this small town, I could walk wherever I needed to go. But the paintings were too bulky to carry on foot.

So right now, I couldn't worry about legalities.

Once the paintings were stowed in back of the car, I climbed into the driver's seat and fastened my seat belt. I remembered enough to keep my foot on the clutch to start it, but I ground the gears several times on the way to the sheriff's office, all the while scared to death of getting stopped. When I finally arrived, I parked where no one would see me getting out of the car.

I had no more time to think. I grabbed the paintings and headed into the station, hoping and praying that someone would help me. That somebody would take what I had and save my mother. I had already waited far too long.

When I walked in, the first person I saw was Brody Carter. Brody had gone to my high school, a couple of grades ahead of me. He'd always been nice to me, but we weren't exactly friends or anything. I'd heard that his father was a high-ranking officer in the army and that his parents had moved here to give Brody a stable home life. I'd also heard that after graduation, Brody had gone to work for the sheriff's department and was on his way to becoming one of their top deputies.

When I saw him, I felt a pang of…something. I didn't understand what it was but didn't care to think about it further. I was in total despair.

Brody was immediately joined by Sheriff Johnson. The state of Kansas has a ton of counties, and ours is one of the smallest. As is our local Arrow Springs sheriff station. It's more like a place for neighbors to hash things out than a place hardened criminals are marched through every day. But our deputies are more than capable of handling a serious crime if one should occur.

In my case, though, they needed a little convincing.

I told the sheriff and Brody that my mother hadn't come home last night. Of course, they were concerned, but when I told them I'd been having nightmares about it, they looked at me in disbelief. But I wouldn't let up. My worst fear had come from my worst nightmare, and they *had* to listen to me. I had paintings!

Sheriff Johnson invited me into his office and tried to soothe me. He offered me water and asked me to tell the story again, with just the two of us. I took a deep breath and recounted everything again as calmly as I could.

When I was done, the sheriff cleared his throat and stood.

"Melanie," he said, "what you've just described is the exact scenario as the serial killings that have been sweeping the state—murders by the Route 66 killer, as the media has called him. If you've been having nightmares about this, I'm sure it's just from images you've seen on TV."

Again he cleared his throat, this time in even more of a "tsk, tsk" way.

"And I know it's scary that your mom fits the killer's profile—brunette, thirties to mid-forties, a mother—but there's no need to jump to conclusions."

Serial killer? Profile? News?

As someone who'd had nightmares my entire life, I avoided the news; I didn't need any extra stimulation. I had, however, heard rumblings about some murders, but that was as far as my knowledge went. I begged him to believe me.

Just then Brody knocked on the door.

"Sir," he said. "I think there's something you should see."

We followed him out to where my paintings were leaned against a wall. Apparently he'd been examining them.

Brody pulled out the painting of my mom's hands affixed to her steering wheel, the killer's gloved hand still resting on one of them. Brody and Sheriff Johnson exchanged a glance.

The sheriff eyed me. "How did you know about this?" he demanded.

What?!

"It was in my dream!" I said again.

He looked at me dubiously.

It appeared he was about to accuse me of something—I had no idea what—when Brody put a restraining hand on his arm. It felt odd that Brody would stick up for me, especially since he barely knew me, but I was grateful for the gesture.

They stepped away and talked quietly for a moment.

The sheriff turned back to me. "We promise to look into this right away," he told me. "But until we get back to you, you must swear to me you won't mention any of this to anyone."

I was confused, but also encouraged by his new resolve. I promised.

"And I'm going to need to keep these paintings," he added.

I nodded.

My help was no longer needed, but since I was technically a minor, they couldn't just let me go. So they called my neighbor, the elderly Mrs. Wayland, who agreed that I could stay with her until my mom came back. Brody offered to escort me.

As we exited the station, Brody asked how I had gotten myself there. I could feel the heat of embarrassment as I confessed to having driven myself with no license, in my dad's vintage Volkswagen that I could barely shift.

He shook his head and snorted.

"You risked a lot to get here," he said. "I really hope that we can find your mom and that she's okay. Why don't I drive you home in your dad's car and then have another deputy pick me up? Where did you say we were going?"

I directed Brody to my house, where he returned the Beetle to my garage. He waited outside while I packed some things, and then watched as I went in Mrs. Wayland's front door.

The reality was that as soon as he left, I'd return to my own house to stay, but the authorities didn't need to know that.

Including Brody.

EARLY THE NEXT MORNING, Sheriff Johnson showed up at Mrs. Wayland's, accompanied by Brody. She directed them over to my house, protecting my cover by explaining that I'd just gone over "to gather a few more things."

Both the sheriff and Brody were somber as they knocked on the door and asked to be invited in. My hands were shaking as I led them to the living room.

I'll never forget that terrible moment when they told me that my mother was dead. Though most of me already knew, hearing the confirmation was a shock. I ran into the bathroom and threw up.

They'd located her car in a far corner of a large multistory mall parking lot in one of the larger nearby cities. My mom was sitting in the driver's seat, her hands on the steering wheel, dead.

Just as I had envisioned it.

That's when the sheriff explained that the serial killer they'd been hunting was obviously a pro. Detectives had determined that his MO was to slickly jimmy the door lock on his target's car, pop the hood, disconnect the battery, relock the car, and then lie in wait, presumably to offer his victim assistance getting into and/or starting her car.

He further explained that the placement of my mom's hands on the steering wheel was a secret hallmark of the serial killer. A detail purposely kept from the public, in order for law enforcement to detect copycat killings.

Therefore, the fact that I had painted that detail meant that I was somehow involved, or…

As the sheriff left the words unsaid, Brody grabbed my hand to comfort me. I could tell he didn't believe I'd murder my mom.

Either way, they decided to use my paintings to hunt down the killer. I don't know just how much the sheriff sincerely believed in my abilities, but he did tell me that he'd heard of other law enforcement agencies—even the Feds—enlisting help from people like me. They didn't have anything else to go on, he added, so why not? What did they have to lose?

It may not have been the strongest endorsement of his confidence in me, but inside I was grateful that even though I hadn't stopped my mother's death, this was my chance to at least find her murderer.

We would begin right away.

A FACIAL RECOGNITION SEARCH on my portrait of the killer came up with a match to a known drug addict named Stan Harris. Harris was from our area but was known to associate with drug dealers and other lowlifes up in Kansas City. He'd served time after being convicted of armed robbery and the slaying of a homeless man in our neighboring state of Missouri, but somehow he'd managed to work the system and get paroled a few years ago.

Now we just had to find him.

Brody stopped by one day and told me he had an idea he'd like to try, if I was willing to trust him. I was willing to do anything to catch my mom's killer.

As he led me out to his patrol car, he explained that he wanted me to think back to the dream and try to remember as many details as I could about the killer's route.

We knew the house was in a rural area, so we'd start out on the highway and see what happened.

As we drove, sure enough, I started to see landmarks that were familiar from the dream. And I started to *feel* which way we should go. Though it was disturbing—and, for sure, I didn't tell Brody—I was able to enter the killer's mind again and decide which roads to take.

Almost an hour later, we were on a country road more than forty miles from town—far outside our Arrow Springs jurisdiction. I told Brody to turn north. He obeyed without question.

I looked down the gravel road and there it was: the broken-down fence, the rustic mailbox, the rusty weathervane spinning slowly on the roof.

Wordlessly, I motioned for Brody to stop. We looked at each other and I could see he knew what I knew.

As Brody picked up the radio to call the local sheriff's office for backup, we saw someone wander into the front yard. The man looked up at me with his scarred face and our eyes locked. Then he turned and ran.

Brody was out of the car like a shot. Screaming at me to "Stay in the car!" he took off running after this man. *This man who had killed my mom.* I was so afraid. I grabbed the radio to try and call for help, but my hands were shaking and I had no idea how to use the equipment.

And then I heard a gunshot.

Though Brody had told me not to, I jumped out of the car and darted toward the house, with no idea what I would do when I got there. I was saved from that decision by Brody stepping out from behind the house. His face was ashen and blood dripped from his left arm. He looked at me with a strange expression. He didn't even chastise me for disobeying "orders."

I'd find out later that Brody had just killed his first criminal.

I started toward him, but he quickly closed the distance between us and grabbed my hand. He told me I didn't want to go back there.

Brody was finally able to radio the local authorities while I sat silently in the patrol car next to him. I think we were both in shock. Waiting for the other officers to arrive, I wanted to ask if he was okay, but he clearly didn't want to talk, so I kept quiet.

ALTHOUGH THE KILLER had been meticulous, leaving no physical evidence at his crime scenes, inside Stan Harris's house, officers found the paralytic substance he'd used. And being a chronic drifter, he'd had ample opportunity to commit all the slayings.

There was no question he did it.

And the ultimate proof was that with him dead, the series of killings stopped.

I wished I could have saved more lives earlier, but it wasn't meant to be. And even though I'd entered the mind of the killer, I wasn't able to even see the other murders.

To make matters worse, the authorities were still suspicious of me. Immediately upon our return to Arrow Springs, I had many questions to answer.

The FBI—now involved because of the interstate crimes attributed to Stan Harris—took me through each painting one by one, questioning me extensively. So here I was, at seventeen years old, traumatized not only by losing my mother but by being treated like a suspect.

During this whole terrible ordeal, Brody stayed by my side. He was extremely supportive and I appreciated his kindness more than he would ever know.

Especially since he'd risked his life for me—and gotten in trouble for it.

The Feds had first crack at us, but Brody warned it would be even worse when we had our "official" sit-down with Sheriff Johnson the next day.

He was right.

Our meeting with the sheriff began with his giving Brody a serious scolding. What had he been thinking going after a known killer on his own? The situation could have ended much differently, the sheriff warned. He also shot *me* a few scathing stares during this diatribe, which made my heart pound several decibels louder.

Brody was finally able to explain that his plan had been a long shot—an experiment, really. He'd mainly wanted to help me feel useful.

I was taken aback by Brody's comment. Not because I took offense, but in hearing he cared that much about my feelings.

Brody went on that even when we found the house, he was going to wait for backup. But the killer ran, and he couldn't just let him get away.

Then it got even hairier.

The killer—this horrible Stan guy—had tried to get back inside the house, but Brody was too quick. He'd pinned the man against the back door. That's when Stan pulled a knife and sliced Brody's arm. As Brody stepped away and unholstered his gun, Stan charged at him with the knife. Brody had to take the shot.

Stan died instantly.

I know the sheriff could see Brody's struggle with having killed someone. So after his initial outburst, he softened his tone toward his young deputy.

And toward me.

In the end, the Feds found no evidence that I was involved in the crimes in any way. DNA evidence did put me in my mom's car, but that was to be expected. They were forced to let me go.

And eventually, after their initial shock, both the FBI and the sheriff seemed to genuinely accept that there are people in the world with special gifts.

But Brody was the *first* believer.

Shortly after all of this, Brody enlisted in the Marines. He said it was to help him get ahead in his law enforcement career, but I always wondered if he was running away from—or trying to process—having killed a man.

Having killed a man for me.

5:44 A.M.

I come out of my memories with the abrupt realization that the water is freezing and shampoo is running into my eyes. *How long have I been lost in my own head this time?* I wonder. *Long enough for the water to run cold and freeze me half to death* is the answer.

I rinse my hair and get out of the shower to dry off. I have goose bumps standing on my goose bumps, and I know some are from the cold and others from memories that *still* cloud my mind with guilt and frustration.

I dress quickly to warm myself and head downstairs for another cup of coffee.

I must have been awake for hours already, I realize, stepping out onto the front porch to clear my head with the now-rising sun. *So how do I not feel tired?*

I enjoy just having some quiet time to reflect. As I stand staring at the dawning light, I realize that I've neglected my yard work again. Weeds cover the garden beds and my grass needs mowing.

Will there ever be enough time between murder and mayhem to live a normal life?

I hope so, but that's not the most important thing.

There is no justice strong enough to take away my feelings of guilt and regret over my mother.

Once I realized what I was capable of—and the agonizing consequence of dismissing my dreams—my gift became something I would never ignore again.

CHAPTER 3

7:22 A.M.

The sun is rising higher.

I go into the house, pour more coffee, and return to the porch.

I also return to my thoughts.

My mother's death is something I've had to live with.

Her death is the reason that as soon as I have a vision or a dream, I work tirelessly to solve it before anyone else is killed.

And although it happened what feels like a lifetime ago, fresh memories of the trauma flood to the forefront every time I dream another murder.

Back then, when the people in town first learned what I could do, they all stayed away from me. I was like a disease no one wanted to contract. My dreams were contagious and everyone was going to be murdered or worse because of me.

So I became more of a loner than I'd ever been. I went to school and I kept my head down. I was smart, so aside from fighting my grief, I did well. But I had no friends and I didn't want any. People didn't understand me, and I learned not to care what they thought. It was just too painful to think about liking—much less *loving*—someone.

My father's death had occurred just a year before my mother's, in a work accident. He was a mechanic at a car dealership, and a separation wall they were building in the service department fell on his leg, creating a blot clot that went to his brain. He was gone within twenty-four hours.

His was the first death I faced in a line of many.

And with my father gone, my mother's murder would have been even more horrible to handle had I been placed into the maw of the foster care system until age eighteen. But an aunt on my father's side stepped in to take care of me for a few months until I was old enough to live in the house by myself. The attorney for my parents' estate also helped handle matters until I received my inheritance and could legally be on my own.

My adoptive parents had gotten me as an infant and, thankfully, they were pretty well off. I was left with the house and enough money to maintain it—even redecorate it to suit me. But I'd rather have had them both back than inherit all the money in the world.

LIFE WITH MY AUNT was hard. Maybe I *would* have been better off waiting out my eighteenth birthday in foster care. It wasn't that she was cruel, but she didn't understand.

No one did.

Throughout town, I was seen as the girl who saw her mother being murdered and didn't save her. Not one person seemed to empathize with my situation. I certainly hadn't asked for what happened—any more than they would have wanted it for someone they loved. I was suffering badly and all I wanted was to be normal.

My aunt wanted that, too. So she determined that I would be, no matter how many shrinks she had to send me to or how many drugs they had to feed me. She would stop me from being the person who had seen and sketched out my mother's death.

I tried to understand that this was just her way of trying to help me—to fix me. But there *was* no fix. Nothing could stop the visions from happening. I was never going to be normal.

I finally just quit taking the drugs and lied that I no longer had nightmares. It was just easier.

As the years went on, though, people became more accepting of my gift. They tried to be kinder, but they still looked at me differently. They probably thought I didn't notice. Except I did, and it changed me.

I don't have many friends and I don't invite people in because there's been too much pain. I don't cry over many things, either.

If a tear is shed, it's during a dream, a vision, or a memory, and it's quickly wiped away and forgotten.

Although my lifestyle doesn't allow for much fun, I focus on showing compassion for others. Life is short, and I know that better than anyone. It's just too bad most have never really gotten to know the real me.

THERE IS ONE PERSON—well, not a person as in someone you see every day, but a "being"—who does know me. Someone I can count on above all others. I call her a spirit source, a guide. I don't how else to explain the unexplainable. Her name is Jamie.

To help you understand, I have never seen Jamie. I can only hear her voice. And no one can hear her but me.

When I first heard her as a child, she sounded like a gentle breeze blowing through my hair. The next time, she was a faint whisper in my ear. I was so young, I thought her whisper was just a bug buzzing around my ear and I tried to swat it away.

Eventually, her voice became vitally important to me. It was like a silky blanket that covered me for security. And not only her voice—sometimes she showed me a picture or a sign of something. Jamie became my teddy bear, my serenity, and my invisible companion.

When my parents first heard me talking with her in my room, they wrote it off as an imaginary friend. Wasn't it normal for an only child to create a playmate? They didn't worry.

As I got older, I knew not to let anyone know she was still part of my life.

Once my parents were gone, it was Jamie who stayed. I could feel her presence. Through the grief and loss was a gentle kindness that brought me out of the darkness like nothing or no one else could. When the town was filled with horror and fear, she was beside me. She would show me a picture of a beautiful meadow or a calm river flowing through a beautiful forest. I would then paint or draw from the visions she gave me.

I believe Jamie is someone who has passed from this life. I don't know who she is or how she came to be with me, but there were times when she was all I had. She comforted me through the pain, just as she had when I was too small to understand.

Jamie has always believed in who I am and what I'm able to do, no questions asked. So many times, she's been the only thing keeping me from losing my mind. How strange it must sound for me to say that someone only I can hear helped me to stay sane. But it was Jamie who kept me from taking my life when things seemed more than I could bear.

I've decided she must be an angel. There's no other way to explain her gentle affection.

Jamie is a big part of my life and I depend on her more than any other. She still sends me visions to paint. I always thank her when she sends me something special, and she acknowledges me in her way.

AFTER THE FIRST PAINTINGS of my mother, I signed up for some art tutoring. Obviously, I hadn't done too badly because my creations led the police to her killer, but I liked art and I wanted more training.

I traveled to the instructor's house, since not many people wanted to venture into *my* home. I knew rumors were circulating that my parents were haunting my house and that I talked to them. That wouldn't have been the worst thing if it were true; in fact, I would have loved it.

I'm not afraid of ghosts at all. If the people in this town only knew that I talk to a voice in my head, imagine what they would think!

My art filled the void of other things I didn't have. I painted to forget. Mostly I painted landscapes, scenery, flowers—happy fluff pieces to sell, which I did in a heartbeat. A local gallery agreed to display them and I also set up a website. I never do public shows, but I've become popular among online connoisseurs, to whom I ship out my pieces. My sole income is now from my paintings.

The artwork from visions revealed to me by Jamie, I keep and hang around the house. These are the striking ones. If I sold them, I could earn thousands per painting. But along with the dream paintings, I would never part with them. The paintings from Jamie are a gift, and the dream paintings are a personal nightmare I don't wish to share with anyone.

Except the cops, that is.

As soon as I have enough to go on, I take pictures of my paintings to the sheriff, who helps contact the FBI on my behalf.

Through this process, I've saved many families from the loss of someone they loved. There have sadly been some I couldn't save; I could only help catch the murderer.

This is not a full-time job—and it's not like I'm even paid for it. But sometimes a grateful family offers up a reward. I don't like to take it, because that's not why I do what I do, but occasionally I can tell they'll be upset if I refuse, so I accept a small token. They've been through enough already.

I've now worked with several different federal agents in different parts of the country, and they all look at me like everyone else does: like I'm a freak.

That's what makes what I do so difficult on many levels. They learn that I *am* a freak, but one who can do what I say I can do. And so, over the course of eight years, I've gone from total dork to valued freak. Wow, I've really moved up in the world!

Still, it's a struggle. I mean, imagine if all this crazy was your life. Sometimes I still don't believe it's mine.

CHAPTER 4

9:08 A.M.

I hear my cell phone ringing and rush back inside. Not too many people call me, so I can only hope that it's Brody. My heart flutters at the thought.

As our friendship grew over the years, I enjoyed learning more and more about Brody and his family.

His father started his military career at Fort Benning in Georgia. After basic training, he was deployed overseas and his career progressed from there.

By the time he met and married Brody's mom, he was of high enough rank to choose his assignments. No longer wanting dangerous deployments, he took a job as a training officer, which allowed them to travel.

When Brody's mom got pregnant, his father asked to be stationed at Fort Riley, in Kansas—the largest military installation in the United States. They wanted to give their child as normal a life as possible.

And they did. They stayed in Arrow Springs throughout Brody's upbringing. His mother was a homemaker who raised Brody to be the best person he could be, and give one hundred percent to anything he undertook. She drove him to his many sports practices and made sure his life was well-rounded. They became very, very close.

His father was strict but fair, expecting nothing but following the rules. With his dad working at the base, Brody considered himself the "man of the house" and took great pride in seeing his parent's joy at his dedication to required tasks. He always wanted to make them proud. His parents paid him an allowance, of which he saved every penny.

Not long after Brody graduated high school, his father's services were requested overseas. But Brody didn't want to leave Arrow Springs. He was old enough to get a job at the sheriff's office and take over payments on his parents' house, which he still lives in. Although splitting the family was heartbreaking, Brody's father's promotion to commanding officer was too good to pass up and Brody could see his parents were excited to travel again. He knew their lives were being well-lived for now at Ramstein Air Base in Germany.

The last eight years brought other changes for him, too. When Sheriff Johnson retired a year ago, his backing helped Arrow Springs' very own Brody Carter get voted in as the youngest sheriff in Kansas state history.

"Hey, Mel—how's your morning going?"

I smile, and then shake my head to clear the remnants of the past—and at least some of the blood from my latest dream.

"Great!" I say.

I'm eager to tell Brody about the woman in last night's dream, but I figure I'll wait and do it in person. Hopefully soon, if he invites me to go jogging.

"You up for a run?" he asks, as though reading my thoughts.

I happily agree.

Brody and I go running together at least once a week. It's my favorite thing to do.

I change quickly into running gear and head outside to meet him.

Brody pulls up almost immediately. Just as he does, I spot a leggy blonde emerging from her car across the street.

Oh, brother. I mentally roll my eyes. *Another chaser.*

Let me explain about chasers. The ratio of single men to single women in Arrow Springs is about one male to every ten females. So certain women in town have made it their mission to nab a guy. Some seem to think a single date with a good prospect will land them a marriage proposal while others just want to play the field.

"Chasing" is a full-time job for these ladies—"ladies" being a word I use very conservatively. Once they catch the scent of a single man, there's nothing they won't do to be noticed. And Brody leads the pack of eligible bachelors. The chasers get all dolled up and show up all over town while he's on duty. It's an embarrassment to females worldwide how they act. Some have even been caught peeking through the windows at the sheriff's office just to get a peek at Brody's ass or pecks.

"Yoo-hoo!" the woman calls out as Brody closes the door of his truck. Having obviously researched his habits, she's clad in full running gear.

Brody shoots me an apologetic glance and then heads over to her.

I cross my arms, annoyed.

I will never admit to anyone how much the chasers bother me. I mean, why can't they act like human beings instead of a bunch of animals in heat? Brody's gone so far as to call them stalkers. He told a couple of them who were hanging around his house that if they didn't leave he was going to have to arrest them. Can you imagine? They probably would have enjoyed being handcuffed by Brody!

I look over and see him still talking to her. *Seriously?*

I suppose it could be worse. One time while we were running, one of them showed up in Daisy Duke shorts and platform sandals and tried to join us! She lasted less than a quarter of a mile before she limped back to her car.

Brody was so embarrassed, he refused to speak to me for the remainder of the run. His face looked like a purple grape! He finally broke into a smile toward the end, after I razzed him pretty good.

Today, though, it doesn't seem funny.

I look at Brody again. His sparkling blue eyes, his light brown hair, his body to die for…I decide I can't really blame the woman.

I remember when we were younger, Brody would spend a lot of time outside during the summer and the tips of his sun-bleached hair looked like professional highlights—though clearly he'd never need to do that. This was before he even knew I existed.

Sometimes I'd watch him talk, reveling in how his full and delicious lips moved as he was speaking. Just like they're moving now.

Stop it! I chide myself. *We aren't kids anymore and you're being ridiculous.*

Brody heads toward me, having shaken loose from his admirer. But for some reason that doesn't improve my mood.

"Sorry about that, Mel. Are you ready to go?"

I shrug and look away. *What is wrong with me?*

Brody seems a bit shocked. It's not like me to act this way.

"What's the matter?" he asks. Then his lips curl upwards. "You aren't jealous, are you?"

I stare at him and snort. "Jealous?" I put my hands on my hips. "Of course not. Who you spend your time with is none of my business."

Before he can answer, I stalk toward his truck. Brody follows.

It's true, I remind myself. It *is* none of my business. Brody and I are just friends. And I'm certainly not the kind of girl he's looking for. Except…sometimes when I think about these women I get so mad. *Oh hell!* I probably am a little jealous. But only because they're stealing Brody's time away from more important things—like helping me solve the dreams.

Brody opens the truck door for me so we can head to our favorite running spot. Again, I feel irritated.

Does he always have to be so damn gentlemanly?

"What now?" he asks instinctively. We've been close for so long, we're able to read each other's moods pretty easily.

"I just had a rough night," I say. "Let's get this run going so I can burn off a little steam."

"Fine," Brody agrees.

The atmosphere in the truck is thick as mud, with neither of us speaking the whole ride over. Brody seems like he wants to say something, but we're both too tense.

We get there and begin our five-mile run, still in quiet solitude. I usually use this time to burn off my troubles and stresses, but today something is different. I feel something pulling at me—an urgency to get to the task at hand and to stop wasting time on trivial emotions. I wonder if Jamie is involved.

I feel much better as we head back to the truck during our cool-down walk and, finally, Brody speaks. "I have to make a trip into Kansas City tomorrow morning," he says. "I was wondering if you'd like to go with me. You could do a little shopping while I take care of some police business, and afterwards we could meet up for lunch."

I smile a genuine smile. That sounds like a great idea. I really love spending time with Brody and I feel bad for being rude to my only real friend in the world.

I need an excuse for my bad mood and decide my dream is as good as it can get. "I'm sorry I was crabby this morning," I say. "I had a new vision last night and it really upset me."

As soon as the words are out of my mouth, I am drawn into what feels like yet another dream. But I'm not sure how that can be, since I'm awake and it's daytime. I don't have "daydreams."

This isn't good.

I'm transported into the mind of a young girl, privy to bits and pieces of a life that is not what any child should have to live.

Huddled in a corner, being beaten, I feel my own body flinch. I can tell the woman doling out the abuse has no love or even the slightest regard for her victim. I'm not able to see the woman, but I sense that she's older—and a relative.

As the woman's wrath continues, the girl wonders if being abused is the way things are supposed to be.

Back in my own head, I try to figure out if the scene is connected to last night's dream. The woman there was fully grown, while this is a little girl. How is it she's never known any true happiness? That her only memories are of the beatings she's lived with since her first moment of recall?

I feel my heart breaking for her.

The abuse progressed. Having started with a quick slap or yelling, the beatings grow more vicious as the child ages. The woman is an addict, feeding her habit with drugs and alcohol. The more she uses, the worse her attacks become. She is sick of looking at the girl. She utters cruel words that should never be spoken to a child: useless, unwanted, nothing.

Tears spill down my face, but I cannot pull myself from the vision.

I feel the little girl's terror as she's locked in a dark closet for no other reason than the woman wanting to go out and party.

"Grandma, please let me out," the child begs, trapped in the darkness with no food or bathroom. "I'll be good! I promise I'll be good."

Her crying seems to go on for hours until she falls asleep from sheer exhaustion.

As one scene after another plays through my head, questions run in and out of my mind, backed by the shouting of the woman and the screaming of the child being punished for her supposed crimes.

How can someone treat a child like this, especially her own granddaughter? I wonder. This person doesn't deserve the title of "Grandmother." I've never had a grandmother of my own, but I've read stories of what they're supposed to be like, and this woman isn't anything like those smiling white-haired ladies who bake cookies and hug and love their grandchildren. Grandmothers don't leave their grandkids locked in closets with no food, blankets, or a bathroom. I can't even think of a word to befit someone who does what this woman has done.

Growing older, the girl senses the woman actually enjoys inflicting pain—that she's defective in some way.

How did she come to be this way? How did she keep the abuse from the police? How was this child not saved by someone? Why was the child left with this woman in the first place? I have so many questions that can't be answered. Not yet, anyway.

As a teenager, the girl calls the woman by name, instead of "Grandma" or "Grandmother." I can't hear it, though—it's garbled, like a piece of a puzzle I have yet to find. But I can tell how much the woman hates it, screaming on and on that it's disrespectful.

Does she actually think she deserves the child's respect? I suppose in her messed-up mind, she does.

Eventually, the girl no longer tries to avoid the beatings, resigned that she'll get one for some reason or another. The only fear and blackness for her now is the dark hatred she feels for the older woman. She vows that one day she will make her pay.

But the girl also has positive thoughts and dreams. She dreams of freedom.

CHAPTER 5

My vision cuts off abruptly and I realize I'm in the cab of the truck, sweating all over Brody. The tears in my dream were obviously real—I can still feel them running down my cheeks.

Before I have time to process what's happened, Brody's voice snaps me back to reality.

"I don't understand you!" he shouts. "How the hell long has this been happening? Since when do you just fall facedown in the dirt? I couldn't snap you out of it. Damn it, Mel. What the hell is going on?"

Brody's venom shocks me. Still lying in his lap, I can do no more than stare up at him in confusion. I'm as taken aback as he is. Also, I'm mesmerized by his expression. Flashes of anger make his blue eyes sparkle. I see something else there, too—something I've never seen. I think it's fear.

And the way he's holding me…it feels as though he wants to protect me from any harm that will come. Oh, that I could stay here forever. Safe.

When Brody first came back from the Marines on leave, I ran into him in town while shipping off some of my paintings. I got that same feeling as when I first saw him in the sheriff's office all those years ago. Except something was different. As he walked towards me, I remember wondering where the boy had gone. He was a man now and had grown into his body in a way that caused my breath to leave me. It was a most inopportune time to not be able to speak. I hugged myself to hide the bumps that stole their way up my arms. He took that to mean I was cold and offered me his coat. But I wasn't cold—I was hot for no reason at all.

Well, obviously there *was* a reason. But I wasn't ready to go down that road. He was and is the nicest person I know in this town, and no way would I screw that up. I'm definitely not going to join the league of chasers.

But now, here he is, cradling me in his muscular arms, and I—

Brody abruptly drops me and gets out of the truck.

What the…

He's even more upset than I thought. I see his face turn a fiery red and I prepare to get yelled at again.

As a rule, Brody's version of yelling is this: He starts to yell, and then stops and starts again. He'll bang his hands on something or stick them in his pockets to try to hide what he's feeling.

He walks around outside the truck for a few minutes trying to cool his temper. Or maybe his embarrassment at having lashed out—I'm not sure which. He's having a very difficult time trying to calm himself.

The whole scene might be humorous if I weren't the one his anger is directed towards.

Uh-oh. Now he's pacing. I know I'm really in trouble.

But I'm not *too* worried.

That day I ran into Brody on leave, he insisted that I join him for dinner (as if I would have said no!). We went to a small diner that had recently opened. Restaurants don't seem to last long in Arrow Springs; there's forever a new place popping up around town.

He made me finish my whole meal because he said he was worried I looked so thin and frail. Back when we dealt with my mother's killer, we were simply acquaintances—two people with a serious shared purpose. But that day in the diner, we bonded into good friends.

He talked about the visit he'd been able to pay his parents before coming home and how ecstatic they'd been to see him. I told him that I'd sold my first piece of art and that a gallery had agreed to take me on as a client. He seemed as excited as I was.

It all happened so easily, I was barely aware of the transition.

The rest of Brody's stay, we spent hanging out together. We realized that we both loved running, so he would just show up at my house and drag me along with him (again, like I would have said no!).

A curse from Brody pulls me back to reality and I suppress a giggle that tries to escape. That surely would send him over the edge. It's not that I'm laughing at him, but it's just that he doesn't scare me. No matter how big and strong he is—and he definitely *is*—I know he would never hurt me. Physically or otherwise.

He stomps back over to the open truck door.

"First of all," he says, "why haven't you told me about this dream yet? We've been together for a couple of hours now!"

"Well, I was goin—"

"And furthermore," he interrupts, "don't you think you might have mentioned that you are also having fainting spells along with your visions?"

I sit up straight in the truck and climb out. I'm feeling much better and I realize I need to take care of the worried person in front of me before I can take care of what I saw in the vision. I also need to defend myself.

"First of all," I begin the same way he did, "I think you need to calm yourself a bit. You look as though you're going to be the next one who needs to be picked up off the ground."

Brody glares at me. "This is no joking matter, Mel. I'm the one who just lifted you up out of the dirt and brought you to the truck. You were unresponsive, and I was terrified something bad was happening to you. Do you understand me?"

I take a deep breath and try to gather my thoughts. I'm going to have to tread lightly on this one.

"I don't know, Brody," I say. "I mean, I'm not *having* fainting spells. This has never happened to me before."

It's true. I sometimes go into a trance while following clues—like when we were searching for my mother's murderer—but I can still hear what is going on around me.

"I can tell you I had a vision," I continue, "and that it was different than the dreams. I didn't feel it coming, so I had no time to react."

While I occasionally get dizzy and need to sit down, with this, I had no warning at all—hence, falling flat on my face!

"It wasn't my fault," I finish up.

"I see." Brody nods. "Well, *that* makes it all okay."

This is said with the most direct sarcasm I've ever heard from Brody. Man, he must really be messed up by this. I feel as though I'm missing half the discussion he's having with me.

"So," he continues, his sarcasm thickening, "let's say you had been driving your car and this happened. Then you would be dead and we wouldn't be having this conversation."

What?!

"Brody, I honestly don't believe that whatever forces give me the dreams, or visions, or whatever, would give me one while I'm driving."

Brody snorts. "Are you willing to bet your life on that? Do you honestly think this couldn't just happen to you at any time of day?"

I'm not totally sure he's wrong about this, so I try to steer the conversation in another direction.

"Can I have some water?" I ask. "I feel like I have dirt on my face."

"You *do* have dirt on your face!" he cries. "You went down flat on the ground before I could even grab a hold of you. And then when you started crying, it turned to mud running down your cheeks. And now—well, I can't tell you what you look like because that would be just downright rude of me."

I take a deep breath, chagrined that my diversion tactics are backfiring completely.

I try another tack.

"Have you calmed down enough to hear about the vision?" I ask.

Brody grunts and hands me a bottle of water. I clean my face the best I can and then take a long drink. Brody digs a towel out of the backseat of the truck and hands it to me so I can dry my face. Then he stows the towel and comes back over to me.

He grabs my hands and looks into my eyes.

"So tell me," he says.

I take a deep breath. "First, I want to thank you for being here with me and taking care of me. You are the only person who understands what I go through when the dreams are happening."

Brody nods slightly but doesn't speak.

"And I'm sorry that I frightened you," I add. "I have to admit I was a little bit afraid, too."

I suddenly realize that we're still holding hands and that I'm talking way too fast. I feel my face flush and drop his hands.

This causes Brody to get riled up all over again.

"Why do you always look as though you're having a good laugh with yourself at my expense?" he asks. "I don't know why you always think you have to handle everything on your own."

He claps his hands together. "You know what? I have to go get cleaned up and head back to the station. We recently hired a new officer and I want to get in some more training time with her today."

"You're training a female officer?" The question jumps out.

Brody smirks. "It's nothing like *that*, and you know it. Her previous captain in Kansas City told me she's a good cop but she's a bit self-conscious and always thought the male officers were making fun of her. And some were. He suggested she might be more comfortable in a smaller town."

Brody stretches. "And so, as much as I don't want to wait to finish our talk, I really have to get back to the station. You can tell me about this new dream and today's vision tomorrow on the trip to Kansas City."

"Fine," I say. "I'll meet you at the station in the morning."

Brody reddens again. "I. Don't. Think. So." He draws out the words like he's scolding a child. "You won't be driving for a while. And if I catch you, I'll be writing you a ticket for driving under the influence of visions."

My mouth falls open and I almost choke on the water I'm drinking.

"Is that even a thing?"

I guess we aren't discussing it, as he drops me off at home and speeds away in a cloud of dust. I watch until his truck disappears.

Seems I'm getting really good at pissing him off.

I WALK INSIDE, back into the loneliness.

The house is filled with all the things I love, and I'm surrounded by my paintings. Not the dream paintings—the ones from Jamie.

But something is missing.

I think back to when Brody was home on leave. When he returned to the Marines to finish his tour of duty, my loneliness was the greatest I've ever felt. We sent each other emails, and I'd ask him to share how he was. I was tired of talking about murder. He would tell me of his adventures and how he enjoyed most of what he was doing in the corps. He loved traveling and meeting people, and I wondered if he would ever come home. I worried that Arrow Springs would never be enough for him after seeing the world.

Being friends with Brody made me want to feel something—anything—besides the devastating loss of my parents that I felt every day. Brody was the smartest, bravest man I'd ever known and I found myself eagerly checking my inbox for a new message to arrive. I was lonely, and there was no one in town who could make me feel as happy as Brody did.

I go upstairs to take another shower. It suddenly seems weird that I have to take a shower before going running and another shower after running. I mean, I suppose I could skip the first one—except there's no way I'm going to show up to see Brody as a smelly, sweating mess like I was this morning. Sure, he sees me as a smelly, sweating mess after we run, but somehow that's different because we are *both* smelly and sweaty. Sometimes I confuse the hell out of myself.

Back in the shower, my eyes tear up as I think about Brody's final return home from the Marines. He gave me a huge bear hug along with an "I'm so happy to see you" type of peck on the lips. But I felt that contact in every nerve of my body.

Not that there's anything between us. I'm not saying it's like a brother/sister relationship, either—that would be well, ick! I'm just saying he's the best friend I have in this town, and I'd be mostly alone without him.

And now I feel really bad about being jealous and angry, and for not telling him sooner about the dream.

Damn it, though! He probably really *would* give me a ticket if I drove to the station in the morning.

Hopefully he'll be in a better mood tomorrow.

CHAPTER 6

Stella Ford lets the warm water soothe her sore body as she stands in the shower, smiling. She's not the type to have sex with a guy she just met, but she's glad she took a chance last night with Pete. Her mind still in a daze, she picks up the shampoo bottle, trying to remember if she's washed her hair once, or twice already.

Except for being teased about her chubby figure and her practical but not-so-feminine haircut, Stella isn't used to getting attention from men. Sure, she had some flings when she was younger, but now she can't remember the last time a guy even looked at her romantically.

She sure doesn't care about doing the things "normal" girls like to do. Stella's favorite pastime is fishing, a passion she shared with her father since youth. He taught her everything she needed to know, from finding the best fishing holes to baiting a line to casting to preparing a fish. Her father used to tell her: "No sense in fishing if you aren't going to eat it. And in order to eat it, you need to know how to clean it." She can now filet, debone, and de-scale with the best of them, and she never freaks out at the sight of a worm or lurches when a fish jumps out of the water.

Although still relatively new to Arrow Springs, Stella has already discovered some prime spots here. She often wonders if all that time spent with her dad in the peacefulness of streams and lakes and rivers is also the reason she likes solitude so much. She never had girlfriends when she was younger because she had no interest in that "normal" stuff they liked to do. Malls, shopping, and sleepovers couldn't compete with rods and reels in the world of Stella Ford.

Stella sometimes wonders if she should have been born a boy. She has boring looks and boring hair and her body has always been on the larger side. But her dad never cared about that. Nor did the calm water or the creatures beneath it.

But yesterday afternoon while shopping at Fish N' More Bait Store, Stella hooked more than she planned.

She made her way up to the door, dreading the tussle she inevitably had with it whenever the wind caught it. But suddenly a man reached from behind her and grabbed the handle to open it for her. Though grateful, she felt a slight affront to her feminist sensibilities. She instinctively turned around to see who had committed this dubious act. The perpetrator flashed her a smile. She smiled back.

Hmmm…chivalrous and easy on the eyes.

As much as Stella was a strong, independent woman, there was something about a man taking care of her that she relished. It had been a long time since she'd experienced that.

She retrieved the bait she'd come in for and was making her way to the register, when she noticed her white knight pacing back and forth in one of the aisles, holding what looked like bobbers and some hooks. She watched as he picked up one rod, put it back down, and then picked up another. He looked totally lost.

She found it oddly endearing how he examined everything with a scowl on his face. But at the same time, she felt bad for him. She could see that he had no inkling what he was supposed to buy.

Stella was usually very shy, but the man's awkward attempts to shop somehow made her feel more in control. Fishing was something she knew well, so she confidently decided to help him. She figured on offering him some quick tips and then continuing on her way. Her real goal for the day was to get out to her favorite stream for some quiet time.

When she neared, the man glanced up at her and she saw a *look* in his eyes that she wasn't able to decipher. She was intrigued, though, and decided to see where things went. Knowing her life, it wouldn't be very far.

The man's "look" turned to confusion as he lowered his head and glanced from one hand to the other. When he lifted his eyes back to Stella, something about his gaze made her squirm. But her intrigue remained.

"Is there something I can help you with?" she asked.

"Well," the man replied, "I'm guessing you can tell I've got no idea what I'm looking for here."

Stella almost let a giggle slip out, but she wasn't sure how that would go over. "Tell me what your budget is," she said, "and we can pick out what you need. I've been fishing for a long time and, well, I don't mean to be rude, but have you *ever* fished before?"

"Honestly, not really," he answered with a slight smile. "But although I'm no fisherman, a friend told me that there are some good spots in the area so I thought I'd give it a whirl."

"So, you're not from here," Stella noted as she began gathering some simple gear. "I didn't think I'd seen you around. What brings you to our little town of Arrow Springs?"

"Eighteen wheels!" he replied. "I drive a truck and I've got a few days layover while I wait for my next load. I decided to kill some time trying this whole fishing thing out. Looks like it'll be more trouble than I thought, though."

"Don't you worry." Stella smiled. "I can at least start you off on the right foot by helping you get the proper supplies."

"I wonder…" The man looked thoughtful. "And tell me if I'm being too forward…but maybe you could do more than that. Maybe you could go fishing with me—teach me a thing or two? Obviously, you know your way around bait and hooks and things and—" He cut himself off and hung his head. "Never mind. I'm being *waaay* too presumptuous. Just load me up with what I need and I'll try to find the fishing hole my friend was talking about."

Hmmmm… Stella barely knew this individual—she didn't even know his name. Given her track record with men and not being in the habit of picking up random strangers, she felt very hesitant. But what harm could come from just going fishing? After all, she *was* a cop; she could handle herself. So, why not take a chance? Chances had been so few and far between lately.

"Hey, you still there?" the man asked with a smile.

Stella realized she must have been lost in thought longer than she supposed. Apparently he'd continued speaking and she hadn't heard a word. She must look like a real ditz.

"Yeah, sorry," she said. "I was trying to think about what you need to get. Let's get a couple of lures and some bobbers. A pole is gonna set you back a little bit, but there's really no way around it. This one over here is pretty good and it doesn't break the bank."

"Oh yes, that one's a fine pole. Thank you."

"Okay then, let's go over here and if you could hold my bait, I can grab the rest of what you need and we can check out together. And you know what? I'd be happy to take you out fishing with me."

"Excellent!" he said. "But before we do, I should at least introduce myself. I'm Pete. And thank you for letting me tag along with you."

As he said this, he looked down at his hands—both full of the items she'd helped him select—and realized he had no way to shake hands with her. They both laughed it off.

"Well, hi, Pete. I'm Stella. I was going fishing anyway, so what's one more person along for the ride?"

Pete did have one more request. "This may be a lot to ask, and I hope you don't think I'm taking advantage, but the only vehicle I have here is my rig, which is staged right now at YRC Freight Company waiting on that load. Would you mind driving us?"

"Of course not," Stella answered. She paused. "But, then, how did you get *here*?"

"Oh, I walked over," he said. "It wasn't far and there aren't a lot of places in town to legally and comfortably park a big ol' Peterbilt and a fifty-three-foot trailer."

She smiled again, thinking it endearing how shy he looked asking her for another favor. And again, what harm could come from it? She had her gun stowed in her car for easy access, but she had a feeling she wouldn't be pulling it out. Pete seemed nice enough and she was excited to have a man notice her for a change.

"I want to thank you for being so helpful," Pete said as they left the store. "I didn't come over here expecting to meet an expert angling instructor! This makes the idea of putting that hook in the water a whole lot more pleasant."

Stella felt the same. She was also happy that it was Friday, which was the reason she'd decided to do some fishing. She finally had a Friday off and was excited to spend it relaxing. What she *wasn't* happy about was that she had to work tomorrow morning, on a Saturday. Like her license plate frame said, *I'd Rather Be Fishing.*

Stella put their purchases into the trunk of her car. She knew from experience that she didn't need earthworms spilling all over, which is why she kept a special bucket back there to hold them. After catching some fish, she'd then use the same bucket to stow her prizes until she was ready to start cleaning them.

As she headed toward the driver's side of the car, she looked around for Pete, only to find him holding the door open for her.

Her first thought was that never in her whole life had anyone ever held open a car door for her. At least not anybody interesting.

As she drove them out of the parking lot, Stella had a thought. "If we go fishing now, we may be out there awhile," she said. "Maybe I should order up some subs or a pizza to bring with us, and there's a store on the way where we can grab some drinks…if you're interested, that is."

"I think that sounds great." Pete smiled. "I feel bad, though, that you're going so far out of your way for me. Let me at least pay for the food."

Stella smiled back at him. "It's no trouble—I'm grateful to have a fishing partner again. So how about if we split everything? That way neither of us feels put out."

Pete agreed.

Stella called in the order, and they stopped to pick it up. Since the restaurant knew her, they sold Stella a six pack of beer she could take out with her.

On the way to the fishing hole, Pete asked what Stella meant about having a "partner" again. She explained about all the good times she'd shared with her father.

It didn't take long to drive to the spot along the river that she'd chosen, and they loaded up everything from the car that they would need. Stella had stashed the food and beer in a cooler she also kept on hand, which she asked Pete to grab along with the blanket.

Once they got situated on the bank, Stella suggested that they have lunch first. As they sat on the blanket eating, Stella asked Pete about his truck driving, which he mostly shrugged off. He seemed more interested in knowing about *her*. Boy, that was a switch from what she was used to!

She told him more about growing up in Kansas City and about how she'd lost her father—and fishing partner—ten years ago in a convenience store hold-up. He'd just been in the wrong place at the wrong time. The guy who killed him had been apprehended, and he was a simple druggie wanting money. The conversation died off a bit after that until lunch was finished and it was time to start fishing.

Stella helped Pete prepare his pole as she did her own. As she showed him how to cast the line, she caught him watching her with a slight smile on his face. Feeling the heat creep up her neck, she turned away to get her own line into the water.

As they fished, they kept the conversation going.

"I never did ask you what type of job you do," Pete said.

Stella felt a tad uncomfortable sharing her occupation. He might not like that she was a cop. So it was with much trepidation that she revealed being a deputy at the Arrow Springs sheriff's office.

"After my father's death I went to the Academy," she explained.

"Wow, I never would've guessed that about you," he said candidly. "And that's not a bad thing. It's just that you don't seem like a cop to me."

Stella took no offense—she was just grateful that he didn't seem put off by the idea.

Pete went on to explain that she was "too sexy" to be a cop. Now *that* was a shocking revelation! She almost slipped right off the bank into the river. Thankfully, Pete grabbed her arm before she fell in the water. As she reclaimed her footing, she looked up into his eyes. She wasn't sure exactly what she saw, but she *clearly* felt a tingling all the way down to her hoo-ha.

They continued to reel in the fish. Both caught several that would make a nice dinner for a future night.

And he continued to want to know even more about her.

Stella told him how she had just moved to Arrow Springs a month or so ago and explained the problems she'd had at her last job. Her new boss here was much better to work for, she told him.

She was surprised at how very attentive Pete was, listening to the complaints of a female cop from the big city. She saw absolutely no judgment in his eyes.

By now, the bucket was getting full and the sky was getting dark.

"I think we should get going," said Stella. "It's getting kind of late and I have to be at work early tomorrow."

She did a quick cleaning of the fish down by the water while Pete gathered up the equipment and carried everything back to the car. Stella made her way to the driver's side of the car to find Pete was once again holding the door for her. As she was busy thanking him, he grabbed her and kissed her.

"Thank *you* for taking me with you today," he said. "I had a great time. You're a good teacher and great company."

The only response in her mind was *Wow!* The kiss was amazing and she wouldn't forget it.

On their way back to town, they picked up their conversation—again about *her.*

"So what made you pick this area to move to?" he asked.

"I did my research," Stella proudly explained. "Iroquois County is a beautiful place, with the river flowing through, lots of outdoor activities, and everything moving at a slower pace than in the city. All of that, I figured, added up to a nice place to live. Like I said, I knew I needed a change. A quieter life with fewer frustrations—and I was more than done with the big-city attitudes about my weight and looks."

When Stella finished, she could sense that he'd been paying close attention. *And* that he was checking her out from head to toe.

"Everything looks good from where I'm sitting," he said. "I don't think there's anything wrong with your weight or your looks."

Was he really saying these things? Stella felt such a strong connection with this man. The desire she felt from him when he kissed her was strong and extremely seductive. She decided then and there that she had needs that had to be met in any way possible. She was tired of taking care of herself sexually, so if Pete could be the one to do it, then so be it.

As they reentered town, Pete asked Stella if she was familiar with where the YRC Freight Company had its yard—the place where his rig was parked.

Instead of answering, Stella pulled her car over.

"I was wondering if you would like to…uh…*continue* the evening?" she asked Pete. "We could go for a drink, or even back to my place. We have a couple of beers left in the cooler."

In response, Pete grabbed her and gave her another searing kiss. "*That's* a great idea," he said. "And if you can't tell already how interested in you I am, then maybe I can show you a little more." He grabbed her hand and placed it on his crotch. She could feel his erection bursting through his jeans.

From there, it was like a switch had been flipped—for both of them. Suddenly he was touching her breasts and fondling her crotch. She could feel the heat coming from his body through his clothes.

She finally started the car to drive them to her house, but she was so distracted, she was forced to pull over several more times. Finally she begged for mercy, assuring him her place wasn't far away. He relented a little.

During her slight reprieve, she took a moment to reflect on her struggle to find a home to purchase. She liked the privacy of a residence, which she knew from experience she wouldn't get in an apartment. Thankfully she'd found a house to rent, and that privacy would come in real handy right now.

Once they finally made it to her door, they stood outside and kept kissing and touching each other. She giggled that he seemed so anxious to get inside—of the house *and* her.

"No one has ever made me feel like this," Stella told him.

"Baby," he smiled, "I haven't even got started yet."

Once the door was opened, there was barely time to make it inside. Pete kicked it closed and shoved Stella up against it. He was kissing her from her neck to her mouth and back again and he obviously couldn't wait to get her clothes off. He didn't give her a chance to say yes or no before he proceeded to remove her shirt. It didn't matter, because she wasn't saying no to anything.

He massaged her breasts through her plain white bra with one hand as he pinned her to the door with his leg. She could feel her nipples harden as she felt his rough hands on her body. Kissing her as if he would never get enough, he rubbed her down below with his other hand. She felt the flush of desire rise up in her cheeks. She was burning for him.

He turned her to face the door and grabbed her around the waist. Then he reached around her middle and unhooked her pants, quickly pulling them down her legs in a way that said he'd removed the pants of many women. Then he tore her panties from her body. She fleetingly worried if she had shaved recently but with everything he was doing, she couldn't think about anything except his hands on her.

His hands came around front, fondling her to see if she was ready. *Oh, she was ready.* Giving her no more than one second to worry about whether he'd use a condom or not, he rammed himself into her.

Stella stifled a cry. Her body wasn't used to be taken so forcefully. Hell, it wasn't used to be taken at all. She was no virgin, but it had been so long it almost felt as though she were.

All thoughts were forgotten once he started pumping in and out of her. She had to brace her hands against the door to protect her head from bumping it—but she didn't want him to stop for anything.

He pumped hard and fast, and before she knew it, he had pulled out and she was being flung onto her back on the couch. He eagerly removed her bra and cradled her breasts with both of his hands. Then he suckled her distended nipple between his teeth, nipping it hard enough to make her cry out. Everything he was doing was a shock to her but it made her feel so desirable, her own need only increased.

Suddenly, he shoved his fingers in the place his member had already been. It felt like several as he worked them in and out with great dexterity. He was rubbing her nub with one coarse finger while the others went in and out, in and out. She was so hot, she felt she would explode.

Finally, he removed his fingers and she thought she would die from pleasure when he entered her again. He rode her so hard, it was like he was trying to jump inside her body so they could be as one.

She couldn't breathe. She was getting ready to let go and she wanted him to come with her. She didn't have any time to discuss it before they both shattered in unison.

Stella couldn't remember ever feeling such an intense, much-needed release as this one.

Both of them were still panting hard when they looked down and realized they hadn't even gotten their pants all the way off and that they both still had their boots on. They laughed aloud.

Once her heart rate calmed enough to move from the couch, Stella excused herself to "freshen up."

"I don't think I'll be able to walk again for a while," she said, still laughing.

And she was right. Walking certainly wasn't easy as she eased her way to the bathroom.

"Hurry back!" he called out. "I have plenty more where that came from."

"Holy shit!" was her response.

Stella hastily removed her pants and boots and then found a washcloth and quickly rubbed down her entire body. Then she sat down on the toilet lid, trying to figure out how to brace for whatever else he had planned. She had enjoyed the intensity of their first encounter, but she wasn't sure how much more pounding she could take. I mean, she didn't want to hobble into work tomorrow with a limp. At that thought, she let out a snicker, imagining the expressions on everyone's faces if she did.

When she looked up, Pete was at the door. Stark naked now, he was watching her with eyes that seemed almost black. His private part was in his hand, and she felt her eyes widen as he rubbed himself up and down. She could see now that he was very well-endowed.

Damn, she thought, *I AM going to be walking funny tomorrow.*

But she didn't care. As her body heated up again, she resigned herself that it was going to be completely used up by the time this night was over.

"Let's go to your bedroom," he said to her. "I can't wait any longer to be inside of you again."

Well damn, she barely had time to stand up before he grabbed her and started kissing her. She'd never liked being naked in front of men, but he gave her no time to cover herself or to care. He had her so hot that by the time she got to the bed, she felt the urge to do something she rarely did.

She wanted to be in control this time.

She touched his chest and then slid her hand and body slowly downward. Looking directly into his eyes, she held his member in her hands and took him into her mouth. She sucked him harder and faster until he couldn't hold it any longer; he pumped his release into her mouth and she swallowed it.

When she looked up, she saw a gleam in his eye like he wanted to eat her alive…and damn if he didn't do just that. He moved down her body, licking and nipping all the way—not hard enough to leave bite marks, but she didn't care anyway.

He panted about how wet she was and told her he couldn't wait to put his tongue inside her. Then he probed every inch of her with it. Then he directed her to get on her knees so he could enter her from behind again. She liked the way his balls slapped against her as he pumped in and out. He kept wanting her over and over. She couldn't keep track of how many orgasms she had, but when they were done, she was completely spent. She fell asleep shortly after he finished her off.

Waking up this morning, she indeed felt a little sore down there—okay, a lot sore. But her desires were completely satisfied. She's not sure if his were, though—or could ever be for that matter.

Before getting in the shower, she watched Pete head to the bathroom completely naked. Seeing a man undressed wasn't something she was accustomed to. She enjoyed seeing him comfortable with his nudity and wondered if she'd ever feel like that.

She sure was comfortable watching his hot ass walk around.

Stella hasn't had any company since moving to Arrow Springs, and she decides having a guest is so much better than being alone.

Finally finishing her shower, she walks back into the bedroom to get dressed. But Pete grabs her arm and drags her back on to the bed. Her words come out before she can stop them: "Whoa—I don't know how you could possibly be ready to go again so soon!"

"Actually," he says, "right now I just wanted to spend some time with you. We will definitely get back to that shortly."

She breathes a sigh of relief.

"It's been a while since I had a lady as interesting as you want to be with me," he continues. "I don't want you to think I just want sex. Let's talk for a while."

Stella feels a blush steal up to her face. She's more than okay having a conversation with him.

"What do you want to talk about?" she asks.

He shrugs. "How about a little more about you?" he says.

Of course, thinks Stella. But she is far from complaining.

"Tell me about your life as a cop," he says.

Stella snorts. "I think I told you almost everything there was to tell last night!"

"That can't be true," says Pete. "How 'bout this: What's the most interesting case that has happened in these parts?"

Stella thinks back through the cases she knows about—the ones big enough to be newsworthy in Kansas City, or that she's heard about during her short tenure in Arrow Springs.

One, and only one, rises far above the rest. Pete will surely find it interesting!

"Well," she begins, "there was a big case some years ago where a serial killer murdered several women along the Interstate."

"Around here?!" Pete sounds shocked. "You wouldn't think a small town like this would have had something so terrible happen."

"I think every place has its shameful secrets," Stella replies. "But this one was all over the nationwide news. I'm kind of surprised you never heard about it."

Pete rubs his chin. "Hmmm…being on the road all the time, I don't get to watch much TV, and I usually have my XM tuned to country stations. I'd rather tap my foot to Kenny Chesney than get depressed by the news, if you know what I mean. But now that you mention it, maybe I *do* remember hearing a little something about that." He begins to slowly knead her breasts one at a time as he continues speaking. "But tell me more. Just what exactly happened? I think I remember something about a local woman somehow helping catch the killer?"

Pete's touch is getting Stella going again, and she doesn't know how much more *work* she can focus on, while feeling so wet and wanton.

But Pete persists. So between breaths, Stella explains that it's someone her boss knows but whom she has yet to meet.

Pete continues to ply her with questions—probing her mind as his fingers probe her body. And with each of her replies, his ministrations became more intense. She's never been this responsive to a man before.

"Do you know how the case finally turned out?" he asks. "What happened to the guy?"

"I don't know specifics," Stella pants, "but the murderer was killed in a final showdown. I'm sure I can find out more today at work," she offers. Hell, she'd find out anything to keep him interested and in her bed. "If you *let* me go to the office, that is!"

"Mmmmm…" Pete responds noncommittally, continuing to rub her and touch her and lick her.

Stella moans. She can't think straight with all the things he's doing.

He then explains in no uncertain terms that they're not done having sex and details out some things he still wants to do to her. He says she'll be begging him to come see her every day of his trip.

He then asks if she'll give him a ride back to his truck so he can get some sleep.

She can't believe the words are coming out of her mouth, but she replies that if he wants to stay with her until his freight is ready, she'll be okay with it. She tries to make the offer casual— she doesn't want to sound too eager and scare him away.

He grins broadly. And after that, he goes back to manhandling every part of her body with renewed vigor. He even convinces her they needed shower sex before she leaves for work.

"Your pulsating 'magic massage' showerhead's got nothing on me, doll!" he says as he soaps up her back and then slowly bends her over in the sensuous flow of warm water.

CHAPTER 7

I'M SO EXHAUSTED, but with all the dreams I've been having, my subconscious fights the urge to slumber. Finally, as I toss and turn and fluff my pillow over and over, I succumb to my body's needs…

It's as if the dream has been lying in wait for me in the darkness. I'm in the mind and body of a man—a killer.

He knew before coming to town he'd need a suitable vehicle for transporting his victim. He leans into his recently acquired van, reveling in his own brilliance.

He'd carefully checked the area before making his move. No sense giving the coppers a free pass to catch his ass. As he walked toward his unsuspecting target—some idiot trying to sell his van online—he'd wanted nothing more than to kill the stupid bastard. Didn't the asshole know better than to invite strangers to his home? But a bash over the head with a tire iron had been enough for the job. He reveled in making sure the poor slob was dead before loading him into his own van.

The killer then drove to a remote spot to change the plates—and dispose of the body, of course. But those weren't his biggest concerns. Devising a way to get the woman into the van without detection or risk of her escape, was.

The killer opens the rear doors and admires the large grab handles he installed there. Once he gets her in, he can shackle her to them—he has plenty of handcuffs. Although she'll be drugged, the substance can affect different people in different ways. He'll take no chances.

The killer pulls his bag of tools out of the back with a wicked smile. He always gets excited when he thinks about his tools. But he mustn't get off track. He has a lot to do before he can go to the bitch's house and get her. Everything must be perfectly planned.

He thinks about how much he likes planning ahead. It increases the anticipation—and it's kept him safe so far.

His next step is to find a really good hideaway to do what he enjoys most. Because this bitch, he's sure, will give him the greatest pleasure he's ever had. She <u>deserves</u> to die.

Finally the day is here. He's more than prepared. He's been casing her place for a week. He knows the house and he knows her routine.

Climbing into the driver's seat, he marvels again at his own ingenuity. He's a pretty good house painter and got himself hired last week to do a job for her neighbor a few doors down. He needs the neighbors not to question the presence of his van or of him now that he's ready for the real job.

He's worn contacts while doing his paint work and a cap with a wig. He's good with disguises. He also knows how to keep a low profile. He's made himself someone you wouldn't look twice at—or remember.

The plan is simple: Go up to the house carrying a clipboard and wearing a painting cap, as if he's giving a quote. Then sneak in and do what he came to do.

The killer keeps himself calm as he knows that's required. But he becomes more aroused as he makes his way closer to her house. All he can think about is what he will do to her…

The dream shifts again. The man is upstairs in a steamy room—obviously a bathroom. He stands outside the shower's view but as he listens to the water run, he can barely contain himself from opening the door and grabbing the woman wet and naked. He enjoys the anticipation. There's no escape for her. She will fall, like all the others.

The shower turns off and he braces himself. As she steps toward the fully fogged mirror with her back to him, he grabs her from behind with his hand covering her mouth. She tries to fight him without success.

Wanting her to feel his excitement, he pushes his erection into her back. This makes her struggle more, but he is much stronger and smarter than she is. Another pathetic victim to be destroyed. He's so excited about what he'll do to her that his arousal is almost to the point of pain. But for him, pain is excitement.

His needle is ready for her. He sticks it in her arm and her body succumbs immediately. As she sinks to the ground, he replaces the cover on the needle and stows it safely in his pocket. Then he quickly rolls her into the painting tarp he's already laid out and throws her over his shoulder.

In a flash, he's back at the van. He opens the doors and lays her not-so-gently in the back. He removes the tarp enough to place the handcuffs on her wrists and hook her up to the handles. They are perfect.

He starts the van and looks on the seat beside him at his carefully wrapped tool pouch. He unhooks the three clips holding it together and slowly unfurls it to reveal his greatest love. Each tool has been placed in a separate pocket and wrapped so that one will not touch the other. He strokes them as he would a woman. What these items have done to the flesh has brought him some of his greatest sexual pleasure.

The killer also thinks of his tools as an extension of himself. He spends a few minutes rubbing his handheld blowtorch, his most favorite tool of all. Reliving the screams that have been ignited by the small flame at the end of it, he almost loses it.

But no—he mustn't.

He needs to get away from the neighborhood as quickly as possible. He's planned exactly where he'll stop to give the bitch another dose of drugs to keep her out until he reaches his destination.

The killer drives away, feeling ecstatic. This is what he was born to do.

I WAKE WITH A START and feel my whole body trembling. The woman I've been dreaming about is going to be kidnapped and tortured!

I need to paint.

As I set out my supplies, my hands continue shaking. I'm used to sick murderers by now, but this guy may be the worst. I shiver, like you do when you're so grossed out you feel dirty. This guy is messed up.

It's hard for me to go back into this dream. I have an innate sense of fear. But I need to so I can see what the painting brings.

I close my eyes. Immediately I'm lost in reliving the dream, and my paintbrush is steady as the image takes form—a life of its own, filled with fear.

The killer chokes the woman from behind, wrapping his arm around her throat. From his vantage, I see the woman's hands clawing frantically to stop him—her long fingers the same ones I know from the other dreams. But she scratches and fights to no avail. I wish I could tell her it's useless.

I can feel the fear pulsating through her as he pushes his erection into her back. The horror turns my blood to ice as the needle again goes into her arm and I feel the joy he derives from it.

I watch her body fall to the floor.

I'm pulled out of the dream as if attached to a large rubber band that has snapped me back to reality. I have goosebumps from fright, and nausea rolls in my stomach.

I need to take a shower…but I'm jolted by a car horn outside.

Crap! Brody's here to pick me up! I've completely lost track of time.

I scramble around for my phone and text Brody that I'll let him in to wait while I get ready.

I run to the bathroom in a panic. I quickly brush the snarls of sleep out of my hair. Though short, it sticks out like a haystack when I first get up.

I used to wear my hair a lot longer, but in one of my murder dreams, a victim was grabbed by the hair. It frightened me enough to cut off my own so no one can use it to catch *me*. I now wear a short pixie cut—I think that's what the style's called. I chose it from a random magazine, but it turns out I like it this way. It's so easy to deal with. Just throw in a little mousse, and I'm ready to go.

But I don't have time for even that right now.

I take a large gulp of mouthwash and swish it around. I don't want Brody to smell my morning breath, but I don't have time to brush my teeth right now either.

I need to get downstairs.

I open my front door and there stands Brody in all of his handsome glory. Facing him in my old-lady pajamas, I feel my face heat up. Hopefully he thinks I'm just embarrassed by my behavior yesterday.

"Just give me a few minutes to freshen up," I say.

He tilts his head to examine my face. "Did you get *any* sleep at all? You look like hell."

"Why, thank you so much," I respond. "You sure know how to make a girl feel special with your gleaming compliments."

Brody crosses his arms. "Ooh, I guess that answers my question! You're even crankier than yesterday." He walks past me into the house. "While you get ready, why don't I make a pot of coffee? Perhaps that'll improve your mood before we go."

I have no complaints about that one! I can sure use it. Plus, I like the idea of Brody in my kitchen.

I run upstairs and take the fastest shower of my life—and then another minute to brush my teeth and mousse my hair. I throw on a pair of recently acquired jeans and one of my nicer t-shirts. I need to keep my look casual so Brody doesn't realize I'm "dressing up" for him. I pull out my mascara and run a couple of swipes over my lashes.

I look in the mirror and shrug. This is as good as it's going to get with such a short amount of time to get ready.

I return downstairs to find Brody standing at the stove making an omelet. He somehow found enough ingredients in my fridge to make a sizeable breakfast we can share. Seeing that he's prepped bread in the toaster, I walk over and pop it down to start. I grab two plates from the cupboard and silverware from the drawer. Then I set the table for two. The torture of having him so close and yet untouchable is almost more than I can bear.

"I see you know your way around the kitchen," I say.

It's a joke. I know Brody well enough to know breakfast is pretty much the only meal he can handle.

"Ha, ha, Mel," he says, knowing himself well enough, too. "Why don't you sit down and eat? You'd better hope I didn't throw a few eggshells into the mix to try and cut the edges off your irritable attitude!"

I'm tempted to make a face behind his back, but I don't want to get caught.

I follow his instructions and wait for him to join me. After dishing us food, he pulls up the chair across from me. Realizing he hasn't served anything to drink, I get back up and retrieve a carton of orange juice and some glasses.

As I rejoin him at the table, my stomach growls—I had no idea how hungry I was. I take a bite and the food tastes delicious.

"Didn't you already have breakfast before you came to pick me up?" I ask him.

"No, I actually have less food in my house than you do. I was planning to stop on the way for coffee and donuts or something, but this works out way better."

I couldn't agree more.

"So, tell me about the dreams," he says, "including yesterday's vision and what obviously kept you awake last night. I barely slept myself, worrying about you. I felt bad leaving, but you were seriously miserable."

Ignoring that comment, I continue scarfing down my breakfast, filling him in on everything between bites: the first dream, yesterday's vision, and last night's dream.

When I'm done, I throw up my hands in frustration. "These dreams seem to be all over the place. I'm so confused. How can I help anyone from my first dream—the one with the woman holding a knife—when I don't know who or where she is? And how can I stop a kidnapping when I have the same problem? I mean, we know he's using his house painting as a cover, but it's not like we can hunt down every freelance painter in the world and question them!"

"And not like he'd be a registered contractor anyway," agrees Brody. "We need to figure out a few more clues on our own before contacting the Feds."

I sigh in frustration. "I know—and I have no idea where he plans to take her or where to start with solving any of this!"

Brody gets up from the table and starts clearing away the plates. I stop him.

"Let me take care of the dishes at least, since you cooked."

As I do, I wait for some sort of response to what I told Brody about the dreams. But I can't read his expression this morning any more than I ever can.

He walks by me and ruffles the back of my hair like I'm his kid sister. I've recently taken to cutting my hair myself, so I wonder if he thinks I'm doing a bad job. I wonder what sparked this action at all.

"Mel, I know we'll figure it out," he says. "We always do. But for now, we need to get going. I need to make a quick stop at the station to make sure the new deputy doesn't need anything before we take off. Plus, this'll be a good chance for you to finally meet her."

I prepare two to-go cups of coffee, since the brew at the sheriff's office is like sludge. Brody sometimes drinks it, but it upsets my stomach. I have enough to worry about as it is!

Jamie, who has been pretty much MIA for the last couple weeks, makes her presence known as soon as I've relaxed inside the truck cab. I get an odd tingling feeling whenever she's around. She's not speaking yet, so I wonder what's going on with her.

I wish she would give me some better clues about where these dreams are leading. Sometimes she gives me signs of where I need to look to solve the dreams, but other times she's no help at all. As I'm waiting raptly for her to chime in, Brody interrupts my thoughts.

"Hey, Mel—where'd you go?"

Oops!

"I'm sorry!" I say. "I guess I'm just tired."

"Phew!" he said. "I was worried you were having another one of those visions like yesterday. I'm happy you're at least sitting down; you sure don't need to face-plant into the dirt again."

"True," I say, chiding myself to stay focused on reality.

Brody is so supportive of my dreams and I've told him almost everything there is to know about me. But talking about Jamie is the one thing I've never done—with anyone. People think I'm crazy already. If they find out I talk to someone I believe is a ghost…well, I don't want to know their reaction!

AT THE SHERIFF'S OFFICE, Brody enters first and holds the door open for me. As soon as I pass the threshold, a woman rushes in behind me. To avoid running into me, she stops so quickly she almost trips.

"Oops, oh my gosh! I'm *so* sorry." Once the apology is out, she giggles.

Then she notices Brody.

She comes quickly to attention like a soldier. Her body is stiff and her uniform is impeccably ironed. It must be his new-hire—I can't imagine anyone else reacting like that to Brody.

I think her brown hair is about shoulder length, but I can't be sure because it's pulled back in a ponytail with her deputy hat over it. Her eyes are also hidden behind dark sunglasses.

"Sir, Sheriff Carter, I'm so sorry that I'm late." Although she seems sincere in her apology, I can tell she's stifling another giggle. "It— It's not like me," she goes on.

Her demeanor seems a bit odd, but I decide to give her the benefit of the doubt. She's new here, after all.

"Don't worry about it," Brody reassures her. "I understand things happen. I just stopped in to let everyone know that I'm headed up north to KC today, so I'll be out of radio range. If you need something, call my cell. But, as always, for most things you can check in with Daly."

Daly was originally hired as a receptionist, but over the course of her long tenure at the station, her role has expanded and she's now trained in dispatch. Brody always says the place would fall apart without her. I know he thinks of her as family.

"I also wanted to introduce you to Melanie Morris," he tells his deputy. "She's a good friend of mine who helps us out from time to time with…uh…special projects. Mel, this is Stella Ford, the newest member of our team."

Stella removes her sunglasses and offers me a handshake.

I suspect the reason Brody feels an urgency to introduce us is because as a newbie, she might need some home-cooked hospitality. And I'm okay with that; I also have a hard time making friends. So I vow to put in an effort with her.

"It's nice to meet you," I say, taking her outstretched hand.

As our palms connect, I hear a whisper inside my head.

Jamie.

But her words are so soft, they're indistinguishable. I suddenly wish I could read people by touching them rather than dreaming murders, because I would very much like some ethereal insight into just what there is to know about Stella Ford.

Brody gives Stella a few instructions and then addresses the entire office. As he's speaking, I move over to Daly and give her a quick hug. I haven't seen her in a while.

Daly nudges me and tilts her head toward Stella. *"It appears someone has met a man!"* she whispers. *"That sure didn't take long."*

I look at Daly in surprise. *"How do you know these things?"* I whisper back.

"The only time a woman is that happy is when a man is involved," she says. "She hasn't been this perky since she started working here!"

Having no experience in this area, I decide to contemplate Stella's adventurous sex life another time. It's far too early in the morning for *those* types of visions.

Then I remember Brody's words about Stella being self-conscious and having been teased at her last job. The person I just met seems more self-confident than self-conscious and, according to Daly, to be experiencing more titillations than teasing.

Daly shrugs as if to say it isn't her business and goes back to her work.

I turn my attention to the rest of the staff as Brody continues to instruct them.

Barney, Daly's son-in-law and the most recent recruit before Stella, is listening intently. He has the name, but this small-town Barney is no Barney Fife. *This* Barney is built like a grizzly bear and has the heart of a puppy. He recently finished his Academy training and Brody is slowly molding him into a street cop.

Barney's already become a good friend to Brody and will be a strong asset to the team once he's fully trained. His size alone would deter anyone.

And, unlike Barney Fife, I'm sure he carries more than one bullet.

Finally Brody is ready to leave. As I turn to follow him, I feel a tickle at the back of my neck. I look back to find Stella staring at me. Her expression makes me uncomfortable. I try to smile back, but something just doesn't feel right. Between that and the whisper from Jamie, I decide I'd better be on my guard with her.

But I'm reluctant to tell Brody something might be off about his new recruit. He might accuse my green-eyed monster of rearing its ugly head again. Oy!

CHAPTER 8

BRODY AND I GET IN THE TRUCK and finish our coffees. I marvel again that as competent as Daly is at running the station, she makes the worst coffee in the world. I love the woman, but since she doesn't even drink coffee, perhaps she shouldn't be the one to prepare it. I don't know why I'm dwelling on it, except that I love my coffee.

I haven't asked Brody what his business up in KC is. When it comes to his police work, I'm not accustomed to prying unless it somehow relates to a dream.

"I'm excited about our trip," I say brightly. "I haven't been out of Arrow Springs in a while."

Brody eyes me speculatively.

"You sure everything is alright?" he prods. "Is there anything *else* you haven't told me?"

Damn! He knows me too well.

There are a few things I haven't told <u>anyone</u>, I think. Aloud, I say, "Of course not."

Hopefully there'll be a time when I can tell Brody about Jamie, but that time isn't now.

"Maybe someday you'll feel comfortable enough to tell me everything," he replies, looking straight ahead out the windshield.

Seriously? Is he reading my mind now? I wonder if he knows exactly how well he understands me.

"Was that a question?" I ask him.

"No, it was me talking out loud hoping someone would be listening."

"Ha! You're the sheriff of Arrow Springs. You'd better hope *someone* is listening to you!"

"I'VE BEEN DOING A LOT of thinking about the first of these recent dreams," says Brody as we drive. "It's interesting that you felt sympathy for the person—for someone who will attempt, and possibly succeed in, committing murder. I wonder what the vision of the abused girl has to do with that—maybe that little girl is targeting her abuser."

I purse my lips noncommittally.

"But what I'm most concerned about," he continues, "is the kidnapping scenario. We both know from solving murders the level of evil that can come from an abduction. So the most pressing issue is to stop that from happening."

"I agree," I say. "And I'm so anxious to dive in. But I'm just not sure where to start."

"You know…" says Brody thoughtfully. "I hate to even say this, but—"

"What?" I demand.

"I mean, this is different in so many ways, but, well, your mother's killer also injected his victims."

I fall silent. I have no idea what to make of Brody's statement.

"How could my mother's murder have anything to do with any of this?" I ask. "Her killer is dead."

"It probably doesn't." He sighs. "It just seems like a big coincidence…and I don't like coincidences."

I stare at Brody, whose jaw is set as he stares straight at the road.

"So, what did you think of Stella?" He abruptly changes the subject.

Welcoming the new topic, I shrug. "It's too soon for me to have an opinion of her." I look away from him. "But Daly remarked she seemed especially perky this morning—said she might have had been with a man last night!"

Brody raises an eyebrow at me.

"Good grief, Mel! I certainly don't want to know about the private activities of my new officer. Why'd you have to put that picture in my mind?"

I let out a small giggle. "I'm sorry. It was Daly who brought it up—I have no idea about any of it. Come to think of it, though, I don't want those images in my head, either."

"What I do know," says Brody, serious again, "is that she has street experience, which is a point in her favor, especially since Barney doesn't yet. I want to start him off in the office handling the paperwork that usually ties me up for hours, and when he does go out, it's going to be with me so I can teach him what he needs to know. But I need someone else who can go out on a call on their own—especially if I need to miss a day or want to take a vacation. So that's why I hired her." He looks at me sternly. "No other reason."

"How do you feel about hiring a woman?" I ask.

"I certainly don't have any prejudice against working with a woman, if that's what you mean."

"I don't mean anything of the sort," I say. "I know you better than that. But the fact that you're defensive makes me wonder if there's some problem you *are* worried about."

Brody hesitates. "I guess I'm concerned about the other males—*or* females—in this town giving her any sort of grief. As I told you, her former commander said she has some confidence issues."

"*Ohhhh…*" I nod in understanding. "So you're concerned the 'cats' will get their fur ruffled over a newcomer, eh?"

I smirk, amused at how much of a problem this is for Brody.

"You aren't going to start that again, are you?" he says. "I hired a cop. I don't care if that cop is male or a female as long as he or she can do the job. I'm not even going to address that other subject—those *chasers*, as you call them—which you seem to find a way to jab at me often enough!"

I smile. "Well, I hope Stella works out for you," I say sincerely. "I know that running a small station, you've needed more good help and backup for a long time. So…what type of vacation are you thinking of taking?"

Brody shoots me a sideways glance. He's obviously on to the fact that I'm trying to keep the conversation going in order to clean up the strain on our friendship, which is entirely my fault, having acted like a jealous jerk. I really need to cool my jets.

"I'm not really planning anything," he says. "I just know I need a break now and then. Maybe a day to go fishing or just sleep in. Come to think of it, a day away from the office with no plans sounds great."

Is he saying he needs time away from me?

I can't let that thought fester too long. He has the right to take some time off just like everyone else. But what if it's to take one of the "cats" on vacation?

God, Melanie, you're pathetic!

"Hey, Mel, you seem to be off in your head a lot these days." He smiles. "I mean, even more than usual!"

"Sorry—I'm just thinking, that's all."

"Is there something else going on with you? You haven't been yourself lately."

Shit, I'm a twenty-five-year old virgin who's suddenly hot for her best friend—that's what!

Thankfully, he doesn't press the question.

We remain fairly quiet for the rest of the ride, sharing just occasional small talk, comments about the scenery along Route 69, avoiding the heavy stuff.

Brody drops me off at the center of town, near a plethora of shopping opportunities. There's an ice-skating rink, too, but I've never learned to skate. I wonder if Brody would try it if I suggested it. Of course, any entertainment plans will have to wait until the dream is solved.

I'm glad Brody asked me to join him. Not only am I enjoying our alone time doing something other than running, but I desperately need some art supplies. I haven't purchased any clothes in a while either, other than this pair of jeans. So I check out that little indulgence first. I end up with two more pairs of jeans, a couple of tops, and a light sweatshirt. That's my favorite go-to outfit: jeans and t-shirt with sneakers or flats. I never feel the desire or the need to dress up—except, of course, for my *slight* primping for Brody.

Next, I head to my favorite art supply shop. Since I don't get up here all that often, I grab several painting pads and canvases, to be ready for my newest dreams, as well as some paints and brushes. I have the clerk put the larger items into a handled shopping tote and I stow the smaller items in my mini-backpack.

I've never carried a traditional purse, but I'm also never without some supplies. I need to be prepared to sketch any time the need arises. I also like to feel that I have a good grasp on my belongings, and a purse doesn't offer that comfort. If someone were to steal a drawing, it would be a huge setback to deciphering my dream. I always take photos of my works as backup, but the originals provide so much more intensity of feeling, useful for revealing truths.

My bag also holds a spray can of bear mace, which Brody insists I carry. Imagine my eye roll when he gave *that* to me!

After exiting the store, I encounter a quaint little antique shop, which I've passed on previous visits but have never entered. I've always liked its name though: Gone But Not Forgotten.

The window display is perfectly arranged with a charming antique dining set. I admire the flatware's delicate vintage lace pattern. A bouquet of fresh garden roses sits in the table's center, obviously placed with care to avoid damaging the wood. I don't know much about antiques, but it's a very welcoming window.

Suddenly I feel a nudge—an idea of, *Let's go in and check the place out.* I know it's Jamie. She always guides me toward finding a good bargain.

I open the door and am greeted by a lovely woman with hair the color of a burnt orange sunset. Speaking with a slight accent, she introduces herself as the shop's owner, Alene, and lets me know she'll be around the store if I require any assistance. Then she leaves me in peace.

Feeling at home, I browse for what seems like hours. I don't wish to spend a lot of money, but if I find something I like, I'll buy it.

As I wind down my perusal, I check my phone. Brody has texted that he's finished, and I text him back with my whereabouts.

I've identified several items that I'd like to purchase or consider buying later. One definite is a glass angel that caught my eye. I envision hanging it from a small nail I'll hammer into the center of the wooden frame of my kitchen window. I have a special affinity for angels.

I head to the jewelry case for a final look there.

I'm just starting to wonder where Brody is, when the bell over the door chimes and there he is in all his glory. *Whomp.*

When I turn back to the jewelry case, it's like a smack in the face when an antique ring grabs my attention. It's so beautiful. I'm drawn to it like a moth to one of those bug zappers that people hang on their patios. Of course, I'd never use a zapper myself—it just seems cruel. I don't know where these thoughts come from sometimes.

The ring is hexagon-shaped with a round diamond in the center. Each side of the ring holds three smaller diamonds and a long rectangular emerald. Surrounding the stones is intricate filigree scrollwork. The ring is sparkling so brightly, I look up— almost in slow motion—to see if some sort of light is shining directly on it.

I find the shop owner staring at me and Brody trying to get my attention. This shakes me out of my spell, and I'm completely dumbfounded by what just happened.

Back to earth *again*!

Brody leans over to see what I've been looking at.

"Wow, Mel, that's a beautiful ring."

I feel a flush rise in my face. "It's very unique, but I don't know what pulled my attention so much. I don't even wear jewelry!"

"Maybe someday one of your many suitors will come here and get it for you," he says, obviously razzing me. The twinkle in his eyes that he gets when he's feeling mischievous is as blinding as the ring.

I must look forlorn because Brody takes my hand and turns serious. "That would look beautiful on your finger," he says.

I realize my hand is sweating and pull it away from his. He smiles but it doesn't quite reach his eyes. *Damn.* I keep doing things to make him think I don't like him.

By this time, Alene is behind the counter and her glowing green eyes are shimmering with what look like tears. But she quickly resumes a professional air.

"This ring has been here a very long time," she tells us, "and I can't seem to sell it. Every time someone is interested, they change their mind and move on to something else. I think it must be waiting for the right person."

"Well, unfortunately, that isn't me," I say. "I was quite taken with it, but I really have no need for a ring like this. It's beautiful, though, and I hope it finds a good home."

"I'm sure it will," she says. "Is there anything else I can help you with?"

I realize she must have noticed the glass angel I'm clutching.

"Yes, I'd like this, and a couple more pieces I wonder if you could hold for me."

"I'll need a small deposit to hold any items. Do you know when you'll be back to purchase them?"

"Oh, I want to pay in full. I was just thinking we could find somewhere nearby for lunch and then come back for them."

"Of course. Just let me cash you out." She smiles. "And if you're looking for a recommendation, I can tell you the best place in town for lunch. My daughter owns a wonderful diner within walking distance and I promise you won't be disappointed."

I look at Brody. "Does that sound good to you?"

"Absolutely!" he says. "I'm starved. Were you in this shop the entire time?"

"I did stop a few other places," I say. "Oh, and I left my bags somewhere. I think they're on the chair I want to buy. What time is it?"

"It's about one o'clock," he says, looking at his watch. "Which is probably why I'm starved."

"You're right. I didn't realize it, either." I turn to Alene. "You have a lot of beautiful items in your store."

"Thank you. My daughter and I adore antiquities. When we moved here from Ireland, we decided that we would open a shop and then later she would open a diner. We love it here, and you'll love her place, too. Let me tell you how to get there."

AFTER SETTLING UP with Alene, who also offers to stow my previous purchases, Brody and I easily find the quaint eatery. From the outside, it's a slim, silver-bullet-style diner like you'd see in the fifties. When we enter, I'm stunned at how beautiful it is. The whole interior is brimming with flowers. Some are potted and others are freshly cut in water. I'm reminded of the garden roses in the antique store window. Hanging from the ceiling are exquisite glass-winged fairies, strategically placed so that no one will knock into them.

The place is packed, which isn't surprising. A sign says to seat ourselves and I'm grateful we find a table by the window.

A striking waitress comes over. She has the blackest hair I've ever seen. The bright lights shining down on it make it appear almost blue.

"I'm Flora McConnell," she says in a sweetly melodic voice with a gentle lilt of Ireland. "Can I start you off with a beverage?"

Her accent indicates she must be Alene's daughter, but I never would have guessed. Their coloring is like night and day. Alene's eyes were the color of the grass in summer. This woman's eyes are sapphire-blue, not unlike another ring I glimpsed in the jewelry case. She appears to wear no makeup but her long eyelashes and thick brows make her eyes stand out even more. She is so stunning, I'm unable to break my gaze from her. Her eyes sparkle back at me in turn, as though we share a secret. I wonder if that's usual for her. She obviously doesn't know me—unless maybe her mother called to tell her we were coming.

Brody seems to notice the look we're sharing and remains silent, though I can see him taking in her beauty.

I seem to have the power to shut him up today, I marvel. *What an amazing new gift! Maybe I'll practice back home and see if I can work it on anyone else.*

Right then, Jamie decides to make the moment more awkward by inserting herself into my already messed-up mind.

I feel an especially intense tingle.

"She's very special," comes Jamie's voice. *"I think the two of you have a lot in common."*

This isn't the first time Jamie has spoken to me directly, but it's so rare, I'm momentarily speechless. And I'm quite sure I look as dumbfounded as I feel. As I try to work out what she's telling me, I take care not to appear too crazy to Brody and Flora.

"Don't worry, Mel. Things have a way of working themselves out."

It takes all my willpower to draw my attention from Jamie and address the woman in front of me.

"Um" is all I can manage without stuttering. "Could I get a glass of water with lemon?"

"Sure, would you both like that?"

"That'd be great," says Brody.

Still feeling awkward, I add, "I'm sorry—I don't mean to stare! It's just that this place is not at all what I expected from the outside. It's like stepping into a wonderland. Everything is gorgeous!"

Flora's face lights into a beatific smile. "Why, thank you! It feels so good when my customers appreciate the atmosphere I'm trying to create. When I bought this place, it was because I wanted something different. The flowers I grow in my small-but-beloved greenhouse and the fairies I make with blown glass in my workshop. I love being able to combine my various passions all in one place."

Well, that's one thing we have in common, I think to Jamie. *No, not the flowers or fairies. But we're both artists, just with different mediums.*

"I will tell you it's gorgeous," I say aloud. "I sure could use help with my garden! It's too bad you don't live closer to me—I bet you could do wonders with my unkempt yard."

First I couldn't speak and now I'm running at the mouth. I feel like she and I have known each other for a long time.

"I'm sure your yard isn't near as bad as you think!" She laughs. "Gardening is hard work, so you have to enjoy it immensely for the love to really shine through. I'd enjoy giving you some tips on that." She looks around the crowded diner and smirks. "Though maybe not today."

I smile.

"Hi, Flora." Brody finally cuts in. "I'm Brody. I believe we were directed here by your mother—from the antique store down the street?"

Flora laughs again.

"That was definitely my mum. She loves to brag about this little place. Sends over anyone looking for a good meal—or even if they look even slightly *ocras!*" At our confused looks, Flora giggles. "Oops—that means hungry in Gaelic. It's so hard to lose the language of home. Speaking of hungry, I better get back to work! I'll take care of your drinks while you look over the menu."

Once she's gone, Brody looks up at me. "It's amazing how the two of you seemed to really connect!"

"I know," I agree. "I feel like we're going to be friends."

"That's great." He tilts his head at me. "But I can't help feeling like something strange is going on."

I laugh. "Brody, do you know me at all? There's always something strange going on in my life."

We laugh together, acknowledging the truth of it.

Flora returns and places our drinks on the table.

"So, what brings you into town today? Are you local?"

"Actually, I'm the sheriff of Iroquois County," explains Brody. "My office is in Arrow Springs, but I had a few matters to take care of up here today."

I wonder if Brody is purposely throwing out his job as a warning. It seems a needless gesture, as Flora appears to be a very genuine person.

"We always welcome out-of-town law enforcement," says Flora. "But I won't ask what your business is, since I know that's none of mine. How about you, Melanie? What brings you to Kansas City?"

"The shopping, of course!" I laugh. "I needed to replenish my art supplies. I also bought a few items from your mother's antique store."

"Ohhh! Maybe I'll get to see some of your art sometime." Flora waves a hand around. "Especially now that you've seen mine! Do you have a card?"

As I rummage through my bag, I realize that Flora called me by name even though I never mentioned it. Did her mom tell her that, too?

"Let me take your order," says Flora, "so I can put it in to the cook. I stole her straight from Ireland, and she can whip up great American food or Irish dishes. You'll have to come for breakfast sometime. Our full Irish is not only delicious but filling."

I finally locate my card and hand it to her.

"I don't know what a full Irish is but I'd love to find out!" I say. "But this time, I think I'll stick with an American favorite: burger and fries. Well-done on the burger. Oh, and ranch dressing to dip my fries in. What about you Brody?"

"I'll have the same. But I'd like my burger medium-rare, please, and just ketchup for my fries."

"Sounds great," says Flora. "I hope you enjoy it. And if I get too busy to see you off, it was very nice meeting you both!"

Brody and I soon dig into our burgers, agreeing that the food is as wonderful as Alene promised. I have a feeling we'll be back here again. Someone else delivered the meal and the check, though, so I'm disappointed we won't get another chance to talk to Flora.

But suddenly she's beside me, just as Brody is already out the door.

"You have a very expressive face," she says. "Has anyone ever told you that?" She leans toward me conspiratorially and rests her hand on my shoulder. I feel an electric current run down my arm. "You should be careful he doesn't notice you're in love with him before you're ready to tell him."

Once the statement is out, she smiles and walks away.

"What was that all about?" Brody is beside me again.

Oh, god. I definitely need to watch my facial expression now. I put on a smile. "Oh, nothing. She just wanted to say goodbye."

Before heading home, we make our way back to the antique store and pick up my purchases, thanking Alene again for the recommendation to the diner. It's been a very nice day and as my thoughts wander, I fall asleep on the ride home.

Before I know it, we're at my house and Brody is gently shaking me awake. He helps me inside with my new treasures and I thank him for taking me along.

Then I think back to what Flora said about my being in love with him. *Am I in love with him?* I have no idea what love even feels like. And I have so much more to worry about right now than my love life.

Mel, I admonish myself, *you really need to pull your shit together.*

CHAPTER 9

THE DREAM CREEPS IN like fog, sliding mysteriously across the ground. There is nothing my subconscious can do to stop it.

I am a young girl reliving my own life. Except that it isn't my life. It's like a horrible remake of the life I was blessed with until my parents died. Almost like an alternate reality.

When the dream begins, I'm living with my grandmother, even though she clearly doesn't want me. I realize I'm the little girl from my previous vision whose life is filled with screaming and beatings. Again, I'm forced to relive them.

I keep wondering what I have done to make my one and only family member hate me.

My biggest mistake seems to have been being born. My grandma says no one else wanted a useless piece of garbage, so she was forced to take me in. Raising me is a huge burden, so I should just be grateful she puts up with me.

Grandma makes sure that the signs of abuse never show. Ever since Child Protective Services was called by what she deemed a "nosy neighbor," she never hits me in the face, instead brutally assaulting my arms and legs. I never wear shorts or skirts, or short sleeves.

I need some way to escape this harsh reality, if only in my own mind.

As I weep silently in my sleep, it feels like someone is hitting a fast-forward button.

I am now in my early teens, standing at the window of a small antique store, looking at a violin. It's the most beautiful thing I've ever seen. It calls to me.

It costs a small fortune, but I must have it. I somehow know this is the reason I've suffered so much and survived. That playing the violin will be my salvation. I imagine myself holding it in my arms and making beautiful music until the darkness that is my life disappears, leaving only light.

So I decide to get a job and save every penny I earn.

Grandma works weekdays until 5:30 and then she goes wherever she goes to get her fix. So she usually she doesn't come home until after 9:00 p.m., some days not till morning. Sometimes she's drunk or stoned enough to leave me alone, but other days she's not. Either way, I can secretly work before she gets home, and deal with her abuse afterwards.

I take an after-school job nannying for a family with two young children. The kids get home about the same time I arrive, so the timing works, and the parents pay me cash. If Grandma were to find out I was making money, she would beat me for every cent.

I've learned to hide everything from her. I stash my money under a loose floorboard in my closet and keep a huge stack of textbooks on top of it, which I know Grandma will be too lazy to lift.

I never tell my employers about my life. I'm good with the kids, so they don't probe too deeply.

Finally, the day comes when I'm ready to purchase the violin. The owner says she's seen me stare through the window at it and has known I'll be the one to have it. It turns out she's quite versed in the violin herself and she offers to teach me in the store after school. She obviously senses I need help. Thankfully the kids have karate twice a week, so I'm able to get them off the bus from school, drop them at their dojo, and pick them up after my lesson. It works out perfectly.

I leave the violin at the store between sessions at first. I don't want to risk Grandma finding it. If she knew I had something bringing me joy, she would surely destroy it.

But I want to practice more. I've indeed uncovered a special talent beneath my insecurities. So I take the violin to the home where I nanny and I practice while the kids do their homework. They tell me it's relaxing for them. Their mom, Mrs. Anderson, loves to listen when she can, too. Leaving my instrument at their house is the perfect solution to keeping my secret safe.

I play as much as I possibly can. The violin is my greatest love, because playing is the only time I'm able to fully escape from my pain and sorrow. I put everything I have into being the best musician I can be.

After several beatings for not finishing my chores at home due to my secret job and lessons, I can't take it anymore.

I REALLY can't take it anymore.

My mind turns to ways that I can kill Grandmother. I don't even care if I'm caught or go to jail. At least she'll be out of my life forever.

My only fear is that I'll lose my violin. And that fear is huge.

So, instead, I learn to fight back. And she doesn't like that one bit. She's getting older and I'm getting stronger.

One day she asks why I can never get my chores done, and I tell her I've started playing sports. She looks up and down my body and laughs. Then she starts hitting me because she thinks I'm lying—which of course I am. This beating will be the last she ever gives me. This is a promise I make to myself and one I absolutely plan on keeping.

I tell her that if she tries to touch me again, it will be the last thing she ever does.

I go to work the next afternoon, and I haven't worn the right clothes. One of the children notices a bruise—not just a bump-against-the-coffee-table bruise but a nasty, discolored violent bruise. I try to explain it away. Mrs. Anderson gently confronts me, asking if there's anything I want to tell her. I'm frightened, but this is my chance and I need to take it.

I tell her reluctantly about my home life. She tells me she was also abused as a child, which made the signs easier for her to spot. She tells me she never had anyone help her and that she wants to help me. We sit and cry together for a while. She offers to call CPS, but I beg her not to.

I try to explain my feeling that if I do not take care of this myself, I will never be able to move on from a life of abuse. She understands better than anyone else ever could.

Still, she urges me to get out of my situation before I'm severely injured. She offers to let me stay with them as a live-in nanny. But, she warns me, if my grandma comes for me, she'll have no choice but to send me back with her. I tell her that my grandma always complains about having to raise me, so I doubt that will be a problem.

I go home and pack my few belongings. My tiny wardrobe is from the Salvation Army, where I've gotten quite good at finding bargains. And I've figured out how to configure my garments into a variety of outfits to make it less obvious how little I have.

Being a teenager is hard enough, but when you have nothing and are trying to hide the signs of abuse, it's brutal. On top of the physical pain, I know I can't handle being mentally tormented by bullies, so I've done everything in my power to stay off of their radar at school. It isn't too hard—I'm virtually invisible.

I never talk to anyone. The abuse has made me shy beyond other kids my age. I try hard to seem normal, but I'm certainly not.

As I'm preparing to leave, I'm hit with worry about my grandma's reaction. As much confidence as I expressed in her not caring to come after me, I want to make absolutely sure that she NEVER bothers this loving family who's taking me in. They don't deserve that.

So I print out some photos of my bruises—which I've been documenting for a while, just in case—and write her a letter, assuring her there's more where these came from and threatening her not to come looking for me. Ever.

I lay it all out on the kitchen table and then, without looking back, I walk out the door of the only home I've ever known.

I feel a rush of joy at being free. It seems like a miracle. Growing up, I never knew there could be a life outside abuse. Now I know. And I relish it.

But as my outer bruises fade, inner turmoil rages on in my subconscious. I have brutal nightmares in which my grandma finds me and then beats me for leaving. Worse, I worry that I'll become like her and hurt the children I nanny for the same way she hurt me. But it doesn't take me long to realize that I could never be like her. No matter what has been done to me, my heart still carries love. I cherish the children in my charge as if they're my own. This family is all I have outside a lifetime of abuse.

With their help, I begin to heal.

The fast-forward button is hit again, and I've lived with this family for two years. I can't believe how much my life has changed in that time.

My new "mom" has instilled in me that I am not responsible for the horrible treatment from my grandmother. What she did to me was wrong in every way.

I've continued my violin lessons, practicing and playing every minute I can. I sit first chair at school and have performed solos in the annual concerts. After I receive the top score in the statewide music evaluations, my symphony instructor sends my name to a prestigious music school, where I'm granted an interview. Thanks to her and to my mom, who helps me apply, I receive a full scholarship to study there and do the one thing in life that makes me happy.

At just eighteen, I have everything I could ever want. I have a family who loves me, I'm living my dream of playing violin, and I'm set to attend a school that will allow me to do so for the rest of my life. Everything is perfect.

My family helps me move and gives me enough money for expenses until I get on my feet. As we cry and hug each other goodbye, I vow to show them how much I appreciate them. I wouldn't be living this dream without them!

I'm so excited. I can't wait for my first class to begin. I work hard and listen to every critique given to me by the instructors. I flourish. There is nothing in life that can take away the happiness I feel when I play my violin.

Except at night, when I'm alone in the dark and the memories continue to creep in through nightmares. So I sleep only when absolutely necessary. Sometimes I call my mom just to hear her voice and talk to the kids, who are getting so grown up.

I make a few friends in the city, but I don't care to party like they do. I saw so much of that with my grandmother, I'm afraid of ending up on the same destructive path she took. Plus, I'm still too shy to meet guys and have no desire to. So when I do go out, I drink soda or water, and I never let socializing interfere with my studies or practice time.

I'm determined to never take for granted the gift I've been given to go to this special place and become the best violinist I can be. So although my schedule is grueling, I love every minute of it and I maintain a 4.0 grade point average.

After about a year, I'm given a solo in a concert. It's the most exciting thing that's ever happened to me. But I fear my shyness won't allow me to perform in front of all those people. This isn't high school anymore.

I call my mom to tell her about the concert, and she laments that my dad isn't well and they're sorry they'll have to miss it. I ask her what's wrong, but she just says he'll be fine and that she wants me to go out and play with everything I have. I hang up feeling a deep seed of worry, but I can't let it overtake my joy. So I put it aside, deciding that I'll call them after the concert and maybe go home for a visit.

The concert is held in a large, ornately decorated auditorium. Heavy red curtains hang on either side of the stage and, looking out to the audience, I see that the seats match the curtains. Each row rises higher than the last, the first situated close to the stage, continuing up to the highest point in the balcony, which stretches all around the upper section of the venue. Embedded in the woodwork at the bottom of the mezzanine and up the steps are lights that twinkle as if filled with excitement waiting for the music to begin.

When I step forward to perform my solo, I'm more nervous than I've ever been. I wish my family was here. Giant butterflies flap so violently in my stomach, I feel like I'm going to wretch. And my hands and legs shake so uncontrollably, I wonder how I'll be able to play. I must find a way to calm myself.

I've been practicing meditation for just such a situation, so I breathe in deeply and look out over the crowd to center myself.

And that's when I see her.

She's in the back, just standing by one of the doors. I have no doubt who it is. I'd know her anywhere, just by the slight hunch of her shoulders and the way she carries herself.

The school advertised greatly for this concert, so she must have found out about it and traveled all the way here to attend.

I thought she must have forgotten about me. I prayed and prayed for that. But maybe she's known where I've been all along and has just been biding her time.

The fear I feel in this moment removes all the joy from my years without her. And yet, I can't let her ruin my performance. I've worked so hard for this!

I close my eyes and imagine myself in my apartment with the doors locked so no one can come in. I fantasize that I'm the only person on stage.

Then I start playing.

And there, in my music, I release all the years of pain and suffering I've endured. Every ounce of fear I feel in seeing her, I put into the piece. Every painful beating I endured goes into the music. All I feel is the violin in one hand and the bow in the other. I play until my fingers feel raw and I'm dizzy with emotion.

I can't hear the music—I can only feel. I feel my body swaying to the beat I feel in my heart. I sense the bow as it slides across the strings and then the notes slowly trickle into my body. They leak into every fiber of my being. The music seems to go on forever.

When the performance is complete, I stop swaying and stand in the hushed silence with my eyes closed.

Slowly I open them…

The crowd goes insane. Everyone leaps to their feet, roaring their approval, including the orchestra of my peers. Flowers land at my feet.

But I feel removed from everything happening around me. My feelings are everywhere at once.

I look out to the back of the audience. She is no longer there.

I AWAKE SHAKING from the intensity of what I just experienced. The music was so penetrating, I still feel it in my pores. I need to paint.

I go to the bathroom first and examine myself in the mirror. I look like hell. I—*she,* I correct myself—had so much sadness at the beginning of her life, but it seems like she made her way out of it. So how does this relate to murder?

I have no way of knowing who she is. The dream felt so much like she was me!

I splash my face to wake up and head into my art room. I know I will paint with the same passion I felt in the music.

First, I paint a girl who has a body covered in bruises and a face that looks startlingly like my own. Although I never saw her look in a mirror, this is how my brush was guided.

I didn't see any faces in the dream, or in my previous vision. Not even this girl's grandma. I saw only hands and arms as she inflicted beatings, and then a shadowy figure at the back of the auditorium.

I start another painting and completely lose myself. When it's done, it shows a large crowd of people gathered around an orchestra on stage. The girl is in the center, playing her solo. A spotlight is shining on just her and her violin, and it's the most beautiful thing I've ever seen.

I bring myself back to reality and look around the room.

It's filled with several paintings now, but I'm not sure how they're connected.

I look at the first painting of the hand with the knife. Could this be the girl's grandma, seeking vengeance? Or is it the girl once again feeling driven to murder her grandmother? If so, why now? And why is some sicko trying to kidnap the would-be killer? I'm trying so hard to understand.

Maybe the kidnapping dream is like last night's dream, not of the future but of the past. I can't begin to comprehend until I have more clues.

After snapping my usual cell phone shots of the canvases, I check the time and see that it's now 6:00 a.m.—almost late enough to call Brody and ask him to come over. But…I shouldn't. I'm relying on him too much. I'll wait until he's at the station and then go ask for help.

I take a long shower to calm myself and to kill as much time as possible. Once I'm dressed, I head downstairs and make toast. I don't feel like eating, but I need something to fill the empty hole inside of me. The toast tastes like cardboard and my coffee, like water. But at least it gives me a much-needed boost of energy. I'd better solve this mystery before I go crazy or starve.

I decide I need to talk this through with Brody. I want to bring the paintings but some aren't even dry yet, so I'll just show him photos I've taken. As I locate my car keys, I know he'll be seriously pissed at me for driving myself, but hopefully he'll forget about that when I tell him about the dream.

I MAKE MY WAY to the sheriff's office in my dad's trusty old VW Beetle. This little ride may not win any races, and I should have purchased a new car long ago, but it's one of my last connections to my parents and I can't bear to part with it.

I pull into the parking lot at about 8:00 a.m. Brody's truck is there alongside another car I don't recognize. I feel a moment of nerves about the backlash I'll take for driving, but I can't worry about it.

I enter the office and see Stella working at a desk. That must be her car outside. I peek behind her and see Brody on the phone in his office. I'll have to wait.

"Hi, Stella," I greet her cheerily. "How are you?"

I try to ignore the fact that even though Brody is on the phone his eyes are boring a hole into me. *Yikes, I really am in trouble!*

"Oh, hi—it's Melanie, right?"

I have a fleeting feeling she remembers exactly what my name is, but it's odd—sort of like the ideas Jamie puts in my head.

I nod. "How's the new job going for you?"

"It's great!" She smiles. "Much quieter than Kansas City. Just what I was searching for, as far as changing my life. I apologize about your name—I've met so many new people I'm having a hard time keeping them straight."

That feeling again…

"I was looking through some files Brody asked me to sort," she goes on, "and I came across the one about the big serial killer case in the area. It was you, right, who I read about helping catch him?"

So here it is: the reason for saying she didn't remember my name. The reason everyone in this town wants to know Melanie Morris.

"Yes, I gave the police information that helped them catch the killer," I say.

She tilts her head. "If you don't mind my asking, how did you know what to tell them?"

She's fishing for information, but since she has access to the police files anyway, I don't see any harm in giving her a bite.

"I don't know exactly what you've read or been told about me," I say, "but I dream murders before they happen."

She doesn't even bat an eyelash at this comment. So, in addition to knowing who I am, she already knows full well what I can do. Like many, she probably just wants to probe into the mind of a psychic.

I fill her in on the killer's MO and how, through my dreams, I had a premonition of him killing my mother. I look up at her then, showing her the pain in my eyes so she can see how traumatic it is to discuss this experience. It isn't just some party trick.

I continue to detail for her how Brody and I drove the streets searching—feeling—for the right roads, and then eventually found the old house I'd painted from my dream. I recount the killer's reaction and how Brody was forced to shoot him.

"Wow," Stella says, shaking her head. "That's an unbelievable story."

"Yes," I agree. "And back then, Brody was still a pretty new deputy. Not long afterward, he left to serve in the Marines before returning to the department here."

Her mouth lifts in a half-smile. "Does he know how you feel about him?"

My head snaps up. "Excuse me?" I glance surreptitiously at Brody to see if he heard her. He's absorbed in his phone call.

"Listen, Melanie, I'm a cop and I'm good at reading people. There is definitely something between you two. I'm just trying to figure out when you and Brody are going to realize it!"

This is now two people in two days who have commented on my feelings for Brody. But Stella also inferred that Brody has feelings for me. Is that even possible?

"What about you, Stella?" I ask, diverting the subject. "Is there someone special in your life?"

She hesitates, but then her words come out in a rush—as though she's been dying to talk to someone about it. "As a matter of fact, there is. I just met him but we had an instant connection. I'm usually very shy, but with him I feel like I'm a different person!"

"That's *so* nice!" I say. "I'm happy for you. Maybe we should all get together for dinner or something?"

I'm not at all into socializing, but in addition to demonstrating to Brody my commitment to befriending Stella, I figure this might be a good way to learn more about her and figure out why she has so many questions about something she already knows most of the answers to.

She looks a bit uncomfortable. "I don't know…he's kind of a loner type. I'll ask him, but I don't think he'll want to do it."

I shrug, somewhat relieved. "That's okay. It sounds like you're in a fairly new relationship, so if he's not ready yet that's understandable. Just keep it in mind for the future."

"I will." She smiles again. "And thank you for being so nice to me. It's hard to start a new job in a different town. I hope that we can be friends."

"It seems to me like we're already on the right track," I say genuinely. I glance behind her. "I see that Brody's free now. I'll talk to you again later?"

"For sure!" she says. "Bye, Melanie."

I knock on Brody's half-open door and he gives me the go-ahead to come in. His expression confirms that I'm still in major trouble.

"So," he says, crossing his arms. "It appears you and Stella had quite the conversation."

"We did," I say with feigned breeziness. "I know she can use new friends." I frown. "She's asking questions about my mother's murder, though. I know folks in this town talk and curiosity gets the best of most people, so I hope that's all it is with Stella. I'm giving her the benefit of the doubt."

Brody unfolds his arms and starts to speak. "Now—"

"I know you're going to ask how I got here," I interrupt, "but it was very important that I talk to you this morning."

Brody rises from his chair and walks around his desk. He goes past me and out the office door. When he looks out the window at my car in the parking lot, I wince. He comes back into his office and points sternly at the visitor chair. I don't feel like sitting, but the look on his face tells me I'd better.

"I'm sorry," I say. "I know you don't want me to drive. But, look, I'm here, all in one piece, and I have something important to tell you."

He doesn't say a word. He just goes back behind his desk, sits down, puts his hands in his hair, and then pulls as hard as he can.

I don't dare laugh, but it's pretty funny.

"Okay, Mel, go ahead and tell me just what's important enough for you to risk your life to get here."

"I had another dream."

"Please tell me it wasn't while you were driving!"

"Ha ha, very funny," I say. "I had to come right away because it might lead us to something." I'm being truthful, although I sound more optimistic than I feel.

At least I have his attention now.

"Why don't you tell me about it?"

I lay out the whole continuing saga of the abused girl.

"The concert was pretty large," I analyze, "but the dream didn't give me a location. I'm pretty sure it was near where she was living. I guess we could search all the major music schools in the world, but I don't know. I think we'd have a better chance of finding a four-leaf clover in a meadow at midnight. Why can't these dreams be more specific?"

I take out my phone and show him all the paintings, especially the new ones.

Brody stares at them and then back at me thoughtfully, as he usually does when we sort through my dreams together.

"I have no idea of timeframe or the name of the girl," I say.

"She actually looks an awful lot like you, Mel," he remarks.

"I know. In the dreams, I'm experiencing so much through her eyes, it really *feels* like me. I think that's why the face is mine."

I don't mention to him how much I feel like the girl is me, in a different lifetime or something. That would be over-the-top strange—even for me!

"I heard her playing," I go on. "It was so haunting and beautiful that I woke up crying. I'm so afraid for this woman. In last night's dream she was happy, but also fearful and trapped in the music. Please help me find her. I think I was seeing the past but something must happen in the future to make her change, maybe even kill."

Overcome with stress and emotion, I break into tears. As Brody rushes to close the door, I don't think he's angry with me anymore.

CHAPTER 10

THE DREAMS ARE COMING more frequently than ever. We must be getting close to the murder. I go to bed hoping against hope for a restful sleep, but the dreams have other plans for me. I'm again transported to an alternate reality, living a different life for the night.

THIS DREAM BEGINS at the end of last night's concert. I'm on the stage taking in the applause, looking at the blank spot where the old woman once stood.

I'm not sure what to do next, so I look to the maestro for direction. He bows to me with a flourish. Following his lead, I curtsy to the crowd as they rage on. I don't realize tears are running down my face until someone hands me a tissue.

One of my dear friends in the orchestra gently touches my shoulder and smiles. In her eyes I see a glimmer of tears, and it's in that moment I realize how much my performance impacted not only me but everyone around me. Everyone on stage lines up to congratulate me. Meanwhile, the crowd continues their revelry, not wanting to let go of this moment.

The maestro is the last to come to me and the look on his face says everything. He's ecstatic with my performance. I know this is the beginning of something important. It's the most exhilarating feeling I have ever experienced.

I never see the old woman again after the concert. Who knows what happened to her. Maybe she was just some kind of hallucination; I can't be sure. But I do know that seeing her gave a power to my music it might otherwise not have had.

After that solo, I'm invited to play at surrounding arenas. It feels otherworldly. My life has changed so much in just a short time. I still speak to my family, but with so much traveling I don't have time to see them. I miss them so much. I tour a variety of cities accompanied by the orchestra. This includes the maestro, who becomes quite enamored with me.

I'm not sure about starting a romance, though. I've never been with anyone, and he's much older and more experienced. Plus, between my musical talent and my innocence, I fear he's not seeing who I really am inside.

But let's just say he's very convincing. We date for a long time. But it isn't until our wedding night—after quick nuptials in a small chapel—that we consummate our relationship.

I wanted to have a larger ceremony and invite my family, but he convinced me there wasn't time.

Now we're in the wedding bed. I've always been afraid to cross this line. But the fact that he wants me in this way makes me feel very special. When I'm onstage many people look at me like I'm special, but this is so different. He looks at me like I'm a princess in a fairy tale. I think I will never be happier than in this moment.

But I'm still hesitant. Seeing my reluctance, he comes to me. As he gazes into my eyes, I believe he loves me as he has no other.

He gently removes my clothes and lays me on the bed. I watch as he undresses himself and am shocked at the sight of his manhood.

Sensing my anxiety, he soothes me with sweet words. He is so patient and understanding, knowing this is my first time being loved. He kisses my mouth gently and then moves to my neck. Chills cover my body as it fills with new and alarming desires. Tension is building.

He continues to prepare me for what I know is coming. He puts his hand between us and touches me where no one has touched me before. I try not to jump. I want him, but I fear learning more of him tonight.

There are only a few moments of sweetness before he decides I'm ready and he can't hold back anymore. He gently settles himself between my legs.

His invasion is slow at first. I feel the first bite of pain as he breaks the barrier of my virginity. I hold back a scream so he won't think less of me. But it hurts and I wish for him to stop.

He can't control his fervor, though, and his speed increases. I wonder when this will end, but his pounding of my body seems to go on forever. I assume this is how things are. When he finally empties his seed deep within me, he falls fast asleep.

Never before in my life have I felt loved. So despite the pain in my body, my heart feels full.

Our lovemaking improves the longer we're together and the more instruction he gives me. I want love so badly, I give him everything I have. It's all-consuming.

My dreams are coming true. I have everything I've ever wanted. I've come from nothing and I've made something of myself. I'm finally free, finally able to feel the love I never had growing up.

I AWAKE SLOWLY, clinging to the feeling of being loved, and of feeling wanted. It's something I also yearn for, and now I've gotten to experience it—at least partially.

I'm forced to wonder what has happened to this woman to make her want to kill—or for someone to kill her, maybe. She seems to have everything in the world. She has someone who loves her and wants to spend his life with her.

But a worry niggles in the back of my mind.

I can't help feeling that something's off. For example, I find it odd that she keeps in touch with the family who rescued her, but she never mentions seeing them. Has it not been possible with all the concerts and travel? And why didn't the maestro want them at the wedding?

I enter my art studio. What I experienced feels so private that I don't feel called to paint it. But I must create *something.*

When I'm done, the painting is of what I know is the maestro, but all I could pull were his eyes. And it's as though they're staring at me. The expression is hard to describe. You would think it would be desire, which I saw during intimacy, but it's not sexual. It's a different type of yearning, underlaid by what I fear is anger. It makes me shiver.

As usual, I feel a need to shower. But this time it's to wash off the sensations of lovemaking rather than blood. As I scrub down my body with a loofah, I think about all the different paintings, racking my brain for what clues this dream has revealed.

CHAPTER 11

WHAT'S THE PURPOSE of all of these complex dreams? Brody wonders on his drive to work. *They're unusual, even for Mel.*

His two-way radio crackles, interrupting his mental musings.

"All units, we just received a 9-1-1 call about a major accident with possible fatalities along Route 91, near Sloan's Creek," reports Daly.

Brody forces aside his thoughts of Mel to focus on what's happening right now. As he races to the scene, his mind turns to the families of potential victims, praying for as few tragedies as possible.

The site is on a country road a few miles outside town, an area Brody knows well. When he arrives, he's shocked to see all the first responders standing around looking confused and disorganized. Stella is one of them, apparently quick to the scene and talking with a deputy from the next county over, who must have heard Daly's dispatch as well. Brody quickly turns off his truck and jumps out, making his way to the crowd who has gathered around…*nothing.*

"Just what the hell is going on here?" he asks.

"I don't know, boss," says Stella. "I heard the call and headed straight over. I arrived at the same time as Deputy Tommy Lee Tucker from Grants Landing, and we searched the entire area. There's nothing: no tire tracks, no vehicle fragments. We don't see anything off toward the creek, either."

Watching even more sheriff and emergency units arrive, Brody scratches his cheek. "I don't understand. Where did the original phone call come from? Daly must have a record of that."

Brody peers down into the ravine where he knows the creek is but sees only a cover of trees and tall-growing grass. If a car went down there, he should see tracks and broken branches. Still, they have to investigate thoroughly.

He tries to contact Daly on the two-way, but he gets no response.

He tries again.

And again.

"I'm going back to the office to see just what the hell is going on around here," he tells Stella. "Stay here with Deputy Tucker and re-comb every inch of the area. You're gonna have to go down there to make sure there's nothing."

"I understand, boss," she says. "You know, this is mighty strange, but I'm sure we'll get to the bottom of it."

He climbs back in his truck and speeds straight for the office.

As he pulls up to the station, Brody sees Daly's car, but the place looks otherwise deserted. Every available unit has gone out to investigate the fatal traffic accident. Any not nearby would be running regular patrols up and down the rural roads of the Arrow Springs area. Brody feels the hairs on the back of his neck stand up. This only happens when something bad is going down, and he gets the feeling this is shaping up to be a *very* bad day.

Brody pulls out his pistol—something he almost never does, especially at his own sheriff's station. He puts his ear to the door and listens but doesn't hear anything. He enters the office slowly.

The lights are on, but the place is vacant.

Daly is the one who makes sure everything is up and running in the morning. She's also the one in charge of regular dispatch and disseminating emergency calls. Brody computes that she would have been alone at the office for about an hour since sending out the call.

The station is set up in a large square with two offices on the left, the closest of which is Brody's. The other is for interrogations, with its two-way mirror viewable only from Brody's office. Due to the offices' shared outer wall, from the station interior, you'd barely know the interrogation room was there.

This office needs some serious redirection, realizes Brody. *The interrogation room should be at the back of the building and not require everyone to crowd into MY office to view it. If we ever used it, that is.*

Brody shakes off his musings as he continues his search. The right side of the main room is lined with four desks, the first belonging to Daly, which has all the dispatch equipment. Daly's sweater has slid from her chairback to the floor next to it. Another bad sign. Daly is a stickler for neatness and would never leave anything lying around like that. The second desk is Barney's, which is also impeccable, and the third now belongs to Stella. The fourth is stocked with office supplies and topped with paperwork that needs to be filed. But it's fairly clean as well, thanks to Daly.

Beyond that is a set of bathrooms to the left and, to the right, a small gated evidence room. He supposes that in a larger operation, the gated area would be used to secure drugs or guns collected during a case, but here it's used to store extra bathroom and cleaning supplies, so it's generally left unlocked. However, the door to the storage area inside the cage—used for cold case files and solved investigations such as Mel's mother's murder—is kept locked at night. Daly would have unlocked it upon opening the office. The station also has two holding cells in the basement, each with a toilet and a small cot.

Brody hears a sound outside the front door and braces himself for trouble. Then he hears Barney's voice calling out softly. He exhales a lungful of air he didn't even realize he was holding.

"Damn, Barney—you scared the shit out of me!" he whispers.

At least Barney's learned not to come in fully cocked and amped up, he thinks. For that, Brody's thankful.

"Sorry, boss. I was east of here when I heard the dispatch. I figured plenty of units will respond to the accident, so I thought Daly might need some help at the office."

Such a good son-in-law and diligent cop, thinks Brody, scanning the abandoned office as he speaks softly to his youngest deputy.

"Good thinking, Barney. I appreciate that. The problem is I don't know where she is. Her sweater is over on the floor, but don't touch it! As a matter of fact, don't touch anything. Just follow me."

Heading to the back of the office, they spot one of Daly's loafers lying on its side by the filing and supply desk. A pit of dread hits Brody's stomach. They must find Daly and fast.

He signals to Barney and they quickly check both bathrooms. *Empty.*

"Where the hell is she?" Barney whispers.

That's when Brody hears it. A light knocking sound—so faint, he'd probably have missed it if he weren't on high alert. It seems to be coming from the storage room inside the evidence cage. He opens the gate, which squeaks loudly, adding to the tension, and heads straight for the storage room. That's when he sees it's been zip-tied to the shelf next to it, essentially locking it from the outside. There's no longer any doubt about foul play.

He turns to Barney, who has silently kept pace with him. He wonders how someone so large can make so little noise.

"Barney! We need to get this door open right away."

Instead of reaching for a tool, Barney grabs the door and wrenches it open, snapping the zip ties in two through sheer force. Shocked at Barney's strength, Brody recalls Barney once using his brawn to save someone else he loves—Daly's daughter, Molly.

Daly is lying on the floor with her hands and feet bound. She appears to be unconscious—or worse.

"Get on the radio," Brody commands Barney. "We need paramedics, now!"

"You hold on, Daly," Brody says, checking her over.

Thankfully, she appears to be breathing.

"We're getting you help," he continues. "Do you hear me? And rest assured we will find out who the hell did this to you."

Brody doesn't think he's ever been this angry and panicked at the same time. The fact that she hasn't moved since they burst through the door is disturbing. She must have used up her last ounce of energy banging for their attention and then passed out as soon as she knew help had arrived.

Brody calls out to Barney to get the camera and photograph everything, from Daly's sweater on the floor, to her shoe, to the zip ties. Then he tells him to check if the front door locks have been tampered with. Barney informs Brody that they haven't; whoever did this must have come in after the emergency call went out.

"Check it for prints anyway," Brody says. "And the padlock, too, even though I touched it."

As Barney documents the crime scene, Brody fetches gloves so he can remove Daly's binding without destroying evidence. But first he asks Barney to photograph her.

"I'm so sorry, Mom," Barney pleads, quickly taking shots from various angles. "This'll only take a minute. You know we have to do it." He pauses. "We *have* to catch who did this."

Leaving Daly bound as he waits for his deputy to finish tests Brody's resolve as well. Daly is his friend. More than a friend, she's family. And as her boss, it's his job to protect her. He feels that somehow he failed.

Brody banishes the thought—he has no time for regrets. Once Daly is unbound, he carefully bags the zip ties that had held her wrists and ankles. He doesn't move her, as there's no way to know what injuries she's sustained.

Hearing a commotion at the front door, Brody peeks out to see Flora standing in the entrance way.

Flora? This is the last thing I have time for right now! What the hell is going on around here?!

Pretending not to have seen her, he turns his attention back to Daly.

Daly is still unconscious when the ambulance arrives—a returnee from the non-existent accident scene. The EMTs check her vitals and find a large bump on the back of her head.

They administer oxygen and brace her neck before loading her onto the gurney.

By this time Stella has arrived back at the office and Barney has placed a call to Molly. The office is anything but empty and quiet now; *everyone* is returning from the non-existent accident scene trying to find out just what the hell happened. It's chaotic, and Brody still can't spare a moment to talk to Flora—though he's seen her try to get his attention several times.

She finally approaches him. "I need to talk to you, Brody," she pleads. "It's important."

"I'm sorry, Flora," he says. "I've got a mess on my hands here, and I really don't have time for anything right now."

"You need to find time," says Flora, "because I think Mel is in trouble."

Brody freezes. "Why? What's happened?"

Flora looks uncomfortable. "I'd rather not get into it here, but I think you should call her right away and find out if she's okay."

Eying her speculatively, Brody grabs his phone and calls Mel. *Voicemail.* His adrenaline spikes. Mel always answers his calls. He tries again. Same thing.

He puts down the phone and grabs Flora's shoulders. "Tell me what you know," he demands. "Now!"

Flora backs away from him. "I promise I will. But I think we should go look for her. I can tell you on the way."

Brody looks around the office. Could the issue with Mel be connected to all of this? It seems like a stretch. But…

He looks back at Flora and then barks at Stella that she's in charge. He runs to a cruiser and motions Flora to the passenger seat. She has some explaining to do.

"How did you find me, anyway?" he asks as he floors the accelerator, sending the car screaming out of the parking lot onto the main road, sirens blaring.

Gripping the door handle tightly, she glances over at him. "At the diner, you told me you were a sheriff headquartered in Arrow Springs."

Okay. One mystery solved.

"So what is it that makes you think Mel's in trouble?" he demands.

Flora hesitates.

"Seriously?" shouts Brody. "You lure me out of my office during a shitstorm, and now you're clamming up? Spit it out, already!"

Brody rarely loses his temper but right now he feels justified.

"Okay, okay." Flora takes a deep breath. "I have psychic abilities."

Flora pauses. She's probably waiting for Brody to argue or burst out in laughter, he guesses. But he knows better. He glances at Flora sideways but keeps his eyes on the road, still driving like a madman towards Mel's house.

"Go on!" he snarls.

"I— Uh…events in my life have made it ne-necessary to keep my gift a secret." Flora pauses as the car jerks over a pothole. "But when you came to the diner, I felt Melanie might be psychic as well. Plus, I don't usually get involved unless I fear someone's life is in danger."

Flora falls silent.

The entire car is silent, except for the screaming wail of the siren.

Flora seems like she's still waiting to be ridiculed, but all Brody can think about is her last statement.

"You're right about one thing," he finally shouts above the roar of the siren. "Mel is psychic."

Flora nods. "I'm quite relieved she's told you about it."

"Actually, her secret is a lot less private than yours!" he says. "She dreams murderers' intentions and she—*we*—work together with the sheriff's office to stop killings before they happen."

Flora appears stunned. "Wow, I…I can't wait to hear more about it."

"So," Brody asks, "did you have a dream about Mel?"

"My abilities are different," explains Flora. "I get a read on things through touch. This time, though, I did have a vision. I'm guessing because that's Mel's gift."

Brody glances in the rearview before replying. "Since knowing Mel, I've seen a lot of strange things. I have to wonder if you two were meant to meet so you could help her in some way."

Still gripping the door handle, Flora pauses. "You may be right. Of course, I'm still hoping she's safe at home and has just turned off her phone or something."

"I hope the same thing, Flora." Brody shakes his head. "But although I'm no psychic, I had a feeling this day would be bad, and so far it's just gotten worse and worse."

CHAPTER 12

As soon as they come screeching up in front of Mel's, Flora urges Brody to let her take over.

"If I'm able to touch things first, I can get a better reading. Because if you've touched it, I may pick up on what you're feeling, and that won't help us find Melanie."

Brody eyes her. "I won't touch anything, but we need to follow policy. I—and this gun—are going in first."

Flora begrudgingly agrees, but there's something she must know.

Before Brody can unholster his gun, she leans in and hugs him. She's immediately overwhelmed by the strength of feeling coursing through his taut body. Worry for Mel is the most prominent, with concern for Daly and their own safety running a distant second and third. The morning he's had has obviously taken its toll. She briefly worries that if Mel *is* in trouble, he won't be at one hundred percent to help her. Then she picks up on a deeper feeling in the recesses of his mind…but she decides to let it go. It's not something she feels the right to delve into.

Brody pulls away from her.

"What was that for?" he demands. "You getting some kind of 'read' on me?"

"Actually, yes," she retorts. "Have you forgotten what you brought me along for? Besides, in most cases, a hug calms a person, and if anything is wrong here, you'll need to be relaxed." She winks. "And don't worry: your secret is safe with me."

"Secret?" Brody pulls at his hair. "Are you talking in riddles now? How about we save the hugs until after we find Mel?"

"Fine!"

"Good!"

As Brody steps away from Flora, he looks at her as if she's taken something from him. She's slightly amused at his consternation, before the reality of the situation hits her again.

The main reason she hugged Brody was to find out the kind of person he is. Despite his understandable concern for Mel, she was struck by his underlying bravery and limitless strength. His is a humble kind of strength she's never felt before—one that exudes a tough exterior but is warm inside. Something so much a part of him, he might not even recognize it. She knows it will be enough.

Flora briefly feels envious of Mel—that she's able to share so much with Brody and everyone else in Arrow Springs. She wishes she had someone she could share with.

But right now she needs to focus on finding Mel.

Immediately!

As they approach the front door, everything appears normal.

Brody pulls his gun and levels it. The door is unlocked—which isn't strange in a small town like Arrow Springs, but is a bit unusual for Mel. He eases the door open, looking from side to side. He makes his way into the foyer, calling out for Mel, but is met by an eerie silence. After "clearing" the area, he nods to Flora, who slips in quietly behind him.

Flora takes an immediate liking to Mel's house. The first thing she notices are the beautiful paintings hung on the walls. Mel mentioned being an artist, but Flora could never have imagined her new friend being this good. She feels a strong desire to thoroughly explore each piece, but obviously there's no time.

They search the first floor. Flora feels nothing as she touches several items. Then they head up the stairs.

Flora senses Brody's panic rising.

After Brody clears the master bed and bathroom, Flora enters, desperate to find something they can use to find Mel. Brody's mounting anxiety makes Flora feel like she's torturing him by not being able to tell him anything.

"She definitely took a shower," she finally says.

"Did you see that in a vision?"

"No, the walls are still wet."

She looks up at Brody with immediate remorse. She's trying to help, but her witty yet perhaps-too-swift comments are obviously not doing it for him right now.

"I'm sorry. I know I can be sort of a smartass."

"Sort of?" Brody raises an eyebrow. "But I think this *is* an important spot. Mel would never have left it such a mess. There may have been a struggle."

"Can I have a minute alone in here?" asks Flora. "I may be able to get a reading off something."

"I don't know…" Brody hesitates. "I need to preserve any fingerprints."

"But I *have* to touch things to have any hope of finding out what's happening," pleads Flora. "What do you want me to do?"

Brody quickly tugs at his hair. "Aww, hell. Go ahead."

Flora walks around the bathroom, touching potential sources: the countertop, the mirror, the shower. She knows her desecration of the crime scene must be killing Brody, but she appreciates his remaining silent. She bends down to pick up a towel from the floor—and freezes.

Bingo!

"A man was here," she says. "I can't see him; I can only feel the presence he's left behind. He took Mel, but I don't know where or why. I see him put a cloth over her face and then use a needle to give her a shot of some sort. I can strongly sense Mel's fear."

She looks at Brody and sees that his face is pure white.

"Wh-What?!" He seems barely able to get the words out. "Mel—she had a dream about a kidnapping. A kidnapping just like that. We assumed it was about a stranger…this woman she's been dreaming about. But apparently *she* was the intended victim."

Flora's own breath catches in her chest. "Oh my god!"

"I'm going outside," says Brody, jumping into action. "I have some investigating of my own to do!"

He runs past her down the stairs and Flora follows him outside to the cruiser. He's obviously in full cop-mode now.

Brody grabs the radio and she hears him call for all units to begin canvassing the neighborhood—something about a painting service. He then puts out an APB for a stolen van.

Flora realizes she's underestimated Brody's abilities, just as he underestimated hers.

Brody scans the houses next to Mel's. He sprints toward one that appears freshly painted and rings the doorbell several times. No answer.

Clawing his hair again in frustration, Brody runs back to his cruiser and grabs some items out of the trunk, including a camera, gloves, and evidence bags.

He carefully checks the lock on the front door.

"There doesn't seem to be any sign of forced entry," he concludes. "I'm going around to check the windows and back door. You can wait here if you want."

"I'll come with you if that's okay," says Flora, now more than a little scared.

"Sure. Just don't damage any evidence. In other words, don't touch anything else."

Flora doesn't reply—because she knows she can't promise that. She'll do whatever she must to find Melanie.

Walking around the house, Brody points to a window he says has been smoothly pried open. Below it, in the dirt, is a footprint.

Brody snaps a photo of it and then calls the office again. Flora hears him directing his listener to gather what's needed to come make a cast of the shoeprint, to determine the size and style.

Flora knows there's a faster way.

She steps into the footprint.

"Stop!" shouts Brody. "What the hell do you think you're doing?! You just stepped on the only piece of hard evidence we have to help find Mel."

Flora is already in a vision and doesn't process what Brody is saying. She doesn't even realize that she has begun speaking. But apparently Brody does, because he stops yelling and starts listening.

"I see a place that looks like the inside of a barn," she says. "There are items hanging on the walls—most of them sharp and dangerous. I think the man intends to take Mel to this barn, or whatever it is…but I can't tell where it's located."

As she comes out of the vision, she looks at Brody.

He grabs his hair and pulls it as hard as he can. She fears he's about to lose it.

"I can't believe you just did that!" snaps Brody, stepping past her. "Stay here and don't touch anything. I need to research barns."

"That's no way to talk to someone who just helped you!" Flora calls after him. "You wouldn't even know to look at barns if I hadn't stepped in the footprint."

Brody stops and turns back around.

"You have me there," he says. "Let's go."

Flora knows Brody is only behaving this way because he's frantic about Melanie, especially now, with her murder dreams pointing to her own kidnapping.

They may have little time left.

CHAPTER 13

I TRY TO OPEN MY EYES but the pain in my head is excruciating. I can't figure out exactly what's happening. I try to remember the last thing I was doing, but thinking makes me nauseous. I close my eyes and try to move my arms, but they feel heavy and sore.

Everything feels in slow motion. It takes a while for the fog to clear from my mind. Fear creeps in as I start to remember…

I had just taken a shower and was feeling peaceful. Last night's dream was more positive than my usual: *Beautiful music… lovemaking…* But as I was drying off, I saw something out of the corner of my eye. I turned to look, and someone was there—a man. He put something over my mouth. It tasted horrible. Then I felt a sharp prick in my arm before I passed out.

I'm now fully aware and scared out of my wits.

And naked.

This is exactly like the dream I had about the kidnapping, I realize. *Only this isn't happening to someone else—it's happening to me!*

I hear movement and pray that if I keep my eyes closed, the kidnapper will think I'm still unconscious.

"Bitch, I know you're awake. I'm well aware of how long the drug lasts. I gave you just enough to keep you out until I could get you tied up and ready."

Tied up! Did he say tied up? I'm consumed by pure panic.

I try to sit up and realize I can't move. I'm bound to a cold steel table with my arms affixed to handles up top and my feet secured to the bottom, my legs spread.

My thoughts run wild.

My throat is dry and very sore. Probably from whatever chemical he used to knock me out. It may have been chloroform but that really doesn't matter much.

When I speak, the words come out in a croak. "Who are you?"

"You suck at being a psychic," he says. "That is, *if* you truly are one. I've heard all the stories, but if you're for real, you'll know exactly who I am. Let's see if I can look into your eyes and see you know true fear."

He leans in so close, I can smell his breath. It reeks of bad coffee and even worse alcohol, all mixed with a lack of brushing. My stomach rolls.

Most horrific, though, is looking into the blackest eyes I've ever seen. I have a strange feeling that I *do* somehow know this man. But I also know that I've never met him before. Because I *would* remember.

"You want to know who I am?" he goes on. "Well, here's a hint: You remember that killer who took out all the women along old Route 66 and I-44? I'm sure you do. Well, that man *wasn't* your pal Stan Harris."

He bursts out laughing.

My breathing is heavy and deep. My lungs burn from fear. I'm not thinking clearly. I know that Stan Harris killed my mother; I have zero doubt of it. I also *know* that her killer, the man Brody shot, was the Route 66 murderer.

The psycho laughs and laughs.

He may be having a wonderful time, but I'm sick.

He finally stops.

"Oh, I apologize for being rude." He smirks. "I need to introduce myself. My name is Pete Decker. I already know who you are, sweetie, and the only reason I'm telling you *anything* is that you're gonna die anyway, and *I* want to be the last thing you see, know, and feel."

My terror spikes.

I want to fight him, but my limbs are not only bound, but they're still unresponsive from the drugs. I have no way to run and nowhere to go.

I try to scream, but I can barely get a whisper out of my dry mouth.

Why does he want to kill me? What am I missing?

I hear him talking again, and at least talking is better than killing.

"So, you wanna know how I *know* your man Stan wasn't the serial killer? It's 'cause it's me! Yup, yours truly, I'm the *real* 'Freeway Freak' and 'Parking Lot Liquidator' and all the other cute nicknames the media gave me. God, I loved that!"

What the heck is he saying? Could I have been wrong about who killed my mother? No way on earth.

My thoughts are ravaged and I have no answers.

His mouth lifts in a twisted grin. "You know, I've killed a shitload of women in my life and I've enjoyed every minute of it. But, sweetheart, I think I'm going to enjoy our little time together the most."

I come out of my repugnant reverie and see that whoever this guy Pete is, he moved away from me while I was ruminating. But now he turns to come back; flashing me that sick smile again.

He's carrying some sort of bag. He gently lays it on the table and I shiver to know what's in it.

I don't have to wait long.

He unfolds it to reveal some very nasty instruments—tools I know won't be used to build anything. In the bottommost pit of my stomach I know they're going to be used to tear me apart, piece by bloody piece.

I let out a blood-curdling scream.

"Please, oh please!" I start to beg.

All rational thought leaves my mind as terror takes over. I know he relishes my outburst, but I can't hold my emotions at bay.

I scream and I scream, until I have almost no voice left.

God! Oh, dear God! I pray. *Please don't let this happen to me. I don't want to die…not like this! Oh, God!*

He just calmly lays out his tools, like a surgeon preparing for a complex procedure.

The fact that he doesn't seem worried that someone might hear me raises my fear to a whole new level.

Tears flow freely down my face. He hasn't even cut me or burned me or raped me or whatever he's going to do to me yet, but I can feel myself going into shock.

He sees it, too.

He douses me with ice-cold water—which he apparently has on hand for just such a purpose. I'm jolted back to reality and to looking into those evil black eyes. I try to scream again, but now nothing at all comes out.

"Welcome back, bitch. I need you awake and aware, screaming and feeling pain. I'm going to hurt you and hurt you until you can't stand it anymore, and then I'm going to fuck you. And when I'm done with that, I'm going to hurt you some more. I'm going to have plenty of time because lover boy—you know who lover boy is, right? I see you do. Well, he and the entire local sheriff's station are going to be so busy trying to figure out who whacked the bitch who works at the station house that they aren't even going to know you're gone until it's way too late."

Now I'm frantically trying to process who the hell he's talking about "whacking." I don't want anyone who works at the station to be hurt.

When he continues his monologue, things start to click.

"My new bitch girlfriend who works there isn't going to say shit to your boyfriend because I fucked her fat ass so good she's practically in love with me. Once I'm done with you, I may go back and get her. This time she's gonna pay more attention to what *I* want. I could have done anything I wanted to her. It wasn't such a problem to fuck her because she was as desperate as shit. Who the hell goes fishing with a guy she doesn't even know and then spends days letting him have his way with her?"

As he speaks, he leans down and touches my face seductively with his hands. I shudder.

"You see, bitch, I'm a planner. Getting to this point with you was always the main goal. But I had to put all the little soldiers in a row first."

He looks down and caresses his tools again, examining one that looks like a torch of some sort. My panic is unspeakable.

"Getting a van to carry you away in was just the beginning of my master plan. When I got to town, I started casing your place. Painted your neighbor's house, to provide a cover story for today. But I also got to watch you for days. You and running boy." He laughs, seeming to enjoy the sound of his own voice. "What a hoot watching the two of you together."

I feel sickened at the thought of him spying on me and Brody. Then I realize he's still talking.

"Next I cased out the sheriff's station and overheard Stella and the boss man talking about her being a new recruit. I knew she'd be the perfect mark. What an easy stooge."

I get the feeling he's telling me all this to boost his own ego—and also frighten me more than I already am, if that's even possible. He continues as if I'm not even here.

"All I had to do after that was trail her to her favorite fishing store, and my whole plan fell into place. Bitch is all messed up by men thinking she's fat. Ha, what a crock. Told her I was a trucker passing through—I *did* used to be one before spending time in the can. Then after I schmoozed her with flattery and got her worked up, her mouth ran like a faucet. She told me everything about how you helped the police to catch Stan and why they pinned him as the serial killer."

Despite being paralyzed by drugs and fear, I'm now interested to see where he's going with this story. I'm still dying to know, who the hell was Stan, and how was he not the killer?

"She didn't know much about your psychic ability," he goes on, "which I admit was disappointing. But she was extremely helpful in setting up this little sting today so I could grab you with no problems. Told me what time everyone arrives at the station and who would be alone and when. Of course, she was too sexed up to realize what all my questions were about."

Alone…who was alone…and what did he do to them?

"And now…" he says, "I'm gonna have the same kind of fun with you that I had with her. It's going to be fuckin' great. Then, when I call your boyfriend, I'm gonna tell him I have you but that you've been all used up. I'll warn him to come alone to pick up his trash or I'll kill you." Pete picks up a long, gleaming ice pick and grips it for emphasis. "When he gets here, I'll kill him, too, and anyone else I want to kill."

I'm beyond afraid now. Because I'm dead no matter what. I don't want Brody to come save me. I don't want him to die. I even feel for Stella because I can see the way he's used and manipulated her. She's in love with him and he's nothing but a psychopathic serial killer.

Tears roll down my face as he reaches out and fondles my breast none too gently with his other hand. No one has ever seen this much of my body, but I have no time to be embarrassed. I do know I don't want the touch of this dirty bastard to be the only one I ever feel.

I think of Brody and I regret not telling him how much I care about him. I want *him* to touch me and love me. I guess that's never going to happen now. I decide that I'll fight to the death to stop this maniac from touching me *that* way. If I'm going to die, I want to die a virgin. But if I can't stop him from doing what he has planned, I'll go to a place inside myself where he can't see the pain he's causing me. I feel myself going there now, going back into shock. Maybe *this* is how I'll die, instead of at the hands of this sadist with his spikes and pliers and blowtorches.

In my mind, I continue screaming for someone to help me, but from now on, I refuse to show my pain and fear on the outside. I *won't* give him that satisfaction.

CHAPTER 14

It's only been ten minutes. Ten minutes too long since first arriving at Mel's; Brody's about to explode thinking what this maniac is doing to her. But he knows from his years in the service and law enforcement that losing it won't do her any good.

As he's about to call the office to help research barns, it hits him that a more efficient path may be in the woman he tried to take a break from. They need to get to Mel quickly, and he's done playing around.

Brody runs into the house and up the stairs. He enters Mel's art room and searches around until he finds what he needs.

He goes back outside.

"Flora, come over here! I have an idea I want to try."

"Okay…" she says warily.

"I'm sorry about before, Flora," Brody tells her sincerely. "And I can really use your help."

She walks over to where he stands by the footprint. "Tell me what you're thinking."

"This is a painting from Mel's studio. I'm guessing she made it after the kidnapping dream, as it fits the story she told me."

The work depicts a woman's hands clawing frantically at what is definitely a man's arm wrapped around her throat.

Flora's fear is evident, but Brody has no time to alleviate it.

"In the dream, Mel thought those were the hands of the girl from her prior dreams," explains Brody, "but it turns out they are hers. The weird thing is the girl's hands looked just like this in other paintings."

He hands the canvas to Flora.

"I want you to hold this while you stand on the footprint again," directs Brody. "And while you do it, focus on the barn. Is it a working barn? Is anyone there other than Mel and whoever took her? What does the floor of the barn look like? Are there animals? Also try and see outside the barn. Do you notice anything familiar? Tell me everything you see and feel."

"Any other requests?" Flora snaps, obviously stressed. "Maybe stand on my head while I look at everything?"

"I'm sorry. I know I'm asking for a lot. But please, this may be the only way we can help her."

Flora takes a deep breath. "I'll do what I can, but I can't promise I'll see everything you want me to see."

"Just see something, anything, to help us find her. Please!"

"Of course," Flora agrees, taking the painting from Brody.

She moves over to stand on the footprint as before. This time she takes off her sandal and kicks it aside.

"If I have direct contact I may get a better reading," she explains.

Brody nods. "That makes sense…as much sense as any of this psychic stuff makes, that is."

Flora closes her eyes and is silent for a few minutes. Then she begins to speak. "I can see the inside of the barn. I don't see any animals in it. There's no hay, so even if animals were outside, there would still be hay, right?"

"I agree," says Brody.

That is the only time he interrupts her. He doesn't want her to lose focus on what she's seeing.

"I don't think it's a working barn. It looks sort of rundown and old. Most of the inside is open but there's a section I can't see. I do see some farm implements hanging on the walls. They look rusty, but I'm not totally sure."

Flora opens her eyes. "I'm sorry, but that's all I can tell you."

Brody squeezes her shoulder. "That's okay; you did good. I need to call the office."

Brody runs to the cruiser, leaving Flora holding the painting. His thoughts are all over the place. They're in a race against a killer.

"Stella, it's Brody. I need you to do something for me."

"Anything, boss," says the deputy. "But are you alright? You don't sound like yourself."

"I don't have time to explain. I need you to go online and locate all abandoned barns in the area."

Stella goes completely silent. Brody thinks maybe she has hung up.

"Stella, are you there? What's going on?"

"Umm, I already know all the abandoned barns in the area. My…uh…friend who's, uh, visiting, is obsessed with barns. He's looking for an old barn he can get cheap so he can restore it. So I've been helping him. He's a good guy and I want him to stick around…what's going on boss?"

"Mel is missing, and we have reason to believe she's been taken to a barn. That's all I can tell you right now."

You…you don't think *he* has anything to do with this, do you? I mean, could this just be a crazy coincidence or—"

"I have no idea, Stella," Brody interrupts. He actually has a *really* bad idea about this scenario but keeps his speculation to himself. "What I *do* know is that I need all the information you have on those barns *now!*"

"Sure, boss. I have the details right here. There are three barns within a twenty-mile radius he wanted to check out. One is pretty close to Melanie's house."

"I don't want that one," says Brody, following his hunch. "Tell me the one that's the most isolated."

"The farthest from town is on Old Adams Road just a quarter-mile west of the deserted church, close to the place you two go running near the mountains."

"Sounds like the place," says Brody. "I'm on my way."

He turns the key and roars the engine to life, frantically signally Flora to hop in. Not taking time to return the painting to the house, Flora places it gently in the back seat. Then she gets in quickly and fastens her seat belt as she listens to Brody's one-sided conversation with Stella.

"But now," he says, loudly over the noise, "fill me in on everything there is to know about your *friend*. And make it quick."

She does. And the key words and phrases in her rapid rundown turned Brody's speculation into pretty-damn-sure.

Just met him…from out of town…over-the-road truck driver… Asking about Mel.

"I'm going to need backup," says Brody. "You're closer than I am, so head there now and I'll meet you. On your way, call in deputies from the closest town to the barn. And I need a team to go to Mel's house to search for prints and any other evidence. I'm not letting this asshole get away once we *do* get him. They'll find my and Flora's prints too, but we'll sort it out later. Now, go!"

"Yes, boss. Anything you need."

"But Stella," admonishes Brody, "don't you dare go in there alone under any circumstances…Do you hear me, Stella? We don't know if your *friend* is the one who took her or not, but I do know for sure that whoever's in there is very dangerous and you could get yourself hurt or worse."

Stella doesn't reply.

"For fuck's sake, Stella, that's an order! Wait for backup. I'm serious here."

"Of course, boss."

Brody knows as sure as the sun will rise tomorrow that Stella isn't going to listen to what he's just told her. And he's just as sure that this "good guy" she's been seeing is in that barn with Melanie. If he's wrong, well, he'll eat his hat and apologize later.

In the meantime, no matter who the hell's got Mel, Brody can't and won't let anything happen to her.

Not now.

Not ever.

CHAPTER 15

I'M DRIFTING IN AND OUT and having trouble remembering why I'm here. But the memory is not far behind the fear. I know that I'm going to die and I wonder if I'll be reunited with my parents when I'm gone. I see a bright glow, and think maybe if I go into the light it will all be over.

But my thoughts are interrupted by a vision taking their place. I see Brody and Flora. I watch as they anxiously search my home. I see them arguing with each other but I don't know about what. Now they're in the car frantically racing to somewhere—presumably to come save me. Is it possible they've figured out my location?

I cry at the sight of Brody and wonder how and why Flora is with him. I also feel hope, seeing these two people racing to save me, so I decide I can't die yet. I have to find a way past the fear and *do* something to stop—or at least delay—this maniac.

I know: *Questions.*

He's obviously a narcissistic psychopath who loves to brag, so I'll get him to tell me everything. Not only will that give Brody and Flora time to reach me, but no matter what happens, I need—and deserve—to know.

I feel renewed hope.

And determination to survive.

"Pete," I say, choking through my tears, "I still don't understand…wh— what did I do to make you hate me so much?"

"Well, well, well," he says, not even looking at me, "look who decided to come back to the living."

Good start. At least he's talking to me.

"I just want to know before I d— die, what made you choose *me*?"

He turns and looks into my eyes. And I can see he *wants* me to know. He *wants* to talk about it. He gets off on this.

Good, you bastard. Talk. And take your time about it.

"Well, it's not your feminine wiles, sweet stuff," he says, walking toward me with that horrible ice pick in his hand again. "You aren't even my type. You're too skinny and quiet for my taste. I like screamers—even though shy girls'll scream for me, too. Your friend at the sheriff's office screamed plenty when I fucked her. I wanted to make her scream in other ways, and I may still do it."

I think about Stella again, further understanding the reason for her questions and pretending not to know my name. I trust she isn't actually *working* with this maniac, but I also know she's so enamored with him she was willing to do whatever he wanted.

"But back to the question…" I choke again but keep going. "Why me? What did *I* do?"

"You know what? I'll tell you!" His voice rises. "Here I was…famous…acclaimed for my unstoppable killing spree. Never leaving behind a shred of evidence. But then your buddy Stan Harris swoops in and steals all my thunder!" Pete's look grows even more menacing. "And you know whose fault *that* was? You! It's because of your damn psychic shit they picked up Stan in the first place. *You're* the one who led the police to him."

So, Stan really didn't kill my mother? I'm so confused.

"I'm the *real deal*, sweets," Pete goes on. "The Route 66 killer. But because of you, that damn copycat not only fucked up his own kill but ruined my streak."

Copycat? I'm more lost than ever.

"And *that's* the reason you're in this *uncomfortable* position." Pete's voice has risen even louder. "About to get this nice shiny ice pick run slowly into your right…no, *left*…ear, just for starters."

I'm horrified but my mind is also still racing.

Pete leaves me no time to ponder. "You know what else I've been pissed about for so long? This Stan guy, or whatever his real name was, is dead. Because if he wasn't, I'd like to kill that fucker myself. Even though he was a so-called *man*, not some bitch, I still would've enjoyed it—though not in the same way, of course. But since I lost *that* little golden opportunity, I figured I'd get back at *you*."

I'm floored but still trying to process what this madman has revealed. If Stan wasn't the real Route 66 serial killer, then why did he pretend to be in order to kill my mother?

"Hey, bitch. Are you still with me? Do you understand now, so that I can get on with it? I'm just about done listening to your blabbering mouth, and whatever powers you think you have, they're shit. Nothing's stopping me this time. Before I'm done with you, you're gonna feel so much pain, you'll be begging me to finish you off." He sneers. "But I won't."

I can barely speak through my panic. Somehow, despite his impatience, I have to keep his maniacal monologue going.

"Just a couple more questions, Pete, please," I plead. "I mean, what does it matter? Like you said, no one's coming to find us. I'm…uh, I'm wondering, what took you so long to come back for revenge?"

Pete gives me a long, hard look before he begins speaking again.

"Well, what the hell, darlin'—you might as well know. It'll be more fun shit for you to think about as you bleed and scream to death."

I shiver.

"Right after you and that Stan fuck ruined my rep," he goes on, "I went to prison. Got sent up for five years for some bullshit mistake I made—nothing to do with all the bitches I enjoyed seeing suffer. So I spent every minute in prison learning about what happened. I read every news article about you and your damn dreams, wondering how so many people could be suckered into believing your lies. Then I started planning. Once that was in the works, I spent every remaining minute dreaming about putting a bullet into that hero deputy of yours who offed that motherfucker Stan. You two spoiled everything for me and now you and this entire podunk town are gonna feel my vengeance."

Fascinating as this is, God, I wish Brody and Flora would arrive soon...

"You wanna know something else that's been eatin' at me all these fucking years?"

I nod my encouragement. He's on a roll now.

"The news reports said the cops knew they had their man because the details of Stan's crime—yeah, I'm talking about him offing your Mommy Dearest—matched those 'specific to the case that were not released to the public.' And I'll tell ya—I'll be damned if I can figure out how our boy Stan found out about my tidy trick of putting those bitches' hands on the steering wheels, like they were driving those stupid cars straight to hell as they took their last breaths." He shrugs. "I always figured it was one of those cop bastards leaking to one of their butt-buddies in the media and somehow this Stan asshole caught wind of it, but I never could be sure."

I try to absorb everything Pete is saying, but especially in my current state, following all his logical leaps is a challenge.

"But I *was* sure it wasn't thanks to you, babe. That psychic shit is bullshit and we all know it!"

I'm down to the end here; I can feel it. But I *have* to keep him talking. So why not ask *the* question? The one that will really get him off...

"Why do you enjoy killing, Pete?" I ask softly.

Pete looks startled. It's probably the first time a victim—or anyone, for that matter—has taken an interest in his..."hobby."

"*Why* do I enjoy killing?" he repeats. "*Why?!*"

He bursts out laughing.

Brody and Flora, please hurry!!

"Listen, doll," he finally manages, "I once heard that Ted Bundy said 'I don't feel guilty for anything. I feel sorry for people who feel guilt.'"

He laughs again.

"And he was right. You can't feel guilty for what you're born with. Babe, I enjoy the fuck out of what I do. Because it's my gift. Bundy was kind of a one-trick pony, but I'm an equal-opportunity operator. I'm 'double the fun.'"

It takes everything I have to appear interested in his "analysis" rather than turn away in disgust.

"The news made a big fuckin' deal out of all those older babes being found in their cars in parking lots," he goes on. "And yeah, I guess it was spooky and made for great press: sitting there in the driver's seat, starin' out their windshield at some sort of highway to hell. And damned if I didn't love every second of it. After I shot 'em with the needle, I'd go back to the car I was in—always a car I'd just ripped off—and I'd sit there and watch 'em gasp, and feel, and think, and wonder why, and then die."

"So…so you usually like to kill older women?" I prod.

"Hell, yeah. But I like to kill *young* women, too. In a *different* way. I usually go for the young girls who aren't in the greatest shape. Watching you and the cop jog together, I thought you'd have more fight in you. Guess I was wrong about that. Shit, you were easy to kidnap. You fit right into the mold of my usual targets—the ones that don't fight so hard when I capture them. Or fuck them. Or cut them up. Or burn them. Just like I'm gonna do to you."

I shudder and fight back tears. *Please, Brody. Please save me from this lunatic.*

"'Cause as much as I love to see the cougars and MILFs and oldies die, I like to have sex with young, tight bitches. And sweetie, I'm going to find out soon just how tight you are. But you probably fucked that sheriff a bunch. You're always hanging around together. You're probably not tight anymore and that's going to be a total fuckin' waste of my time. But hey, we're gonna give it a go anyway."

He picks up the ice pick and slams it down on the table next to me. Every cell of my body feels the vibration. Without a flinch, he continues talking.

"Ya know, the news just ignored so many of those young chicks—I guess 'cause they were hookers, runaways, throwaway foster kids, and other disposable shit. The news just wanted more of the spooky old ladies on the highway to hell."

I'm so mortified right now but I continue to listen. I *have* to listen. I have to survive. I have to live.

"But I loved all of it, bitch!" he's now screaming as he slides out the blade of a box cutter. "Young, old—I loved all of it 'cause I hate women! And do you know *why* I hate women, bitch?!"

"No, I don't, Pete," I whisper. "Please tell me."

"My mother," he says, getting very quiet. "*Your* mother is dead and you're upset about it, so I guess you liked *your* mother. But I hated *my* mother. And she hated *me*."

I nod, encouraging him to go on.

"Nobody, especially me, knew who the fuck my father was. My mother was married to drugs. I was the child of all that. I was the fuckin' child that if I did anything like spill some milk, cry, sneeze, or knock over an overflowing ashtray, this bitch would march me out to our cold garage and make me sit in the driver's seat of her old dirty smelly fuckin' car and raise my little arms up to that steering wheel and just sit there. For hours. Cold. Peeing my pants. Shitting my pants. Arms and hands numb. Sobbing.

"She'd come out all the time and check to make sure I didn't move. She'd spit words at me: 'You little shit, this is what you deserve! You drive me crazy, so this is the best place to do that!'

"For hours—cold, cold hours."

"Pete," I cry. "I'm so, so sorry. I—"

"Fuck you," he says. "No, you're not. You're just another bitch and you're all the same. This little conversation is over. You need to shut the fuck up. I have things I need to do."

Out of the corner of my eye, I see that he's choosing from the many sharp things next to me. I don't know what they all are or what they do, but every fiber of my being knows that they have the power to cause more pain than I've ever imagined.

I *do* know what a blowtorch can do and he looks straight at me as he lights it.

"I'm done talkin', bitch."

CHAPTER 16

Stella finally makes it to the barn. Trees line the road and fill the property, obscuring the building itself. She knows it's the right place. She researched carefully to find just what Pete wanted.

Stella feels a crushing weight on her chest. She prays Pete isn't the man who's kidnapped Mel, even though in her heart of hearts she knows he's in there. Their quick connection was too good to be true, but she wants it to be true anyway.

She shuts off her headlights and turns off the main road onto a gravel road leading to the large red edifice. Proceeding as quietly as possible, she pulls to the side of the path and parks along a line of trees. She exits the car and makes her way through the trees. She needs to get in the barn before Brody arrives; if it is Pete, she wants time to talk him out of whatever he's got planned.

She walks silently around the exterior, unholstering her weapon as she goes. She doesn't want to be the next victim if someone comes out during her search.

She angles to look through the broken and crumbling slats of the barn walls, but in the unlit shadows she can't make out anything.

She reaches one of the side doors, hanging half open with only one rusty hinge still attached. And now she *can* see something.

Something horrible.

She's so shocked, she gasps aloud.

Damn it!

She quickly backs out of the doorway and crouches down, wondering if the kidnapper heard her. She holds her breath, fearing he'll answer that question with bullets.

But all remains quiet. She crawls her way back through the rotting doorway, easing inside on her stomach—which may not be the greatest idea because who knows what creatures are slithering and scurrying around this old barn. She tries not to think about it.

Now fully inside, Stella wriggles over to one of the wooden pillars holding up an overhead loft that extends the entire length of the barn. She hopes *that* wood isn't as rotted as the door; she's in enough danger without worrying about being crushed by an avalanche of crumbling cedar.

She grabs the pillar and uses it pull herself to her knees, remaining as hidden as possible as she looks toward the horrible something she glimpsed from outside.

Most of the interior is a huge open space, broken up only by animal stalls and pens fenced apart with even more decaying timber. At the far end is what appears to be a makeshift storeroom or workshop with a light shining inside it.

Unfortunately, from this vantage, she can no longer see inside it as she could from the door.

Stella inches closer toward the room, using each narrow pillar as a shield. She's almost to the doorway, behind the last pillar, when she hears footsteps coming from her right.

It's Pete.

Her breathing increases, cutting through the quiet. But that doesn't matter anymore—it's time to move. She steps out from behind the pillar.

"Freeze!" she commands, aiming her gun at the man she's been seeing.

He doesn't seem surprised at all.

"Hey, baby, what are *you* doing here?"

She is *so* nervous. Maybe he doesn't think she's seen what he's doing. She's pretty sure that's Melanie trussed up on the table like a stuffed pig.

"Don't call me baby."

As she says these words, tears stream down her face. She can't believe that she's been sleeping with a killer.

She needs to pull her shit together. Let him know she means business. She waves her gun toward the workshop-turned-torture chamber, indicating for him to walk that way. She can't lose her sights on him but also needs to check on the hostage.

"Move it, Pete. I mean it. I know you have someone in there and they damn well better be okay. Try anything and I'll shoot you."

He tries to walk toward her. With her gun still trained on him, she removes the safety.

"I mean it, Pete! I *will* shoot you."

"Honey, why would you do a thing like that? We had so much fun together. Remember all those times I made you scream?"

It's obvious what he's trying to do and it isn't going to work. She knows full well she's been played and played hard. It's too bad because she *did* think they had a lot of fun together. She wonders if this is the only kind of man she'll be able to find.

"Come on—nothing has to change." He grins. "You and I have something really special, and this has nothing to do with that." He waves his hand toward the enclosed area.

"What do you mean?" Stella demands. "I'm a cop and you—" Her voice breaks. "You're a kidnapper and a con man. Now, who is in there and what are you doing to them?"

Stella can't decide if she wants it to be Mel or not. They desperately need to find her, but this—well, this doesn't look good at all.

"Oh *that*, baby. That's nothing for you to worry about. Let me have that gun before someone gets hurt. You don't want to shoot me and you know it."

He beams the sexiest grin she's seen yet and sets his hand on the hip of his jeans.

Her anger swells. Doesn't he know she's not going to buy his shit? She's a good cop, she counsels herself, and she's done being played. She's not going to let someone die because *she* made a mistake.

"Move it, now!" she shouts. "I have this gun aimed at the part of your body you admire the most." She smiles as she says it, trying to throw him off, even though she feels anything but confident at this point. "In fact, I'd like nothing better than to shoot it off. Now stop stalling. Walk in front of me and keep your hands where I can see them."

He seems to take her seriously this time because he turns and walks toward the work area. She follows him around the corner through a large dilapidated opening to find it's indeed Melanie on the table—completely naked. Next to her, Stella sees an array of tools. Taking in exactly what Pete is, she feels sick. A sob escapes her throat.

Melanie looks the deputy right in the eyes, as if she knows this is the guy Stella has been telling her about. Stella also sees a glimmer of hope in Mel's eyes—hope that she is saved.

Wondering exactly what Pete has already done to Melanie, a fresh wave of guilt overtakes Stella. *Where the hell is Brody?* she wonders. She knows enough not to try take down Pete on her own—she can't simply cuff him and read him his rights. *No way.*

She needs to stall.

That's when she realizes Melanie is talking. "I think you need to tell Stella why you're doing this, Pete," says Mel. "Maybe she'll be more understanding after you explain everything."

Gosh, maybe Mel really is a psychic because that's exactly the distraction Stella needs. And thankfully, Pete seems totally in the mood to talk. But the more he reveals, the sicker Stella gets…a serial killer…murders in and around the area…even worse acts to young girls along Route 66…then something about a copycat killer and Melanie ruining his life.

When he's done talking, Stella is confused about the facts, but she's *sure* that he's crazy. He wants the recognition for the murders he's committed, and she hopes she can be the one to do that by putting him in jail—and in the process gain back some of her credibility.

But Pete's disturbing diatribe is far from over.

He calmly adds that he plans on killing Brody, too, and that Stella will just be collateral damage.

"It was fun while it lasted, babe," he says with that sick-but-slick smile again, "but not everything lasts forever."

Pete winks at her, and everything inside her starts breaking apart. This is all her fault—for being so stupid and desperate she fell for this sicko's fake charm. Disgusted with both him and herself, her hand begins to shake and her eyes fill again with tears. *How can this be happening?!*

She reaches up a hand to wipe her eyes, and—

It's the opening Pete's clearly been waiting for.

Expecting.

Planning.

He rushes her, sending her body to the ground and her gun flying. She tries to crawl for it, but he kicks her in the ribs.

He pulls out his own gun from the front of his pants—one she didn't even see with his untucked shirt over it—and points it directly at her head.

Oh god, I should have searched him. But, again, getting that close would have been too dangerous, as he just proved. Can things get any worse?

"Sit up, you gullible fat bitch, so that I can put your own handcuffs on you."

She has no choice. She knows he'll kill her.

"I want you to watch what I do to this bitch and maybe if you're good, I'll give you some of the fun treatment, too." He laughs harshly. "Did you honestly think I would be *with* someone like you? The reason I was able to do you so many times is that I was imagining doing the exact same thing to you that I'm about to do to her."

From her spot on the ground, Stella's view is of Pete's lower half, and she sees he has a raging hard-on. She's nauseated and at the same time is breaking into a million pieces.

She pushes aside her own pain and looks at Melanie. The hope Stella saw a few minutes ago is gone. Pete is going to kill them both and Stella has failed in her job and her duty.

Pete leans down and holds the gun directly to her head. "Now, I want you to tell me just how many cops are on their way over here."

Stella stares at him, realizing she has nothing left to lose. Even if Brody makes it in time, her life and her career are over. She doesn't care if Pete kills her now.

So she lies.

"No one is coming." She sighs. "I heard talk at the station about a likely kidnapping and that they'd probably take their victim somewhere remote, and covered. Since I had done your barn research, I had to find out if it was you. I figured it must be a misunderstanding—or that whatever was happening, we could talk. So I directed the teams to other locations without mentioning the ones you looked into."

"Well, well, isn't that noble of you." He laughs. "But too bad for you, bitch, you and your stupid *nobility* were wrong. Now I get to kill you both—a twofer. I never did two women at once. This is going to be fuckin' awesome."

CHAPTER 17

Outside, Brody and Flora pull up to the location Stella provided. *Finally.*

Stella was right, thinks Brody. *This place is definitely remote.*

Brody spots a squad car in the trees—sure enough, Stella beat him here. He exits his own vehicle and walks up to her cruiser, knowing full well she isn't going to be in it.

Damn it, Stella! He mentally kicks himself for letting her arrive ahead of him.

He returns to his sedan, unlocks the squad-car-standard compartment inside it, and grabs two more magazines for his weapon.

He looks at Flora.

"So now what happens?" she asks. He can hear the fear in her voice.

"Stay in the car and lock the doors. You'll be safe here. More officers should arrive shortly." He quickly radios the other county's units to tell them to arrive quietly. "I don't need them coming in here with sirens screaming before I can get in there and find Stella," he explains.

"I don't have a problem staying in the car," Flora agrees. "I'm scared to death right now. But most of the feelings are coming from Melanie, so I'll be fine. Go! She needs you more than I do."

"Alright. I don't know if Stella's 'friend' is working with anyone, but I suspect if an accomplice pulls up, once they see the sheriff's cars they'll keep on moving down the road."

Flora shivers. "Geez, you're scaring me more. Just go."

Brody runs from the car and eases as stealthily as possible through the brush.

It's dark but he's afraid to use his flashlight. He navigates by the light of the early moon, praying he doesn't trip on a rock or something and give himself away. Remembering a technique he used in the Marines, he stops and gives his eyes a few beats to adjust to the darkness before continuing on; before he knows it, he's at the open side door of the barn.

Brody leans in and sees Stella lying on the ground, right in the open doorway of the lighted workroom—handcuffed, a guy with a gun standing over her.

Goddammit! There goes my backup straight to hell. This "good guy" she's been seeing must have unnerved her.

Then he sees Mel. His heart rate jumps by several thousand beats per minute.

He can't tell if she's dead or alive. He barely stops himself from running in, guns blazing. But he knows that'll get at least one of them killed. He needs to calm down and figure out a plan.

And it *has* to be a good one.

Inspired by the old *Dirty Harry* movies he used to watch with his dad, he forms an idea.

He quickly makes his way through the dark back to Stella's car. The keys are in it, which gives him one more reason to kick her ass. But he's also grateful because he'd rather not displace Flora from his own car right now.

He buckles his seat belt—*tight.* Then, with the headlights off, he quickly backs Stella's car out toward the road. He glances over to his car and locks eyes with Flora, whose agape expression tells him she's on to his plan.

There's no time for second-guessing and no time to waste. He pounds on the gas and plows the cruiser into the far corner of the barn, where he thinks Mel and Stella will be safe from flying debris but still close enough to alarm the gunman, who will think it's the end of the world!

The barn is old and the car easily goes right through the rickety wall. And as luck would have it, the asshole appears right in front of Brody through the cloud of splinters and soot, and is hit by the car. He goes flying from the momentum, like a slow coyote on a fast Kansas highway.

Brody tries to open the driver door but it's blocked by wood that's fallen from above.

He draws his gun and flies out of the passenger side like a crazy man. He gets a more complete look at Mel inside the workroom and sees red. It's too bad that the object of his rage is lying on the floor unconscious. However that doesn't stop him from picking up the asshole and giving him one hard punch in the face. It takes all of his control to stop himself quickly so no one gets a whiff of police brutality.

Once he's sure the guy won't wake up anytime soon, Brody handcuffs him to a large, heavy chunk of wood and checks him for a pulse. The motherfucker is definitely alive.

From this point forward, Brody has to make sure he proceeds by the book all the way. No way can this guy be allowed to walk.

Although he's a cop and a former Marine, this is the one time in his life Brody actually *wants* to kill. But if he does that, he'll be no better than the creep on the floor.

As Brody runs over to cut Mel loose, he still must proceed by that book.

"Is anyone else here?!" he shouts at Mel and Stella. "Anyone with weapons? Or does this guy have a partner standing by somewhere?"

They both indicate strongly that he doesn't. Thank god for small favors.

As Brody gently removes the restraints from Mel's arms and legs, he tries not to embarrass her by looking at her naked body. But he must make sure she has no injuries that require immediate attention.

And though it pains him to put her through any more torment, he has to ask more questions: "Do you know this guy's name? Do you know if he's hurt anyone else?"

"Yes...Pete Decker...He's the Route 66 killer...which means Stan wasn't—"

Just then, Brody spots the tools and realizes what this fuck was planning. He looks away so Mel won't see the emotion taking over his features. It takes all his will not to kill the bastard now.

Mel falls silent.

Brody turns back to her and gazes into her eyes as he takes off his coat and covers her with it. He lightly touches her face. He can tell she's on the verge of shock. She needs to get to a hospital. *Now!*

He tells Mel to sit very still until the paramedics get there. Meanwhile, he gets the cuffs off Stella, whom he's been purposely ignoring. He tells her to go out to his car to check on Flora and radio for an ambulance, *and* find out where the hell those local officers are.

Now!

She starts to go but then turns back to him and Mel.

"I am s— so sorry for all of this."

"It's too late to be sorry." Brody is sure she can feel his rage. "Just don't plan on running off. Now, go take care of what I told you! Melanie needs help and that's all I care about. Also, get the blanket that's in my trunk. I want to cover her with it."

As Stella leaves, he sees her sneak one last peek at the assailant. Brody can't read her emotions, but he assumes she'd like to take him out as much as he would—maybe even more. At least the guy's sorry ass will get kicked by the Law.

Brody returns to Mel's side. The fear in her eyes makes him so upset he must turn away again before facing her to speak.

"I'm so sorry, Melanie. I never should have left you alone."

She tries to reply but her voice and energy seem to be sapped. Brody can barely hear her. He does understand she wants water.

He runs over to Stella's banged up squad car and grabs the bottle of water he remembers rolling around the front seat. He tenderly helps her take a sip.

"Damn it. Where is that ambulance?"

"Brody," she whispers, "this is not your fault. Don't try to take the blame for it."

As she says those words, Stella comes back in with the blanket from the car. Flora is right behind her and she rushes over to Mel. They look at each other and Flora starts crying.

"The paramedics will be here in a couple of minutes," Stella tells Brody, "and units from the other sheriff's office have arrived."

"Tell them that once that asshole gets checked out by the EMTs, he'll be going to *my* station. If he has to go to the hospital, fine. But we'll take him back to Arrow Springs from there."

"Will do, Sheriff," she says, leaving the barn again to go relay his message.

Brody understands that his new deputy has been the victim of a master manipulator and that she's devastated about what's happened. But he also knows formal reprimands will be in order.

He can't think about any of that right now, though. Hearing ambulance sirens, relief washes through him. The local county sheriff also arrives, and Brody makes his way over to fill him in on everything he knows.

There will be many more answers to come.

Brody walks back to Melanie as the EMTs rush in.

"Mel," Brody tells her as they check her vitals, "I want you to know that if it weren't for Flora, I wouldn't have found you. She came and told me you were in danger."

Mel looks at Flora, and he watches the two share a moment of understanding.

Stella stays at the edge of Brody's vision for the rest of the investigation and evidence collection, and the lack of being up close and personal right now is just fine with him.

"We're definitely taking her to the hospital, Sheriff," a paramedic tells Brody. "We don't see any obvious injuries, but she's definitely dehydrated and in this…uh, type of situation, it's best that a doctor examine her."

Brody tries not to ponder the implications of that statement.

Brody turns back to Mel, who's motioning for him. He leans in to hear what she's saying.

"I really don't want to go to the hospital. Please."

"I'm sorry, Mel, but we need to make sure you're okay. I'll ride with you in the ambulance. Daly's at the same hospital, too."

Mel's eyes get huge.

"Oh no! Pete told me he hurt someone at the station. It's Daly, isn't it?! Is she alright?"

"Shhh…you just worry about you right now," Brody soothes. "We'll get you checked out and if they say you can go home, I'll take you right there. Agreed?"

Mel nods. Not that he was giving her an actual choice.

He's not about to give Stella one, either.

Brody tells her to take Flora back to the station in his car since her vehicle is rather worse for wear.

"And then," he adds, "get *yourself* to the hospital to get checked out."

"But Sheriff, I'm fine," she protests, obviously ashamed of her role in this entire ordeal and wanting to shrink from any attention.

"That wasn't a suggestion, deputy," Brody says. "It's an order."

"Yes, sir."

"I'd actually like to go to the hospital, too," Flora interjects. "To make sure Melanie's okay. Could Stella just take me with her while she gets…uh…examined?"

Brody nods. "Perfect. Then I can take you back to your car after we have Mel checked over." He pauses. "Remind me: Where the hell *is* your car?"

"Uh…it's still at the station, I think," she stammers.

Brody nods. It seems like forever since Flora came there to tell him that Mel was in trouble.

Mel is loaded onto a stretcher and Brody climbs in the back of the ambulance next to her. He isn't taking any chances from here on out.

Before the door is shut, Brody tells the neighboring sheriff to make sure someone stays with the prisoner at all times. He reiterates that once the doctors clear him, he *will* be transferred to holding at the Arrow Springs Sheriff's Office.

"Collect all evidence from this scene and have your team start working on it," he adds. "I don't want this guy wiggling his way out of a life sentence."

Yes, sir…

As the door closes, Brody adds that his deputy Barney will be at the station to make sure Pete Decker doesn't even *think* about slipping away.

CHAPTER 18

STILL BORDERING ON SHOCK and now sedated, Mel falls asleep on the way to the hospital.

Brody is pretty wiped out himself. The idea of a good night's sleep is like a fantasy. He knows that isn't happening anytime soon; he still needs to make sure Mel is safe and well, check on Daly, and make *damn* sure Decker is booked and charged.

Then he'll have to deal with Stella.

Watching Mel sleep in the ambulance, Brody shudders at what this freak had in mind to do to her. He wonders how long it will take her to heal emotionally. He even wonders how this might affect her dreams—nightmares—to come.

Brody has so many things running through his mind, he puts his face in his hands to shut down for a minute. He needs to calm himself.

As they pull into the emergency entrance, he gives his hair two quick tugs and sits back up.

Once Mel is admitted, Brody races up to check on Daly.

Daly's daughter, Molly, is at her bedside, along with Barney. Looking at the couple, the first thought Brody has is how completely different they are. Molly is a petite blonde, about five-foot-two, with gray eyes that are the kindest he has ever seen.

And then there's Barney. Barney's hair is jet black and he tops out at well over six feet. But his eyes—they're like a loveable Jayhawker hound dog. And no matter the vertical variances, one look and anyone can see how totally in love the two of them are.

Brody thinks back to how Barney tore apart the twist ties with his bare hands when they were saving Daly. He then thinks back to the other time he saw Barney that angry—a legendary story that spread through the area like prairie wildfire. Apparently, *someone* tried to mess with Molly in high school. This guy grabbed Molly in the parking lot and was trying to drag her somewhere she clearly didn't want to go. She was screaming at the top of her lungs.

Then along came Barney.

At exactly the right time.

People said it was like seeing an angry grizzly bear. The guy was picked up, shaken around a bit, and then put back on the ground in none-too-gentle a manner. Brody always wondered if the guy's brains were still intact after that. He must have had some mental problems for trying to attack a woman anyway.

Big as Barney is, lucky for that guy he isn't mean; he didn't even throw a punch. That showed just what type of person he is. And what he did was enough. It was the last time the guy was seen in town and no one seemed to care much where he went. Truth was, he'd been a troublemaker from the moment he moved to Arrow Springs.

Molly and Barney had been inseparable from that moment on. Molly would never forget how Barney saved her from an uncertain fate, and Barney, well, he was more than thrilled to get the girl he'd pined for since elementary school.

But right now, school days are long over and there's another soon-to-be legendary event to deal with.

"How is she?" Brody asks, nodding at Daly.

"The doctors say she'll be okay," Molly tells him. "But she was hit on the head pretty hard and may have some memory loss for a while. They've put her in an induced coma so that her brain can rest. We'll know more in a couple of days."

Brody fights to control his emotions. So much has happened. Daly has been a friend for a long time. He still can't comprehend how all this shit got started and this day became his worst nightmare.

He realizes Molly is still talking.

"We won't really know how bad it is until she wakes up," she continues in a rush. "But don't worry—we'll make sure she's taken care of. You have enough on your mind right now. I promise to let you know if her condition changes. I'm sure you'll want to question her when she's able. I can also help out at the sheriff's office if you need me. I know most of what Mom does."

Damn, that girl talks fast, Brody marvels. He's surprised she has any breath left after all that. Of course, with her mother being attacked and in a coma, she's probably a nervous wreck. He once again feels to blame for everything that's happening. He should be safeguarding this town better. But he doesn't have time to dwell on remorse. Brody fills Barney and Molly in on all that's happened, and obviously, they're shocked.

"Barney, I need you to check in with the doctors. As soon as they release the prisoner, grab a couple of the other deputies and take him back to the station. I know it's not uh…*comfortable*…but make sure he doesn't acquire any more injuries than he already has."

Barney half-smiles at the comment but immediately gets serious again. "Sure, boss. No problem. What about Stella? Is she going to be there?"

Brody hesitates. "Ahh, no. She may be out for a while. Once we convene at the station, I'll fill you in. Did you make sure the crime scene at the station was preserved so we can gather all the evidence we need?"

Barney nods. "No worries there, boss. Already took care of getting any prints and evidence before the station started crawling with cops. What about Melanie?" he asks. "She going to be okay?"

"Yeah," Brody tells them. "Physically, at least. I'll fill you in about that later, too. Right now I need to get back to the ER."

As Barney prepares to leave, he stands up and hugs Molly. Her head isn't even up to his chest. The worried look she gives Barney makes Brody uncomfortable. He has to get out of there. He thanks them and goes in search of Melanie.

BRODY STANDS AT THE DOOR to Mel's private room, watching with relief that she is up and walking around. She seems a little stiff, but other than that she appears okay—especially considering what she's been through.

She looks up at him with overly bright eyes, her lingering fear obvious beneath the brave front she's putting on.

Standing next to Mel is Flora. Brody nods to her, almost afraid to make contact.

"I was just telling Mel how we were brought together today," says Flora.

After describing her vision, she's interrupted.

"Are visions usually part of your gift?" asks Mel.

"No, I've never had one before," Flora says. "I assume it was our connection that made it happen."

Mel squeezes her hand.

"Then when I pulled up to the sheriff's office I feared they'd already found you and something terrible had happened. I'm ashamed to admit I was a bit relieved when I saw it was an older woman."

She inquires about Daly, and Brody fills them both in.

"I truly hope she recovers," says Flora, looking abashed.

"Well, it was quite the day but I'm grateful we're all here to tell about it," says Brody.

"Agreed," says Flora. "Including you, after you drove through the side of the barn in the cruiser! I don't think I've ever been more afraid and yet amazed." She snaps her fingers. "That reminds me—don't forget Mel's painting is still in *your* back seat. You should make sure it gets back to her house."

"What painting?" asks Mel.

They proceed to tell her about using the painting to find her, along with everything else that ensued.

"I still can't believe everything that happened to make sure you came home safe," says Flora.

"Me neither," says Mel. "You both risked a lot to save me." Mel gives Flora a hug. "You look exhausted. You should head home."

Flora nods. "Do you know where Stella is, Brody?"

"She should be waiting for you outside the emergency room."

Flora and Mel hug one more time.

"I hope to see you again soon," says Flora. "But certainly not under these circumstances. Goodbye to both of you for now."

After she leaves, Brody sees fear reignite in Mel's eyes. They both know that without Flora's help, he may not have found Mel in time. It's a hard truth to deal with.

"How is Stella, Brody?" Mel changes the subject.

"Her ribs are pretty sore and bruised," he says, "but she's been cleared to leave."

"Pete gave her quite the beating," says Mel. "Physically and emotionally. That poor thing."

Brody nods noncommittally. He *really* doesn't want to talk about Stella right now.

"How are *you* holding up?" he asks, crossing the room so he and Mel can comfortably face one another. "Can I get anything for you?"

"No, I just want to go home. I'm still in horror imagining what Pete had in store for me."

Brody shudders. "Me too, Mel." He hates to ask but he has to. "Mel, he didn't— I mean, he wasn't able to…"

Brody can't get the words out, but Mel seems to understand what he's asking.

"N— no, he didn't get a chance. You were there just when I needed you."

Mel wraps her arms around his waist and lays her head on his chest, letting her tears flow freely. She needs to release her stress, and if this is the way, it's more than okay with Brody. He holds her for a long time, just standing there in the room.

Finally, she seems to have cried herself out. When she gazes up at him, her eyes puffy and her nose red from crying, he undergoes a moment of complete panic for what might have happened. It's a fear greater than anything he's ever known he could feel.

Perhaps confused by his expression, she tries to pull out of his arms. She wants to talk about her mother's death—about who really killed her mom and why. But that analysis can wait. Mel's day has been traumatic enough. The only way he can think to distract her is by kissing her.

Looking directly into Mel's eyes, Brody sees something. It's as if she knows his intention but is afraid of it. Undeterred by her trepidation, he cradles her cheeks and slowly lowers his mouth to hers.

It starts with a gentle meeting of their lips. Then he sprinkles soft kisses on her eyelids and cheeks before returning to her lips. His goal was to make her forget the day, but it is he who is forgetting.

He wants to be tender, but something snaps inside him and the kiss takes on unexpected fervor. He pries her lips open with his tongue and feasts hungrily upon her mouth. She responds hesitantly at first but then meets his tongue with her own. The two cling to one another, engulfed in the sensations aroused by the kiss, their frenzy of hot mating mouths leaving no room for thought of any kind. It's as if no one else exists in the world.

A fury of pleasure strikes and the rest of their bodies seem to catch up to the heat of the furnace, exploding with a ferocity beyond any passion Brody has ever felt. He reaches a hand to stroke her breast through the flimsy hospital gown. She releases a soft moan and wraps her legs around his waist, climbing him like a tree. They can't get enough of each other. Soon, their friendship will be past the point of no return.

As they grope each other in the hospital room, a blaring horn of reality rings in Brody's ears.

The fact that Mel is still dealing with the terrible events of the day makes him realize it would not be a good idea to start something neither of them is ready for. Although it won't be an easy task, he knows he must pull away. He gently lowers Mel to the floor and releases her. Her lips are swollen from their kisses and her eyes filled with desire.

Meanwhile, Brody is dizzy from the exchange and isn't feeling very comfortable in his tight uniform pants. He needs to think of a distraction. He's thankful that Mel seems as taken over by the kiss as him and doesn't seem to notice his predicament.

He turns away so that nothing further will happen. This is going way too fast. Mel staggers back a little and holds onto the hospital bed as if for dear life.

Brody tries to speak. "I'll…uh…take you home now. I checked on Daly and she isn't awake yet. I really need to go to the station and get the paperwork going. Are you going to be okay at home alone? I'll make sure everything is safe before I leave you."

He feels relief when Mel turns away from him, but he isn't sure what she's thinking and she doesn't answer his question.

They grab what Mel has, which isn't much. She's still wearing his coat, now over a set of scrubs provided by the nurses along with some socks and shower shoes. Nothing more is said about their interlude.

As they walk out, Brody reads a text from Stella that his car is in the hospital parking lot and his keys at the desk. She says she'll be at the station when he arrives. He really doesn't want to deal with her yet, but he decides to get it out of the way first thing when he arrives. It'll be easiest that way.

In with Mel's discharge papers are two prescriptions, which they pick up on the way to her house. One is a cream to rub on her abrasions from the restraints; the other is sleeping pills in case she needs them.

Back to harsh reality.

It's as if the air has been let out of their balloon of passion and its floating ever so slowly to the ground.

CHAPTER 19

Despite my cacophony of thoughts and emotions, the ride to my house is quiet.

When we arrive, Brody helps me inside and checks the windows to make sure they're secure. He finds a piece of wood in my shed to brace the window Pete pried open, and then nails the entire thing shut for good measure.

I can feel that people have been in my house. I can almost smell the fingerprint dust—or maybe it's just my overworked imagination. I'll definitely need to scrub the place top to bottom, but that's a thought for another day.

I turn as I hear Brody. "I'll replace the latch eventually," he says, "but you won't have anything to worry about tonight."

Brody walks over and grabs my hands.

"Mel, I'm so sorry I have to leave you. Decker is locked up and can't get to you, but I've posted a deputy outside anyway."

"I'll be fine, Brody—don't worry. I'm really tired and I'm sure I'll just go right to sleep."

"That sounds like the right thing for you to do," he says gently. "Goodnight, Melanie."

"Goodnight."

I lock the door behind Brody, feeling utterly spent. But I can't stop thinking about the kiss.

I wonder if Brody realizes it was my first real kiss. I mean, we'd shared a peck before, but nothing like this. This was the most perfect kiss ever—at least *I* think so. And since I have no previous experience, I decide that I'm right.

I had *no* idea my body could feel so many delicious things—and from just a kiss. I essentially went up in flames! I feel a rush of embarrassment remembering how I wrapped myself around

Brody like a blanket. God, I hope he forgets that part. He might start acting all crazy about it the next time we see each other.

And why did he pull away? I can't help feeling like he only kissed me because I was upset. If so, I pray our friendship doesn't suffer any lasting weird effects.

I go upstairs, desperate for a shower. I feel dirty and defiled, both inside and out. I thank God that bastard didn't get a chance to use his tools on me. Or rape me. But while I have no external scars, I know I'll have internal ones.

As I enter the bathroom, I'm jolted by fear, hit by the realization that the horrors of my day began right here. It seems so long ago. But urgency to cleanse myself wins out over terror. I get in and turn on the water as hot as I can stand and scrub until my skin is red. Still I don't feel clean.

I stand with the water running over me for a long, long time.

Finally, when it starts getting cold, I turn it off. Before opening the shower door, I peer through the frosted glass into the room. I know no one is out there, but I doubt I'll ever exit a shower again without checking through the door first.

When I get out, I reach for a towel and see it's on the counter. It must be the same one Flora picked up from the floor. The one that Pete—

Banishing the thought, I walk naked and dripping to the linen closet to retrieve a fresh one. After drying off, I examine myself in the mirror. Do I look any different?

I was kidnapped and on the verge of being tortured, raped, and killed. I then had the breath kissed out of me by the one man in the world I've wanted to kiss more than anything. Then he left as if it was a mistake.

I again question if his only motive was to distract me from the unspeakable horror of what happened and from further analysis. Assuming that's the case, I decide not to bring up the kiss the next time I see Brody. I'll just go on like nothing's happened.

Plus, as amazing as it was, I feel frustrated I didn't get to brainstorm with Brody about everything Pete told me. My mind can't stop wondering: *If Pete wasn't the one who killed my mother, and Stan Harris wasn't the Route 66 killer, then who WAS Stan Harris?* I want to know why he killed my mom! But these questions will have to wait at least one more day.

I'm tired enough to crawl in bed without the sleeping pills. I hate taking anything like that—I fear I'll get locked into one of my dreams and not be able to wake up. As I lie down, though, I assume it will take a while to soothe my mind to sleep. But before I know it, I'm in the middle of another dream.

The sound of violin music encompasses me. I'm holding the instrument, playing a piece filled with emotional turmoil.

I hear a car door shut outside and my heart races in panic. The front door slams and his shouts radiate through the house—to the small cracked window in the upstairs gable and out to the large front yard. He hates to come home and find me playing. When he hears it, he flies into a rage. He says I should be cooking his dinner instead of playing this piece of wood.

I don't know what happened, because he used to love it when I played. He was my mentor. Sometimes I think he hates me for gaining too much status. He resents that he only gained fame because of me.

Since we bought this old house and settled down, he says I don't pay enough attention to him. He wants me all to himself, but he also says he needs <u>his</u> freedom and for <u>his</u> life to be what it used to be. Of course, it's <u>my</u> fault he was fired from his job as maestro. It wasn't me— it was his alcohol abuse that gave them no other choice but to remove his status. But I'm the one who pays for it.

As I try to gently place the violin in its case, he storms in, grabs me by the hair, and lands an open-handed slap that leaves me seeing stars. I can't control my scream.

This just enrages him more. Shouting like a raging bull, he makes his way down the stairs, dragging me with him. It feels like my hair is being pulled out by the roots.

When we're about halfway down, he lets go, sending me flying down the remaining stairs and into the front door. I hold in my scream this time, fearing I won't survive any more of a beating tonight.

I need to get away.

He heads back up the stairs. I want to run but I'm frozen in agony over what I fear he's going to do. He returns with my violin. I plead with him to stop, but he holds it up against the wall and puts his fist through the one thing I love in this life.

The pain from his bodily assault is excruciating, but the pain of losing my violin is greater than that. I open the door and run as fast as I can, tears streaming down my face.

I run toward a thick grove of trees, footed by weeds and thick ground growth. I don't care what creepy, crawly creatures are in the undergrowth; what's chasing me is so much worse.

I hear him follow me out of the house, yelling violently. All I can think about are his bleeding hands dripping on the broken pieces of my violin. I wonder if it can ever be repaired.

Although I'm sprinting as fast as I can, he's closing in on me. "You better not hide from me!" he shouts. "When I catch you, I'm going to beat the living shit out of you, you stupid bitch! I'm going to teach you a lesson about who's the boss here."

It feels like the devil is chasing me.

I dive into the cover of bushes, but it's as though he knew where I was going before I did. He is suddenly on me, grabbing me by the hair and yanking me from my hiding place. He slaps me even harder this time and the force of the blow sends me to the ground. I scream with everything I have.

I awake to total darkness, finding that sobs have overtaken me in my sleep. I'm terrified for the woman in the dream—and for myself.

Where are you? I mentally plead. *Please, God, let me find her. He's killing her.*

Then the fear and agony is again taken over with exhaustion, and my mind goes blank.

CHAPTER 20

I FEEL LIKE I'VE JUST FALLEN back into a deep dreamless sleep when I hear excessive pounding on my front door. I open my eyes to the light of day.

The pounding persists, and I'm hit by a flash of terror. Then I remember that Pete can't hurt me; he's in custody.

This is my home, I counsel myself. *I need to feel safe here.*

I climb out of bed and run to the bathroom to grab my robe. Throwing it on over my pajamas, I quickly pause to pee and run a toothbrush through my mouth. Whoever it is will just have to wait. As I make my way downstairs to the continued thumping, I'm getting seriously irritated. Until I open the door and there stands Brody.

"What took you so long to answer?" he demands.

"I was sleeping," I pant, trying to catch my breath. "I had another dream and woke up during the night."

I realize that I must look terrible. But Brody doesn't seem to notice.

"I'm sorry I woke you then," he says, his tone softer. "And about the dreams, we'll figure out everything soon. I promise."

He raises his hand to rest in the door jamb.

"Other than a terrible night of sleep, how do you feel?" he presses.

"I'm okay." I take a mental inventory of my body. "A little sore maybe."

I find myself staring at Brody. He seems to be in a weird mood, his lips lifted in a playful grin.

"Uh-oh, what's happening?" I ask.

My mind flashes to our kiss and I feel heat rise to my cheeks. I'm not sure whether from embarrassment or desire. Probably both. Brody looks so delicious standing in my doorway, clad in a black t-shirt with his always-hot-looking jeans, that I feel like I'm coming down with a fever.

"Are you sick?" he teases. "You seem to be flushed this morning."

Obviously my "fever" is evident, and he's trying to goad me into revealing something. I wish I could hide my expressions better than I do.

"I just woke up." I counter. "I was nice and warm under the blankets until *you* interrupted me from getting the rest I need."

Maybe guilting him will fend him off.

"Are you sure it doesn't have something to do with our kiss last night?" he asks.

Apparently that's not working.

"Oh, that?" I try for breezy. "It's no big deal—we were both just emotional from the events of the day. No need to rehash it."

I don't like lying to Brody, but I'm desperate to protect our friendship by not making this awkward for him.

"What are you doing here so early anyway?" I ask. "You must have been up late last night."

Brody chuckles. "Actually, it's not so early, Mel. It's almost noon."

That jolts me. I can't remember the last time I slept this long.

"So, back to our previous topic: What if I *do* want to 'rehash' it? Was it really 'no big deal,' or did you *like* kissing me?"

"Why are you doing this?" I plead. "Please just let it go. I had another dream I need to tell you about."

I step back from the door, still without inviting him in.

"We can talk about that later," says Brody. "Not that I don't want to get these dreams solved, but first, I *really* want to know if you enjoyed the kiss. I mean, it seemed as though you did, but I want to make sure."

As he speaks, he walks slowly toward me into the entryway.

"Brody!" I try to stop him. Then I look into his eyes and I see something there. I'm hesitant to test it, but at the same time, I want him and I'm tired of holding back. After everything that happened yesterday, I realize life may be shorter than I think; so I might as well take the bull by the horns.

"Alright!" I answer. "I enjoyed the kiss. Is that what you want to hear?!"

Surprise lights Brody's face.

"In fact, it was my first *real* kiss," I confide, "and I enjoyed it immensely. Unless, of course, you count that one time way back when, when you pecked me on the lips. Though now that I think about it, that felt like kissing my brother, which is sort of gross, so it really doesn't count." I'm babbling, but I can't seem to stop myself. "I mean way back when, not last night."

Brody's lips rise in a slow smile. "So…you think that first kiss was gross and if you had a brother you would go around kissing him on the mouth?"

"God, no." I shake my head. "What are you doing?"

The next thing I know Brody is closing the door behind him and locking it. I step back, suddenly afraid of the look in his eyes. Not real fear; more like excitement.

I continue walking backwards as he stalks toward me. Finally I'm up against the staircase with nowhere to go, so I stop. It's either that or topple over. Brody grabs the front of my robe and pulls me into his arms.

I watch as he lowers his mouth to mine. The kiss is so soft and devastatingly erotic. He takes his sweet time doing it and it drives me senseless.

This is nothing like kissing my brother. Gross! I don't even have a brother. Why am I thinking about this?

Once we start, there's no stopping us. We end up lying against the stairway kissing until we can barely breathe.

Reclining on stairs is not really comfortable; I'm still feeling the pangs of yesterday's trauma. Brody stops kissing and looks at me. He starts to move away from me, but I am so hot now, I'm not going to let that happen. So even though I have no idea what I'm doing, I take charge. I scoot out from under him and straddle him on the stairs.

I'm more than a little tentative. Never have I thought I could wield this type of power over a man. I rub my body against his until I hear a quick intake of breath followed by a moan of pleasure.

Encouraged, I have another burst of bravery. For what seems like forever, I've been aching to see Brody's body, longing to touch his bare skin. Especially his chest. So I tug at his shirt, urging him to remove it.

Brody is the only one I could ever be this bold with. I'm eager to share this part of myself with him.

He complies and tosses his shirt to the side.

I get my fill of gazing at him before I kiss his neck and slowly move down to his chest. It's covered with dark curly hair that I need to get my hands on; I'm dying to feel its texture. I place both hands on his chest and stroke them up and down, finding the hair both soft and coarse at the same time. As I'm doing this, I accidently graze one of his nipples. He jumps.

"Mmmm…" he groans.

I bring my lips back up to his and then lay down a trail of kisses to his neck, rubbing against the desire I feel through his jeans. His manhood seems to have a life of its own as it throbs against my body.

Brody abruptly stops me.

Does he not like what I'm doing? I panic. *Does he want to stop?*

One look in his eyes tells me that he does *not* want to stop. His words come out breathlessly. "I would rather we do this in your bed. Don't get me wrong: making love on the stairs is on my bucket list, but I don't want to hurt you, so that won't be happening." He winks. "Not this time, at least."

Oh!!!

With that, Brody scoops me up and carries me up the stairs a la Rhett Butler and Scarlett O'Hara.

In the bedroom, he gently lowers me to my feet.

I rise nervously on tiptoe to give him a cautious kiss. He responds, also hesitant, and then surrenders to it fully. This kiss goes deeper than the kisses we shared on the stairs or in the hospital. A fire spreads through my body.

I pray that the burn I feel is the same for Brody. I want him so badly, I'd be willing to beg.

Though still unsure of myself, I've found that being assertive intensifies my desire, so I push Brody on the bed to finish my earlier assault of his chest. Rubbing myself against the growing bulge in his jeans, I kiss his mouth and then move downwards. Remembering his reaction on the stairs, I flick his nipple with my tongue and softly bite it. He lets out a moan. I feast on first his right and then his left nipple, and they tighten into buds— not unlike my own when they harden with desire.

I look up into Brody's eyes and see them smoldering with need. I slide back up to kiss his mouth, rubbing against his body like a cat. In this position, the throbbing of his member beneath me sets me completely aflame.

I am consumed with hunger to see it, touch it.

As I move to go downward, he holds me in place.

"Easy, Mel. You're making me nuts here." He smiles. "Don't look at me like that! I couldn't stop if I wanted to. Just give me a chance to give you a little of what you've been giving me."

At those words, he quickly takes over and I find myself on my back with Brody's body between my legs, his hands pressed into the mattress. I'm not opposed to this position, as I like the feel of his groin pressed against me. My anticipation heightens over what he'll do to me next.

"You're a little hellcat," he says. "And you're driving me crazy. I want to be gentle, but you're pushing me over the edge. I'm going to do things to you that you could never even think of. I want to give you as much torture as you've been giving me."

"Please, Brody," I plead, "show me how to love you." I look deep into his eyes, trying to gaze into his soul. "I've never been with anyone," I say, "and I want you to be the one to teach me everything."

This gives him pause. He already knows he's my first kiss, but the impact of being my first *everything* seems to hit him in full. So much so, I fear he may stop. But then he stands up and slowly removes his clothing: his shoes, his pants, and finally, his briefs.

I gaze at his naked body through my lashes and almost cry out. Not only because he is beautiful, but also from trepidation. He is extremely well-endowed.

Of course my expressive face gives me away.

"Don't worry, Mel," he soothes. "I'll take my time. You know I'll never hurt you."

I give him a small smile. I've wanted him for so long and I trust him implicitly.

"Then, please hurry," I plead. "I don't know how much longer I can wait."

That kicks him into gear. He walks over, pulls me to a stand in front of him, and gently removes my robe. He drops it to the floor and examines my choice of pajamas. I'm wearing shorty pajama bottoms with a sexy tank-style top. The fabric is silky and sensual. I love the feel of it against my body. The look in his eyes as he takes it in is intoxicating.

He reaches for me, and begins slowly removing each item, making my heart beat a little faster. But inhibition also creeps in. I'm not wearing a bra, so with the removal of my top, my breasts are in full view. After removing my shorts, Brody turns me slowly to inspect my panties, which don't have much in the way of coverage. He gently slides them from my body, leaving trails of goose bumps where his fingers linger on my skin.

Oh my god, I'm about to be naked in front of Brody.

When I look up at him, my anxiety dissipates. Brody is my best friend in the whole world. Who could I be more comfortable with?

When I'm completely nude, he stands back and looks at me. I see him eyeing my abrasions and pray he won't change his mind. I want him way too much to turn back now.

But all he says is "You are so beautiful, Mel."

Hearing the huskiness in his voice, I feel a switch flip in my brain. I've waited so long for him to look at me this way. His next kiss is filled with tenderness but also urgency. My fear of his backing out subsides quickly.

I place kisses on the side of his mouth and neck. I move my way down from his chest to his belly button and then I go lower, leaving small wet kisses as I go. I hear his sharp intake of breath as I take him into my hands. I've waited so long to touch him. He is so warm and firm, yet soft. It's completely unexpected.

I move down lower and hesitantly kiss the top and then the sides of his manhood. I have no idea what I'm doing as my tongue strokes him up and then back down. Desire rushes through me as he moans in pleasure.

I've never felt so consumed yet so powerful. As I take him fully in my mouth, I look up to see his beautiful blue eyes glaze over and turn a deep sapphire. He wants to regain control from me, but I'm not ready to give it up yet.

Brody is like a drug that I can't get enough of. As I suckle every inch of him, I have a hard time catching my breath and my hands shake from desire. I can tell I'm on the verge of...I don't know what.

I finally let Brody pull me to standing, and he lays me down on my bed. His eyes are so dark now, and I see something new in them. Something I can't wait for him to set free.

He makes his way over my body, kissing and touching me, all the while telling me how much he wants me. As he gently spreads my legs, he asks me if I trust him. I do, with everything.

He takes my breast into his mouth and I practically jump off the bed. He runs his hand from my breast to the slight patch of hair between my thighs and rubs me until I'm pushing up off the bed with the heels of my feet. Everything he's doing feels amazing. When he plunges his finger into me, I let out a gasp of pleasure. My body instinctively begins thrusting with the rhythm of his hand. I can feel my own wetness and hear his breath catch with every stroke.

He continues doing things to me that I had no idea even were things. It's a punishment of epic proportions. I'm in big trouble but I have no idea what for. He keeps on until I have no thoughts or inhibitions.

I never imagined that being with someone could be like this. A pressure builds inside me and when I close my eyes, I see a beat pulsing behind them—my very own light show accompanied by a drum pounding with the thumps of my heart. The more excited I become, the louder the pounding. As the rhythm quickens, resounding in my ears, my body is like a volcano about to let loose its lava. I lose all conscious awareness as an explosion rocks my body. I cling tightly to Brody and scream with pleasure.

As my body slowly relaxes, I realize Brody is whispering something.

"I can't hold on much longer, Mel," he pants. "I need to be inside you."

"Yes, Brody, please," I urge him.

"I'll be as gentle as possible," he says, "but I'm about to lose it. You're going to feel some pressure and possibly a little pain, but it will subside."

"You won't hurt me," I whisper confidently.

Brody stands up next to the bed and I'm not sure what he's doing as he picks up his pants and begins quickly checking his pockets. He finds what he wants and opens the package. His hands are shaking as he places a condom over himself. Staring into my eyes, he climbs back on the bed and touches me gently, reigniting the spark that dissipated only slightly while he prepared himself.

My fear is of the unknown as he places himself at the entrance to my body. He slowly penetrates and I can feel the stretching of my most inner self. I close my eyes and wrap my legs around his back as I fight the uncomfortable burning sensation. He starts to slowly pull out and then reinsert himself. I can tell it's taking all the restraint he has; his arms are shaking almost uncontrollably.

Finally, he is fully inside of me, and I'm burning again—but not the burn of pain. I can't believe it's possible, but I am building up to another explosion.

"Brody, please!" I gasp. "I need more of you. Now!"

I feel some of the restraint he's holding onto break and he thrusts completely again and again, burying himself inside of me.

As he invades every inch of me with pulsating glory, my body matches his assault as if it knows what to do. I can barely hear the sounds of our lovemaking as the thrumming of my heart resounds in my head.

His shaft pulsing in and out goes on for what seems like forever. We're doing a mating dance that's as old as time. It's as though we're made for each other, and I'm so thankful that I saved myself for Brody.

The next orgasm feels like a rocket going off inside my body and fireworks explode behind my eyelids. Hearing me release, Brody follows with his own explosive orgasm, clinging to me tightly.

He collapses on top of me, both of us breathing heavily. This has surely been the most beautiful lovemaking ever and I pray Brody feels the same.

When he starts to move off me, I hold him in place.

"Let me feel you another minute," I beg. I want to savor this—him—a bit longer.

"I'm too heavy for you, Mel. I don't want to squish you."

I giggle and it sends a final ripple of pure ecstasy between us. We both laugh in full.

Finally, our hurried breaths return to normal.

Brody slowly pulls himself free from me and moves to the side, keeping me nestled in his arms. After a few moments, he gets up to dispose of the condom and then quickly returns to the same position. Lying contented in his embrace, I'm overcome with exhaustion from the previous day along with the beauty our bodies just shared. I fall willingly into a peaceful, dreamless slumber.

CHAPTER 21

Before even opening my eyes the next morning, I lie basking in what happened between Brody and me yesterday and then over and over again last night.

I had sex, so much sex, I can't believe it—I'm no longer a virgin!

Just thinking about such a perfect first time makes me squirm. When I move, I realize I'm a bit sore—but that's just a happy reminder of all we shared.

I reach for Brody, but he's not in the bed; the sheets are cold. I feel a tug at my heart thinking he would leave without waking me.

Then I shake my head. *That's enough of that kind of thinking!*

I get out of bed and head into the bathroom.

After my post-coital collapse yesterday, we did have to come down off Cloud Nine for Brody to fully debrief me about my kidnapping. I filled him in on everything Pete Decker said about Stan Harris and my mom. After that, I was completely spent yet again, so I rested while Brody went to the station to interrogate Pete.

When he returned, Brody carried me to the bathtub, which he'd filled with perfectly warm water, and set me in it. Watching him step into the bath with me, I didn't care that the water poured over the sides. All I cared about was the smile on his face and the look of desire in his eyes. After that, one thing led to another, and then another, and then another again…

Hearing noises down below, I quietly slip on my nightie and descend the stairs.

Entering the kitchen is like walking into a wonderful dream I've wanted for a very long time. Brody has coffee brewing and, with his back to me, is cooking breakfast over the stove. I stand still, checking him out. Watching him shirtless and in jeans, I feel the urge to run my hands over his back and then down over his very nice, very well-rounded butt.

Sensing my presence, he turns around. But his eyes don't meet mine; his gaze lingers on my body. He tilts his head as if to take in everything that he can. When I look down, I realize that my favorite nightie—which no one in the world has ever seen me in—is totally see-through.

"I certainly hope you don't wear *that* too often," he says, leering.

I smile. "I usually put on my robe, but I guess I wasn't thinking clearly or something."

He finally meets my eyes with a look that makes me yelp. He walks over and kisses me passionately, turning my blood to molten lava.

"You're driving me insane," he says. "I want nothing more than to tear that little number off your body, but unfortunately we don't have time right now."

I stifle another squeal as he takes a gentle nip of my neck.

"There will, however, be plenty of time later," he promises.

He looks at me wantonly one last time, flicks his eyebrows up and down, and then turns to grab whatever he's cooking. "Let's eat. I have some ideas I want to talk to you about then we need to get moving. We need a lot of answers and I'm hoping we can find a good amount of them today."

I bring some plates to the stove and Brody fills them with eggs, bacon, potatoes, and toast—enough for several people. I make a face.

"Ah, I see you're admiring my little feast here. Well, sorry, but I'm hungry! I even looked up what a 'full Irish' is and made the closest thing I could with the food you have. But we'll definitely have to try it at Flora's diner because I don't think I did it quite right."

"It looks delicious!" I smile. "I'm just not used to eating a lot, so I can't guarantee I'll be able to clean my plate."

"I think you may surprise yourself," he says with a wink. "You've burned a lot of energy over the past twenty-four hours."

I feel my face turn what I presume to be a lovely shade of red—*again*. Brody laughs.

We spend the rest of the meal eating and talking over yesterday's interrogation and Brody's ideas for moving forward.

"I spent several hours questioning Decker," Brody tells me. "He gave me the same line over and over, and it's the same story he told you and Stella. He vehemently denies killing your mother and says that Stan Harris is not the real serial killer. He has nothing to lose at this point: He's aware he's headed for death row if the evidence bears out that he's indeed the serial killer. Not to mention the kidnapping and assault charges I filed on your behalf. But this crazy bastard wants his *recognition*. That's what he told us."

I look at Brody quizzically.

"My team and the FBI," he clarifies. "They're here because of the serial nature of the murders and the interstate crimes. We didn't get any of his prints in here, but they're all over the items in the barn. Not to mention your testimony and Stella's. He even told us where to find the still-missing bodies of two of his younger victims. The Feds have a crew out there digging."

"Wow," I respond as a chill runs down my spine. It could have been *me* in a cold lonely grave somewhere. Brody doesn't notice my anxiety and I realize he's still talking.

"I think I believe him," says Brody, "but I'll keep that between us until—I should say *unless*—they find the bodies."

"So, what's next?" I ask.

"Well," says Brody, "I have an idea. And it involves Flora."

"Flora?" I ask in surprise. "How?"

"What if she used her gift—getting readings from objects—on some items from your mother's murder? Maybe that would help us figure out why she was killed. And how Stan Harris was able to copycat Decker's crimes."

I grip Brody's arm. "That's a brilliant idea!"

He smiles. "I thought so. And I already called Flora and she's agreed."

I continue staring at Brody, but I can't read his expression. He's suddenly hesitant and I wonder why.

The answer comes quickly.

"I know this may be painful for you," he says. "You know, to bring all this back up again."

I purse my lips. "I think of my mom all of the time," I tell him. "Just the other day I relived the whole nightmare of her death right after waking from one of my other dreams; so it's not like we're bringing back memories I've forgotten about. It's always with me."

Brody reaches over and strokes my hair. "I'm worried about what happened with Decker, too," he says gently. "You seem okay, but I don't want to put too much strain on you."

"I understand," I say, touching his hand. "But we need to find answers, and the sooner we do, the faster I can start the healing process. For everything."

He lowers his hand to caress my shoulder and then stands to clear the dishes from the table. I realize that as we've been talking, I've eaten *everything* on my plate! I look up at Brody and his smile is huge.

"I told you you'd be hungry!" he gloats. "You have no idea how much energy lovemaking burns."

I shrug. "I guess I do now."

We both laugh and I convince him to shower while I finish cleaning the kitchen. When I hear the water stop, I yell upstairs that I have an extra new toothbrush in the medicine cabinet. *Too late.* He comes to the top landing with *my* toothbrush in his mouth and as much of a smile as he can muster behind a sea-foam of paste. I don't care. We've already shared so much, what's a little more?

A warm, settled feeling surrounds my heart and I love it.

CHAPTER 22

AFTER A LEISURELY SHOWER, still basking in the glow of "playing house" with Brody, I come down fresh and ready to go.

We stop by the station so Brody can check out the evidence we need. I go in with him.

I look around. "Where's Stella?" I ask.

"I told her she needed to take some time to process everything that happened," he says. "I'll keep her on our staff, but she has to make some life changes for herself. I think she learned a hard lesson with Decker, but there has to be some punishment for not following my orders at the barn and for putting you both in more danger."

I can tell he doesn't want to talk about it anymore, and I understand.

After leaving the station, we make the hundred-mile trek to the diner in what seems like record time. This time we park directly in the lot.

It's late morning and a few diehard breakfast fans still linger. Plates filled with delicious-looking cuisine cover the tables. We take a seat at the counter and look around for Flora. She comes over quickly. She takes one look at us and smiles knowingly.

She seems about to hug me but hesitates. I stand and pull her in.

"I'm so happy you're okay," she murmurs.

I'm not used to being this friendly with people, but without her, Brody might not have found me. I squeeze a little harder and I think she understands better than anyone.

Like me, Flora has dealt with treatment from those who don't understand special gifts.

"Thank you, Flora," I say, "for everything. I'm feeling much better today."

"I can see that. Is there anything I can get you?"

"Just coffee, thanks. We had a big breakfast at my house before we left."

Oops…

I've inadvertently confirmed her obvious suspicion that something happened between Brody and me. I'm not ready to go there just yet, but clearly she knows.

Having remained quiet during Flora's and my exchange, Brody enters the conversation. "You'll have to ask Flora some time about hugging people," he says. "She probably just read your life history or something."

Looking from Brody to Flora, I see them share a look.

"I don't read *everyone* I hug," Flora retorts. "Just stubborn police officers who don't want to open up about their feelings."

"Alright, what's going on here?" I ask.

"Never mind" is Brody's answer. "We don't have time for it."

Okay… I drop that subject really quickly. For the moment.

Brody gets back to business. "Are you available to work with us right now?" he asks Flora.

Flora looks around the near-empty diner. While we were talking, the late breakfast bevy cleared and the lunch bunch hasn't arrived yet.

"We should be okay for a bit. I recently hired a new waitress and she's working out very well," Flora says, taking off her apron. "So now should be perfect. Let's meet in my office." She points to it. "I don't want to do this in front of customers."

I couldn't understand more.

As Brody goes out to the car to retrieve the evidence, Flora and I make our way to the office. It's small, with barely enough room for the three of us. Of course, Flora has hung up some of her glass angels in the corner.

As we wait for Brody, I ask her how she and Alene ended up in Kansas City.

"We lived in Ireland for most of my life," she tells me. "It's so beautiful there. But when my father died suddenly, everything changed. My mom and I decided we wanted to live somewhere not filled with so many memories. We eventually landed here. We both love antiques, so we pooled our money to open the shop. Once it started being profitable, we saved enough for me to open the diner. We're finally happy for the first time in a long time."

I can tell she's not revealing the whole story—such as, *Why choose Kansas City after Ireland?*—but I don't ask any more questions. I know Brody could use police resources to find more answers, but I don't want to *investigate* a friend. And I'm beginning to consider Flora a friend.

Brody enters the office with the box of evidence and sets it on the desk. Then he comes over and takes my hands in his.

"Mel, if you don't want to be in the room while we do this, you don't have to. I know some of these items may distress you and I really don't want to do that."

Flora nods her agreement.

"Really, I'm fine," I insist. "But I'll stand back out of the way so Flora can do what she needs."

I watch as Flora sits down behind the desk across from Brody, who's in the visitor's chair. I walk over to close the door.

As Brody pulls item after item from the box, I realize I'm holding my breath. They're all my mother's personal belongings. In the end, they weren't needed to catch the killer since Brody and I unwittingly accomplished that. But I assume they have my mom's DNA—and energy—on them which could be useful for Flora.

Brody hands her a sealed plastic bag containing my mother's purse. I remember the day I bought it for her as a birthday gift. It didn't cost very much, but my dad and I made a special trip to the next town to buy it, and my mom was so pleased with it.

The purse represents two painful memories wrapped into one, but I won't cry. Not today, anyway. I'll save the memories in a part of my heart where I can take them out when I'm ready.

Brody obviously senses the effect the purse is having on me. "Mel, we'll understand if this is too much for you."

"No," I tell him. "I have to be strong now. Finding out why she was killed is the most important thing that we can do."

Now Flora looks at me. She seems to be sad but also knows that I'm right.

"Can I take the items out of the bags?" she asks, looking back toward the evidence box. "I'm not sure I can get a reading through the plastic."

"Yes," Brody tells her, "we've gotten all the evidence we can from them anyway." He glances at me hesitantly. "I'll warn you, we found a little of her blood on the purse. It could have come from when she was given the paralytic."

"I'll be okay," Flora says, now looking at both of us. "If Mel can be strong enough to go through this, then so can I. And it may even help me to get a better reading."

I watch carefully as she handles the purse. She closes her eyes to concentrate. I wonder if it's the way she always gets readings.

She holds on to the purse for quite a while.

"I'm not able to get much from this." She sighs. "Do you have what was *in* the purse at the time?"

"Most contents were given back to Mel," Brody explains, "but we can try something else."

As Brody digs to the bottom of the box, I close *my* eyes and think of what items I have at home that were with my mother when she was murdered. If needed, I can find them for Flora.

"Here, try this one, Flora," Brody says, pulling a small bag from the carton. "It's something we found in the car that Melanie says *didn't* belong to her mother."

I look over and see the tiny clip Brody told me was used to hold marijuana joints. I know for certain my mother didn't use drugs.

"We surmise it came from the killer," Brody explains, "but we found no proof of that."

Flora removes the clip from the evidence bag and holds it in her hand.

"This definitely didn't belong to your mother," she says, eyes closed again. "Someone else was involved here…a woman. She's meeting with a man, and they're passing each other this clip to smoke some sort of drug with each other. His face is scarred or disfigured on one side."

Brody and I share a knowing glance: *Stan Harris.*

"She's contracted him to kill your mother. The clip falls out of his pocket when he reaches into the car to affix your mother's hands to the steering wheel."

Flora opens her eyes and looks at me.

I'm in shock, but this is just the information we need in order to figure out why my mother was killed.

"Did they put their mouths on this?" I ask quickly. "Shouldn't there be DNA or something?"

"Everything in here was thoroughly checked for DNA, Mel, and fingerprints and everything else. People might touch their mouths to joint clips like this but they're more concerned with getting their lips wrapped around what the clip is holding! Also, DNA—especially 'touch' DNA—is hard to get off metal, and the layers of fingerprints on this thing were meshed together and smudged." Brody shakes his head. "And we found only your mother's DNA on her items."

I can tell Brody has another idea, though.

"If we need to, Flora," he asks, "could you work with a sketch artist on the woman?"

Flora shakes her head sadly. "I'm sorry. I could see the man's face clearly, but the woman had her back to me. All I saw was some short gray hair."

I'd thought mine was a good question, but Flora comes up with a better one:

"Brody, do you have any way to find out who this Stan Harris was in communication with right before the murder?"

Without replying, Brody starts digging frantically through the box. After a few minutes, he pulls out a sheaf of papers and lifts them in the air.

"Phone records for Harris," he says triumphantly. "We went through them before, of course, and we came up with all dead ends. But with Flora's 'mystery woman' now front and center, we'll go through them again."

I jump up out of my seat. Maybe *this* is the key.

"Mel, let me get started on this," Brody says, waving the stack of papers. "I want to call the station to get research underway ASAP."

"Mel and I will wait out in the diner," Flora offers. "To give you some quiet for your call."

"Thank you for everything you've done," I say to Flora. "I feel like we may finally have caught a break."

"You don't have to thank me for anything. That's what friends do for each other, right?"

Brody gives me a comforting squeeze before Flora and I head out of the office.

CHAPTER 23

Flora and I sit down in a booth to talk while we wait. It seems like the perfect time to bring up my questions about her gift—and maybe she's curious about mine, too.

I feel suddenly shy. "I— If you don't mind, Flora, I'd love to hear more about how your, uh, ability works."

Flora smiles and glances around. I turn to see what she's looking for and then I realize: eavesdroppers.

"Of course, Melanie. I have no problem talking about it. With *you*, that is—I wouldn't trust just anyone with my secrets."

Mel squeezes Flora's hand knowingly. "If anyone understands that, it's me."

Flora nods. "In just the short time we've known each other, I've come to trust both you *and* Brody. Although, in Brody's case, I'm not sure the feeling is mutual." She glances toward the office door and smiles. "I'm grateful he was willing to come see me today."

"Not just willing," I clarify. "He instigated it! By the way, what did you read from him the other day that he's so worked up about?"

Flora looks down at the table. "I promised him I wouldn't talk to anyone about it," she replies softly. "It's something he has to come to terms with in his own time. When he's ready, I'm sure he'll share it with you."

Now I have even more questions. And confusion. But she's right: If she found—or felt—information from him that he's not ready to give out, it's not fair of her to share it with anyone else.

"Anyway," says Flora, "I'm happy to know he trusts my gifts. And I'll ask *you* a question first: Want to tell me what's gone on between you two since I last saw you?"

I feel my face flush again—I'm getting used to being embarrassed. Flora lets out a strange giggle and raises her eyebrows. Someday I will tell her that she and Brody make the same gesture with their eyebrows. Probably for different reasons, though. I think hers means she's curious.

I know I don't *have* to answer her question, but I could use a friend to talk to and I want it to be her.

"Let's just say that we took the friendship out of the friendship zone," I say. "Brody and I have been close for a long time, and I've always wanted to be more to him, but I didn't think he thought of me that way."

"You know I saw from the first time we met how you felt about Brody," says Flora. "I still wonder that he didn't see it, too."

"I guess I need to learn to hide things better," I gripe. "Brody's so good at it."

"He *is* very private with his feelings," Flora agrees.

"You can say that again!" I cry. "I mean, it took him *how many* years to be with me?"

Eek! Did I just say that?

"Can we change the subject now?" I beg. "I really don't want Brody to come back and hear anything. And please don't tell him I told you anything about any of this!"

"No worries, Melanie. I know how to keep a secret." Flora smiles her wicked smile that I'm beginning to appreciate as part of her quirky personality.

"So, tell me about your psychic powers." I finally get to the heart of my questions. "How did you find out you had them? How old were you? How do they work?"

"Whoa, Melanie!" Flora laughs. "Let's take one question at a time."

I apologize, and Flora shakes her head. Then she becomes serious.

"I first found out when I was very young," she explains. "By accident, really. I wasn't even remotely aware that I had any such gifts until I touched someone I loved greatly and realized they were very sick, even though they appeared to be in perfect health. I tried to tell my family, but as you can imagine, reactions were mixed. Eventually, this person got checked out by a doctor, but it was too late—*I* was too late. After that, everyone in my family stayed away from me, to avoid my giving them bad news."

Flora sighs and I nod in compassion. If only she knew how well I could relate.

"My mother became the only person I could trust with what I saw," Flora goes on. "My father wanted to turn me into a parlor trick—trying to get me to do readings on people to make money. No one except my mother understood that it didn't work that way. My father died not long after I refused to be his circus freak, and a lot of bad things he'd done began to come out. It was embarrassing for my mother, so we moved away from our town and family."

Flora and I both fall quiet for several minutes.

"I'm so sorry, Flora." I break the silence. "Our lives have definitely been similar. I'm glad we've found each other."

I touch her hand and I feel a connection between us—a very strong connection.

"Tell me more, Flora," I probe. "Tell me more about how your gift works."

Flora wiggles her fingers in the air. "It's not magic, Mel, but it's certainly useful."

We both laugh.

"Well, as you know," she replies, "I have to touch something to get a reading. For example, as we looked for you, I took off my shoe to step into a footprint. Of course, Brody was incensed about my defacing evidence—until I started giving him information."

"Oh, you're right about that!" I confirm. "He told me all about it."

But I need to know more.

"Do you have to think about something specific? When Brody was debriefing me, he indicated trying to focus you on certain questions."

"Yes," she replies without hesitation. "Being specific—being focused—helps me to go deeper into the situation. And into myself. That's why I close my eyes—to close out everything around me."

"I kind of figured that, watching you touch items from the box," I tell her.

"What about you, Melanie?" she asks. "How do your dreams work?"

Apparently it's her turn for some questions.

"Please call me Mel," I smile. "I've been meaning to tell you that for a while."

She smiles, too, and I feel our connection growing.

"In all honesty," I admit, "I'm not one hundred percent sure how the dreams work. Usually they just come to me at night when I'm sleeping. Although recently I had a vision during the day after Brody and I went running. I lost all control over myself and fell face-first into the dirt—that scared a couple years off Brody's life! I thought he was going to blow a gasket. He also told me that given the possibility of it happening again, that if I risked driving a car he'd give me a ticket! I guess I understand now why he felt that way."

Flora and I smile at each other again, both appreciating how much Brody cares and worries about me.

"It was actually kind of funny at the time," I relate, "to see him yelling and tugging at his hair."

"Oh my gosh!" She laughs. "I saw him do that hair-pulling thing right after I stepped in the footprint."

"Ha! He does it when he's stressed. Always has."

I grin as I think about all the times *I've* been the reason for his breaking out that habit of his.

"Sorry," I say to Flora, coming back to reality. "I get a little off track sometimes."

I take a deep breath. I know I want to tell Flora *everything* about my gift. And that, by definition, includes Jamie.

I feel a bit bad because I haven't even told Brody yet, but maybe I can start with someone who I *know* will understand.

"So…" I continue. "Sometimes the visions are sort of… *brought* to me."

Flora looks at me quizzically. "Brought to you how? By whom?"

Her second question provides me the perfect opening. I inhale deeply.

"By someone I believe has passed," I explain. "This woman—Jamie—has been with me since I was a little girl. Especially when I was lonely after both my parents died."

"Wow," says Flora raptly. "Tell me more."

"I've never seen her," I explain. "She communicates with me in my head, kind of. That's the best I can explain it. She gives me visions of things, places. Did you go inside my house? Most of the paintings on the first floor are visions from her." I pause. "Sometimes I can hear her voice, but that hasn't happened much lately."

"Oh my goodness!" cries Flora. "First of all, those paintings are amazing. Obviously, I didn't take time to inspect them closely, but I would love to. Secondly," she says, her voice rising, "now that you're telling me this, I think this 'Jamie' may be the one who came to me to let me know you were in trouble. She's also the reason I knew your name the first day we met."

My hard breaths become deep and long.

"I…I…I don't think she's ever made her presence known to anyone but me!" I say excitedly. "And I have zero information on her, like who is she? And why is she with me—what is the purpose? I've always wondered about it."

"Well, I sure didn't get any of *those* answers," Flora says, "but it's obvious she's very protective of you. She seemed hyper-concerned about your well-being; though I admit it would've been nice if she'd given me more information toward saving your life. Oh, I did get the sense that she couldn't intervene directly."

"Well," I respond, "if I've learned anything through all this—these dreams and everything else—it's that if understanding all that surrounds us was easy, you and I wouldn't be so special."

Flora smiles. "That's a very good way to think of it."

Flora looks around and notices that the diner has picked up since we started our conversation. She excuses herself to make sure all is under control, and I watch as she rushes around checking on patrons.

She comes back to stand by me just as Brody emerges from the office.

"Flora," I whisper, concerned she might spill the astral beans, "Brody doesn't know about Jamie, and I need to be the one to tell him."

"I understand," she says, squeezing my shoulder.

"What are you two in cahoots about?" asks Brody.

"Oh, just chatting," Flora says smoothly.

"Well, I have my team tracking down phone numbers," Brody says, "but we really need to get going. Mel, are you ready?"

As we prepare to climb into his truck, I grab Flora into a hug. As we pull apart, we look into each other's eyes and shed a couple of tears.

"Goodbye, Flora," I say. "I hope to see you again soon. Thank you for everything you've done to help me."

"Anytime, Mel. That's what friends are for."

CHAPTER 24

THE DRIVE HOME TINGLES with an air of excitement—as though it's bouncing around in the truck. There's no conversation as we both sink deeply into our own thoughts. Before I know it, we're at my house.

"Do you want to come in for a drink?" I ask. "I think I have some wine—or coffee, if you're going to work?"

"A drink sounds great," says Brody, "but I'm starved."

"Oh, do you want to try that Italian place that just opened?" I ask.

"That's not what I meant," says Brody, his eyes smoldering with desire.

We get out of the truck and make our way to the porch holding hands. Before I unlock the door, he kisses me so tenderly, I could float away.

"I think we should order the food and have some wine," I say.

I feel suddenly self-conscious even after all the times we've been together. My nerves shoot electrical charges through my body in anticipation.

Brody reluctantly agrees. I place the order and pour each of us a glass of red wine. I sip slowly as we wait for the delivery. As we continue making small talk, I notice Brody hasn't touched his at all.

"Don't you like the wine?" I ask.

Brody lifts an eyebrow. "Actually, it's because I have all this pent-up energy, and *wine* isn't what I want right now."

"Oh!" is all I can say, accompanied by a full flush.

Finally the doorbell rings. Brody gets the food and places it on the counter near the oven.

When he turns back toward me, his eyes—usually the most vibrant of blue—are suddenly *dark* blue and travel from my face to my breasts and lower. I've never been so sufficiently stripped naked without even a touch.

I lick my lips.

Brody is suddenly right in front of me. He swipes his tongue over my lips where I just licked them and brings his hand to my breast. I'm instantly awash in heat. My nipple puckers into a hard nub in his palm.

He lifts my t-shirt over my head and ever so slowly removes my jeans. He runs his hands up the outside of my thighs, sending an electric current straight to my center. Then he grabs my panties and pulls them down my body. As he stands back up, he trails one finger along the inside of my leg, marking me with his touch. Staring straight into my eyes, he places his finger on my center and then inside me. My head falls back from the ecstasy of his touch, sending me slightly off balance. He grabs me and hoists me to the counter and then slowly and efficiently begins to send me over the edge of sanity.

He suckles my breast through my lacy bra, but it must not be enough because he rips it down the center. I couldn't care less. Once it's gone, he lavishes me with kisses from my mouth to my breasts. Looking into my eyes, he spreads my legs and begins to fervently pleasure me with his mouth, tugging and licking. Oh my gosh!

"Brody, please."

"Please what, Melanie?"

He gives me no chance to answer as he continues his feast. I couldn't anyway because he's vigorously driving me crazy. My only thought is that he sounds so in control. I hope he's burning up as much as I am.

Now he's talking and I can barely make out his words.

"You thoroughly tortured me during our first encounter," he says, "and I'm going to show you what that feels like."

"You're torturing me now, Brody. Oh my god."

He thrusts his tongue deep inside of me and I push myself into him. He's turning me into a mad woman. He replaces his tongue with his fingers and I ride his hand, moaning loudly, as he masterfully rubs me to oblivion, stimulating the little nub that's my most sensitive spot. The orgasm begins as a slow burn that starts in my core and builds to a fever pitch of insanity that has me screaming his name. When he puts his mouth back where his hand had been, my body lifts off the counter so my center is meeting his mouth. He continues to thrust his tongue in and out of me. Then he puts his fingers back inside of me and uses his tongue in a place that feels like—I can't explain it—but it feels so good, I never want him to stop.

Suddenly he stops devouring me and I whimper. He pulls me to the edge of the counter and removes his pants with a deftness I admire. Gazing at his body, I can't wait for him to make me his again. He isn't gentle as he pulls me down onto himself and thrusts fully into me. It's exhilarating. I can hardly think as he takes me with punishing fervor. I close my eyes so I can fully feel everything there is to feel.

"Melanie, open your eyes," he commands. "I want to see your desire for me; I want to watch you as you come."

I look directly into his eyes and a wave of desire crashes over me. I can't control the fever raging through my body, and I yearn to let go. He holds me and rocks rhythmically in and out of me. The dance goes on for so long that we both drop to the floor and he continues his assault. We look at each other with so much need.

"I'm ready to lose it, Mel. Go over with me."

It begins as a deep throbbing inside me, launching a massive tremor that spreads to my toes, making them curl. The orgasm takes over our bodies and we're molded together as one as he continues to pound into me. There's no stopping the train of desire we're riding, and we're rocked out of control. I don't think I can take much more until another wave of bliss hits me, and I feel like I'm on a rocket to the sky. We cry out each other's names as our bodies explode over and over.

When we're finished, we lie exhausted on my kitchen floor trying to catch our breaths. I wonder how last night and today could have possibly given me so much.

My heart staggers as I grasp *how* completely in love I am with Brody. And always have been. I feel suddenly shy, which is silly considering all we've shared. I sincerely hope he's not able to read my face. I'm still deep in thought about how my relationship with Brody will be moving forward, when he pulls out of me. I feel empty but try not to show it. He rolls over next to me and kisses me hard on the mouth.

"We'd better get up and get dressed, or you and I are not going to be eating that dinner we ordered," he says.

He takes my hands and helps me up off the floor. I have difficulty standing, so he stabilizes me and I rest my head on his shoulder. At least when he hugs me, he's not looking directly in my eyes—he certainly would see and I'm not ready for that. Even with as much as we've shared, is love what Brody wants? I'm too afraid to find out.

He kisses me again, pulls on his pants, and says, "Melanie, you really need to go upstairs and get another bra—it seems this little number is destroyed." He laughs as he holds up what used to be one of my favorites, and I laugh with him, thinking I can always get another.

He spanks me lightly on the ass and then turns to wash his hands. Suddenly his phone rings.

As I walk away completely naked, I look back to find him watching my every move as he answers. I feel the old familiar *thump, thump, thump*—except this time it goes from my heart to my crotch. Oh, I like the feeling!

I come back downstairs fully showered and dressed. Brody is off the phone and the table is set. Somehow he managed to locate two candles, which are lit in the center of the table. Seriously, could he be any more amazing?

"Well?" I ask, staring pointedly at his phone.

"I think we have a lead," he says. "Let's eat while we talk about it, 'cause I'm—"

"Let me guess," I interrupt. "You're starving."

Ignoring Brody's *look*. I fill my plate with food and Brody follows suit. As we prepare to eat, I lose myself again. Sitting side by side, enjoying a nice dinner as we gaze at each other longingly, I wonder why *anyone*—guys like Stan Harris or Pete Decker or any of the killers in my dreams—would ever choose cruelty over closeness.

I have no answer.

The smell of pasta brings me back.

"I've been dying to try the food from this place," Brody says, upbeat. "Here, taste the eggplant parmesan—you're going to love it."

I take the bite into my mouth.

"That is delicious, Brody," I say, "but how about you tell me what you found out—the suspense is killing me."

"Oh, yeah. That." He looks down at his plate as he rolls his fork in the pasta. "Well, it's kind of huge, and I'm worried it'll upset you."

I cross my arms. "The only thing upsetting me," I tell him, "is *you* trying to protect me from information."

He raises his hands in surrender. "Alright, alright." He looks at me. "To be honest, I was just trying to let you enjoy your dinner before we started—"

"Well, guess what?" I tell him. "I *am* enjoying my dinner except that I'm frustrated. Not only am I having dream after dream to save someone I haven't a clue about, but now I have to re-delve into why some psychotic asshole killed my mother. I need answers and I need you to stop trying to protect me. Yes, I've been through hell this week, but you have to trust that I can handle this."

I almost never use foul language, but right now I don't much care. However, as soon as the words leave my mouth, I regret snapping at Brody.

He stands up and comes around the table. He pulls me to my feet.

"I'm sorry," he says. "I guess I'm feeling overwhelmed with everything that's happened as well. I just wanted you to have a few minutes of peace."

I fall into his arms.

"I understand," I say. "But we're in this together. We need to be open and honest with each other about the case."

"Fair enough," he says. "Okay, so here goes. We—*I*—have been digging hard through those phone records. The same dead ends came up again, but in the years that have passed, one of those dead ends opened up. It took some work and some new tech, but my team tracked down a number that Harris called a few times—a number that was disconnected shortly after your mother was killed."

Brody pulls away to look at me. "It belonged to an older woman," he reveals. "And I think we should go talk to her."

"You know where she is?!" I almost scream. "Let's go! Where is she?"

"She's in prison."

I freeze. "Prison?"

"Yep. She was arrested for check fraud—*this* time. And she's got quite the history: petty larceny, drunk and disorderly, drug abuse and dealing, prostitution. Her record goes back a long way. I'm not sure how she's connected to Harris—much less your mother—but it's sure worth checking out."

"Well, let's go!" I demand again.

"Mel," says Brody, "first of all, I have to go back to the office to do more research and arrange the visit. Second, the visiting hours are almost closed for today. Third, you need to get some rest. We'll head out to the 'big house' tomorrow."

I'm a little deflated, but I know Brody's right. I'm exhausted. We finish our dinner, clean everything up, and put away the leftovers in the fridge.

"Soooo…" I ask, kissing him goodbye at the door. "I'll see you in the morning? What, uh, time will you pick me up?"

"Early," he says. "Visiting hours begin at nine a.m. sharp. I'll have everything arranged, so be ready at six."

"Six a.m?"

"Yes." He smiles. "I'll see you then."

I look at him and the words "I love you" are stuck in my throat. I have enough control not to let them out.

CHAPTER 25

I MAY HAVE BEEN ABLE TO CONTROL my words with Brody, but what I can never control are my dreams. Tonight becomes another night of living in another person's psyche—living out another person's scheming.

It doesn't take long to start.

I AM IN THE MIND of an older woman as she rubs her dirty hands together over an open flame in a trash barrel. Homelessness has become just another part of the life she's had to deal with. So are drugs. When whatever money and anything else she once had was gone, she moved to the streets. At that point, any semblance of a "normal" life was also long gone. She now alternates from staying in shelters to finding the cleanest dirty places among the jungle of asphalt and alleys.

And she'll do anything to get her next fix.

But the idea she's concocting in the blowing smoke and fire embers might just change all that. In fact, the more she thinks about it, the more perfect it seems. It's finally time, she decides, to get what she's due.

Thankfully, it hasn't been that many years since she was sort of an upstanding citizen. She still knows a few people who help her keep tabs on that disgusting little secondhand "family." The old man is dead now, so all that leaves is the old bitch.

And if I take care of her, she thinks, I can take care of ME!

Her plan will start with changing her name. Because a strategy like this will be best served by anonymity…less traceability. And it's an opportune time. One of the other homeless women in their "group" was killed recently, so she'll simply become her: Beatrice Thomas. No one will know the difference. And who'll care, anyway? No one will be looking for the real Ms. Thomas. The body taken to the morgue won't have been labeled by that name, either—just another Jane Doe from skid row.

But Beatrice actually revealed a lot about herself before dying—at least enough to establish a pretty solid identity. And it was clear she had no family or even a criminal record. Hers was the ideal identity to assume. And it wouldn't be hard to find someone to make an ID; that was the first item on the agenda. The streets aren't a friendly place to live, but anything and everything is available for a price.

As the woman continues warming her hands, her excitement about her plan has her practically jumping up and down. And if it necessitates the old bitch being killed off to make it work, well, so be it.

She gets more and more animated, cackling and congratulating herself on the brilliance of this slickest of schemes. At the shelters, she's seen recent news reports of serial murders along the old Route 66 corridor and surrounding areas. Some just seem like drifter killings of random young girls, but others seem more planned-out: murders of "older" women, the details of which are "not being released by authorities"…

I FEEL MY MIND wanting to wake up, but I can't. I know I'm swimming in those "hormonal teenage girl" sweats that the dreams produce, and I can feel my teeth clenching and grinding. But I also feel my inability to control this dream. I know I have to live through every demented detail of this person's "plan" before my eyes can—*will*—open. In more ways than one.

IF THE WOMAN CAN JUST FIND out a few of those secret "details," her plan will surely succeed.

She cackles once more, thinking back again to when she was "normal." Back to when she earned a good living in sales and marketing. It might be time to resurrect those skills—along with a few she learned running scams on the streets, amidst the drug haze and hygienic neglect.

Using the shelter's communal computer, she'll explore the identities of some of the serial killer's victims and ferret out their families. Then, leveraging the same persuasion she used to sell people things they didn't need or want, she can surely convince gullible grieving kin that she's with law enforcement and trick them into revealing some of those withheld "details."

Her brilliant plan becomes even more dazzling.

And possible.

But she will need help—someone to act on those "details." More than once, her dealer has mentioned knowing "this guy" who's "always open to a little extra work." She's sure he'll be perfect.

Thinking about her dealer makes her lick her lips. She could certainly use a fix right now. And while she's there, she'll put in word that she'd like to get in touch with the dealer's "friend." This will all come together.

THIS ISN'T JUST A DREAM; it's a long, entangled epic. I feel myself writhing, wrapped tightly in wet sheets, blankets, and bewilderment.

I dread finding out who she's going to kill.

Because I think I know.

But what I don't know is who she *really* is and why she's doing this. What does she have to gain?

Also, am I really having a second set of dreams now, unrelated to the girl with the violin? Or does *all* of this somehow tie together?

It's too much for my muddled mind to contemplate. I lose myself back into the vision.

KANSAS CITY HAS BEEN HER HOME all her life, but this plan could provide the perfect new beginning. For quite a while now, she's felt it's time to move on and try a new town—someplace with new opportunities for a woman like her. She's tired of panhandling and begging and stealing, tired of needing a fix. She shouldn't have to struggle so hard to get what she wants and what she needs. She shouldn't be on these mean damn streets at all.

The fire is burning down, so she decides to get into a shelter for the night. More and more, she's trying to avoid staying on the streets. They aren't safe for someone no longer strong enough to fight off unwanted advances from the others. Someone like herself. Someone like Beatrice.

As she walks quickly to the shelter, her excitement rises again. She'll sleep well tonight thinking of all the money she's going to come into. Anticipating her perfect partnership with "this guy"—a willing, mercenary killer. She isn't afraid to get into an arrangement with someone like that because she herself has wanted to kill before. Hell, if he refuses, she'll pull this off alone. She'll do anything now to save her own skin.

Anything…

CHAPTER 26

6:00 A.M.

When Brody picks me up, I don't know how much sleep I have or haven't had. He was right about my needing rest, but last night provided little in the way of rejuvenation. I'm as wrung out as my tangled-tight bedding.

I have coffee ready. Strong brew is my specialty and right now I need every caffeinated drop.

As I climb into the truck, I think about how much I missed Brody in my bed last night…but also how I might have missed that dream if he *had* been there.

"Good morning," I say—and then cut to the chase. "Were you able to get any more information about today's visitee?"

I might as well hear what he has to tell me before inundating him with *my* news.

Brody smiles. "I'll tell you all about it, but first you're going to have to give me a kiss."

I smile back. Of course I'll give him a kiss! I can't believe *I* didn't think of it first. I need him now more than ever.

I move to the middle of the truck bench and wrap my arms around his neck. Looking into his eyes, I move my mouth over his. I take the kiss a bit deeper and Brody pulls me onto his lap, where we kiss passionately for several minutes until we're both breathing heavily.

I suddenly feel more energized.

"Unfortunately, we're going to need to wait until later for anything further," he says. "Now get off my lap, you hussy."

I turn my usual shade of red and punch Brody in the arm. Of course, this hurts my hand more than his arm.

"Missed you, too, you bully," I say.

"I am not a bully," he argues. "I just know we have a schedule to keep, and if I let you and your wanton ways take over, we won't end up going *anywhere*."

He does his eyebrow-raising thing, and I laugh. It feels good and I realize that I haven't had a good laugh in a long time. After today, it may be a bit longer.

"Let's go," I agree. "I'm eager to see what we'll find out."

WE PULL ONTO WESTBOUND I-44, heading for Mabel Bassett Correctional Center in McCloud, Oklahoma. It's about a three-hour drive from my house.

"Uh," Brody," I stutter a bit, "do you…uh…have any idea who this woman is?" I suddenly realize I haven't even asked the prisoner's name.

"Well," Brody says, "her *real* name is Agatha Hadley. That mean anything to you?"

I think hard. "No," I tell him regretfully. *But maybe…*

"Well, I have a pretty good idea of *what* she is," he interrupts my thought, "if I go by that long and colorful arrest record of hers. But other than that, I'm not sure how or if she's connected to all this. We know she spoke to Stan, but that's not enough to solidly link her to anything. However, it *might* be just enough to let us squeeze her—or trick her with a few half-truths—into providing us details."

I nod.

"I already know she's going to be nothing but trouble the minute she sees my badge," Brody goes on. "And I have to wear it; it's required to question a prisoner. There's no way around that particular truth. And in order to get *you* in, I had to tell them that you were my on-staff forensic psychic. They weren't exactly excited and made a couple comments, but they had to let you in since you're serving in an official capacity."

"That's fine," I tell him, "because it sounds like *you*'re going to look like the crazy one."

I manage a slight laugh, even though I'm not feeling very jovial, knowing what I still must tell him.

"But seriously," I say, "I'm not worried about people's skepticism. I mean, I've been in this situation before and, besides, when will I ever see these people again?"

"Perfect," he says, touching my leg. "'Cause you know I'm with you. I'm not worried about what some other cops think of us, either. What *I* care about is getting to some truths. And maybe that will start with this woman."

That opens the door.

"Uh, Brody," I say, stumbling a little again.

"Yeah?"

"I had another dream last night."

"Oh?"

"And it was about a woman," I tell him. "A homeless woman devising a scheme that involved murder-for-hire."

Brody raises his eyebrows, but says nothing.

"So here goes…"

For the next forty miles or so, I do my best to untangle the sinister story and lay it all out for Brody—*and* myself. When I get to the part about the woman contracting a killer after the "old man" has died, Brody about drives off the road.

"Damn, Mel!" He turns to look at me as I wrap it all up. "With what I know about you and your dreams, it seems that this guest of Oklahoma we're driving three hours to *visit* with is definitely the one who pulled Stan Harris's strings."

"And the one ultimately responsible for my mother's murder," I agree.

Brody reaches over and grabs my hand.

"But I desperately want to know *why!*" I say. "*What* was she going to gain from my mother's death? And what did my father being gone have to do with that?"

"Well," he says thoughtfully, "the pseudonym you mentioned, Beatrice Thomas, doesn't ring a bell with me, but Hadley has a huge rap sheet and with a raunchy recluse like her, some stuff can get lost or overlooked. So knowing this other alias might just help us out with our 'squeezing and tricking.'"

Agatha Hadley…

Beatrice Thomas…

A "raunchy recluse"…

I don't understand any of this. My mom was just a regular person; she wasn't a celebrity or anything. This woman had no reason that I can think of to choose her. But she definitely did. In fact, she was "keeping tabs" on my entire family…

Lost in thought, I'm not even aware that we've arrived at the prison until Brody touches my arm. Back to reality.

I'm more than a little nervous to go in and meet this woman. But to add an old saying to new fears, there's no time like the present.

"Let's go," I tell Brody, jumping out of the truck. "I want to get this over with."

"*And* get closer to the truth," he adds. "But you have to leave your backpack here."

I turn and put it under the seat.

We walk toward the gate. Although this is a medium-security facility, it still has the high fences with razor wire all around it. I can't imagine what it would be like to be locked in a place like this day and night. I certainly don't plan to ever find out. Hell, I didn't even know what a "joint clip" was before all this.

As we near the entrance, Brody stops us.

"You know," he tells me, "let's feel out how the conversation goes with this woman before we throw anything at her from your dream. When we do hit her with some of our surprising knowledge, I'm hoping it'll scare the hell outta her enough to spill everything."

Everything…

My stomach forms into a knot.

We're escorted through the gate and to the first of two security checkpoints. They ask us both for ID, even though Brody has his badge on, and require him to surrender his gun during our visit. He's carrying a file folder, which they look inside but allow him to keep.

I'm glad I couldn't bring my backpack in. It's much easier not dealing with it, and I don't think I'll be doing any drawing during this visit. I intend to be *very* focused on reality.

The warden greets us at the second checkpoint and explains the rules of the prison. It's a nice show of professional courtesy, but I still catch him looking at me like a major league baseball player glances at the local batboy. He tells us that, per Brody's request, he's arranged for us to meet this woman in a private room.

"Stay on your guard," the warden warns us. "She's street-smart and won't hesitate to try and hurt you. Not physically—our guards won't allow that *and* she'll be cuffed—but she's an emotional abuser, too. She's witty and bad-tempered, and if she thinks she can cause you any kind of pain, she will."

I shiver.

CHAPTER 27

WE WALK INTO THE ROOM and I see an old woman ravaged by age and what I assume to be drug and alcohol abuse. She doesn't *look* familiar; in the dream, I was in her head and *we* never looked in a mirror.

But the lack of familiarity is apparently mine alone.

"Well, well, well, look what the cat dragged in," she mutters, looking at me with some sort of recognition. "What the hell do *you* want?"

I'm taken aback. Her tone is abrasive and I wonder just how she thinks she knows me. I shoot Brody a panicked look.

He lays a hand on my arm. "It's okay, Mel," he says.

The woman lets out a squeak of surprise. She seems about to speak but then quickly snaps her mouth shut and crosses her arms over her chest.

I have no idea what caused this shift in demeanor and obviously neither does Brody. He narrows his eyes in suspicion and then launches into his interrogation, leading right off with a "half-truth."

"I'm Sheriff Carter from Iroquois County, Kansas," he starts, pulling out his file folder.

The woman's eyes widen, and I wonder what she thinks we know. *I* know the folder doesn't contain much, but she doesn't.

"We want to ask you some questions about a murder we're looking into," he says.

The woman stares at him stoically. "Ask all you want," she grunts. "Don't mean I have to answer you."

Brody remains calm. "We can make this easy or we can make it hard," he says. "You see, we know a lot about you—even beyond your extensive criminal history in Kansas City and other places." He opens the file and pretends to peruse it. "Your real name, of course, is Agatha Hadley, although you've used many aliases—"

"Like Beatrice Thomas," I interrupt, letting my excitement get the best of me. *Oops, he told me to hold off on the dream stuff.*

Brody turns quickly toward me. Fearing his annoyance, I duck my head, but he actually shoots me a pleased wink.

Agatha looks surprised at my outburst. She whips her head toward me and there's nothing pleased or pleasing about her hateful scowl.

"That's nothin'!" she growls. "The fuckin' cops know all my aliases."

"Hmmm," Brody taps the file. "We actually didn't have *that* one, Ms. Hadley. Until recently. Seems fresh information about you is sprouting up every day from different sources—some you couldn't even imagine."

Agatha sinks back into her seat, crossing her arms even more tightly.

"Anyway," says Brody, "the point is that we now have evidence pointing to your involvement with this murder." He takes a minute to scan the folder more intently. "We know you had conversations with a 'person of interest' named Stan Harris. We have records showing phone calls to and from your number at the time."

I can see Agatha's mind churning, but she remains silent.

"*And* we know," I say—locking eyes with her as I pull something else from my dream that may provide the tightest "squeeze"—" that you used your pre-prison sales expertise to trick family members of the Route 66 serial killer's victims into divulging details of his crimes that at the time weren't known to the public."

"'Hands on the steering wheel,' to be exact," Brody interjects.

Agatha's eyes widen.

"Stan then used that information," I go on, "to 'copycat' those murders and make his own look like a serial killing."

Agatha's mouth is now pursed tightly, like she's ready to boil over.

"So tell us…" Brody goes for the jugular. "Why exactly *did* you contract Stan Harris to kill Helen Morris eight years ago?"

Brody was right: Agatha freaks. She jumps up from her chair and nearly rips her cuffed hands off in the process, screaming like she's being disemboweled and boiled in oil at the same time.

"Who the hell do you think you are coming in here and accusing me of murder?!" she shouts.

I can't help but back away from her assault.

"You know what I think?" she hisses, displaying what's left of her teeth. "I think you think you're better than me, so you came here looking to berate an old lady about a case that was closed a long goddamn time ago. Well, bitch," she says, pointing a bony finger at me, "maybe I *do* have some information to spill, and you especially are gonna want to hear what I have to say."

Again I look at Brody.

Although I'm frightened even imagining what she's going to reveal, I need to hear it. And despite knowing she engineered the death of my mother, I need to keep my cool as we fish for answers.

I pause to make sure that I sound strong and sure.

"Is that so?" I ask her. "Please do tell."

Her mouth lifts into a twisted smile. "*Somehow* you idiots have concocted *some* kind of ridiculous scheme that involves a serial killer and you and me and this Helen Morris bitch." She glares right through me. "Well, I don't know how you came up with that fuckin' fantasy, but me and you, bitch, *are* connected. Because I knew your birth mother."

Her words knock the wind out of me. I take a step back, but not of my own fruition. I feel Brody's hand on me, but he's outside my inner turmoil.

"I see I've hit a nerve," she says, clearly delighting in my distress. "Yup, I knew your loving mother when she was a two-bit drug-down whore who didn't have a clue which John she fucked may have been your no-good daddy. So she gave you up. She didn't care about you, so she sold you for money to keep her habit going. Some crooked adoption agency threw a few bucks at her and you were history. You were nothing when you were born and I can see that you're still nothing now."

I feel sick. "H-How do you know all this?" I ask.

"And why should we believe anything a miserable old witch like you says anyhow?" Brody chimes in.

"How do I know all this?" She laughs. "Because you look exactly like that rotten bitch!"

I see Brody trying to quell his anger. He shifts into cop-mode and his eyes narrow.

"Oh, really?" he says softly. "Well, if you know so much, prove it. Give us the name of this so-called mother that she looks like."

Agatha instantly claps her mouth shut and folds her arms across her chest like an indignant child. Except there's nothing endearing about her at all.

I feel like I've been punched in the gut and gonna throw up right on the floor. I'd felt a small surge of hope I would learn my birth mother's name, but this woman has done nothing but cause me grief. Out-of-control heart palpitations are added to my nausea. I can't catch my breath and I can't get out of this place fast enough. So I guess *her* squeezing wins.

Brody shoots Agatha a look that causes her to sink back into her miserable self and then he yells for the guard to come "take this bitch back to her cell!"

He grabs my arm and helps me to the door. But he's not quite done. As Agatha is escorted past us, he warns her that he'll be back, and that when he comes, she'll be out of her cushy "medium-security" cell and headed to a tiny sterile room in a scream-filled psych ward for the rest of her life.

I guess he hopes that will either shut her up or make her confess something, but it has neither effect. Strong for her age, she fights the guards and yells obscenities until we can no longer hear her tirade in the distance. But I'll remember that voice for the rest of my life.

WE BARELY MAKE IT back to the parking lot before I break down in tears. I want to be brave in front of Brody, but it's not working. This woman is exactly as the warden described her, and I've never met anybody so horrible—except for Pete Decker, of course.

Standing outside the truck, Brody wraps his arms around me. "Mel, come on, honey. You know you can't believe everything she just said in there."

Brody speaks so softly that I barely hear him call me honey. I'm too upset to register much of anything right now.

"She probably just made that stuff up," he soothes. "That's what addicts do: They lie and make stuff up. And hell, telling someone—*anyone*—that they look like their mother doesn't prove anything. *Everyone* looks a little or a lot like their mother! And did you notice when she decided to say all of that shit to you? After we'd already gotten the upper hand. It was like the synapses in her head short-circuited and she found a weapon of words. She enjoys hurting people, just like the warden told us."

I'm crying hard now and trying to get words out between sobs. "Yeah, but she must know s-something!" I argue.

Brody rubs my back.

"Of course there must be a connection between the two of you. You told me how in your dream the old woman talked about how she 'kept tabs' on a 'secondhand family'—*yours*, the Morrises. Maybe she was an old friend or acquaintance of your adoptive parents, so that's how she knew you were adopted."

"But why would she want to kill my adoptive mom?" I ask.

"I don't know," says Brody. "But I promise we'll find out."

I nod. "Let's go home," I say.

He opens the truck's passenger door.

"I think we should do some more research," he says. "We *will* find out the truth for you, Mel." He puts his hand on my arm. "I know that you've never really cared about finding your birth parents, Mel, but I think we definitely need to look into that now. It may give us some answers to the questions eating at us—as well as questions we haven't even thought of yet."

I look into his eyes and, in this moment, I fall even more in love with him. More than I ever thought I could love someone. His ability to give me such support as I stand here crying like a baby proves what kind of man he is.

I wipe the tears from my eyes and kiss him softly on the mouth. I love him and I know that he…desires me. I have *seen* that desire. I have *felt* that desire. I *love* that desire.

But would he ever love me like this?

If not, how will I deal with it?

"Thank you," I tell him softly. "With you beside me, I can handle whatever we find out. This is what I want to do and I'm so glad you'll be here to help me."

We drive back home in complete contemplative quiet.

I have a lot to think about.

As I strategize about how to *seriously* start the search for my birth parents, I still feel bruised by what the old woman told me. I can't even begin to escape her words. They just get more and more painful.

CHAPTER 28

It's late afternoon when we arrive home and Brody walks me to the door.

"I did pick up that new latch for the window," he tells me like a proud handyman. "I'll install it as soon as—"

"It's fine just nailed shut for now," I interrupt. "Fixing the window isn't my main concern."

He looks at me. "Mel," he says quietly, "you've been through a lot in the last couple of days and—"

He's apparently hoping repair work will distract me from what happened with Agatha. But I have a better idea to take my mind off it. I grab his shirt, pull him in through the door, and kiss him with everything I have. I put all the love I feel for him into the kiss.

He kicks the door shut behind him, and we continue kissing as we move inside the house. We don't realize that we're near the stairs until Brody backs into them and falls onto his butt. A burst of laughter escapes us, but laughter is not what I'm after right now.

I grab his shirt again and pull it over his head. He's now reclining across several steps. Gazing at his bare chest, I slowly strip myself, watching him. The desire inside me increases just from his expression.

Once I'm completely nude before him, I step in to complete the removal of his clothing. I start with his shoes, proceeding slowly so that he can take in my every movement. Next, I remove his socks, realizing that I've never noticed his feet before. He has long toes with the same curly black hair as his chest.

I want to know every inch of his body intimately.

I move on to his pants, wondering, *Who is this woman stripping a man on her stairs?*

I know the old Melanie—that shy, virginal girl—is gone and that Brody is responsible for it. I reach for the waistband of his briefs. They aren't the utilitarian tightie-whities many men wear. His are dark and cotton and go about a quarter of the way down his thighs, which are covered in hair as well.

His member is at full attention by now, peeking out over the waistband like a soldier awaiting instruction. A trail of dark hair leads directly down to the object of my obsession. I notice the small wet droplet on the tip only because I am completely focused on it. I instantly become more aroused than I've ever been. As I bend over to lick it off, I can feel the wetness between my legs. Brody moans loudly.

Once he's fully undressed, I climb on top of him and kiss him fully on the mouth.

I can't wait any longer to have him inside of me. I'm so ready, and gazing into his eyes is driving me to the brink. I spread my legs and insert him. Then I press down hard, enjoying the sensation of his invasion. I wonder if the length of him can touch my core.

I move up and down with a leisurely rhythm designed to make him wild. He grabs my hips, prodding me to speed up a little. I shake my head. *I* am leading this soldier the way I want him to go.

I slide completely down on him again and moan as he fills me. Then I rise up to the very tip of his rock-hard manhood, almost removing him from my sheath. I then glide down to once again take him all the way in. Watching me intently, Brody reaches up to knead my nipples, which are at full attention and begging to be touched.

At Brody's caress, I can't control my movements any longer. I quicken to increase the building inside my body. Despite our being on the stairs, Brody flips himself on top of me. He suckles my breasts, each of them in turn, and then kneads my nipples until I think I'll explode with ecstasy. He pulls out and I cry out for him to continue, but he puts his fingers in me instead.

"You're so wet for me, Mel," he says, bringing me easily to my first orgasm.

Still catching my breath, I watch intently as he removes his hand and replaces it again with his penis. I gasp in surprise as he seems to lose all control and lifts my legs over his shoulders.

Piercing me with his gaze, he plunges straight into me. I scream—not in pain but in absolute bliss as he goes deeper and deeper. We ride each other as if it's the last time we will come together. It seems to go on forever until he screams my name and, as though he read my earlier thoughts, seemingly touches my core with his final thrust. I lose all thought as we call out each other's names and explode in harmony.

I continue to drift in euphoria as we lie there, panting.

Finally, Brody kisses me hungrily, as if he can't get enough. It sends a shiver all the way down my body, causing my nipples to stand at attention again. He pulls out of me, but I don't feel empty this time because I know this will happen over and over in the future.

"Well, scratch that off my bucket list!" Brody says, smiling.

I reach up and tousle his hair. "Happy to oblige, sir," I say. "I believe I might enjoy hearing about any other items on this list that we can work toward crossing off."

Brody smirks. "Well, ma'am, I won't be telling you about any of those for a while, as I believe I have a stair tread embedded in my back."

I laugh. "Me too; but it has been well worth it."

Brody kisses me again. "Yes, yes it has," he agrees.

I WAKE EARLY the following morning, feeling rested. Yesterday's "release" was certainly therapeutic! Brody and I ate a light dinner together afterwards and then he went home.

So now it's time to get back to reality—*again*.

Who am I?

I need to find my adoption papers. They *must* be somewhere in this house, right? I've looked before but not with this kind of passion. And all the while, that gritty voice continues to haunt: "*She sold you for money to keep her habit going…*"

I wonder if my parents destroyed anything, hoping I would never find my birth mother. Did they know all along that she was who and what the woman in prison said she was?

So many things are coming at me now: Pete Decker, my mother's murder, this mystery woman in prison, a disjointed assortment of dreams…

I'm spinning.

I've already had several cups of coffee and I desperately need a shower—especially after yesterday's stairs interlude.

On top of everything else, I can't stop thinking about Brody. It's all happening so quickly with him. After fearing my whole life that I would never find love, everything's moving at lightning speed now. For me, at least.

I keep searching for the documents. There must be *something* here that will tell me about my birth and—like Brody said—give me a hint as how it might tie in to all the other clues. If I have to tear out the floorboards to find it, I will. No, no I won't tear out the floorboards…unless, of course, I find one that squeaks.

Who am I kidding? Most of the boards squeak.

I smile to myself. I guess I'm in a much better mood than I thought, even with everything going on.

I decide to take that much-needed shower so I don't spend *all* day smelling Brody's scent on me. First, though, I'll take a long soak in the bath to relax my muscles. I can throw in some of those scented bath salts that make my skin so soft and then I can—

Whoa! I stop myself. *Do I have time for all that—with all I need to accomplish?* I spend several minutes in self-debate.

Finally, just a shower wins out.

I turn the water very hot so I can clear my mind. The warmth streams onto my body like tiny fingers gently stroking my breasts and stomach.

Visions of being with Brody on the stairs flood my mind and I'm very stimulated again. I've never felt quite as desirable as when Brody gives me that blazingly sensual look, like in the kitchen when I had on my see-through nightie. And now the water seems to have awakened the need I feel when he looks at me like that, his eyes bright with desire.

How is that even possible?

Timidly, I touch my breasts as Brody touches them. I pluck the hardened nubs with my fingers. Then I let the hot water stream over them and it feels almost like the inside of Brody's hot mouth.

I'm shocked to realize I've been taken over by some sort of visceral connection with Brody. I can actually smell him. Could it be his lingering scent from yesterday, or is it that I'm somehow with him now? As I contemplate if that's even possible, sensual desire overtakes me.

As erotic memories of our sexual encounters float through my subconscious, I become so hot I can't control my hands. I'm not sure if it's the heat of my body or of the water cascading down my breasts, but I'm on fire. I rub my nipples until they're super hard and then I hesitantly run my hands down over my stomach and to my center. As I touch myself, my head falls back from sheer ecstasy.

The inside of my body is soft and slick and feels like a raging inferno. I remember Brody telling me how wet I was when he touched me.

I can't believe that I've never been aware of the stimulation I can give myself through my own touch. But although I'm alone, it feels as though Brody is in the shower with me, with his hands over my hands, guiding me.

A flood of sensations take over as I slide my fingers into and over my sex. I have no idea what I'm doing, but it's as though Brody is directing me, instructing me. I rub the length of my torso, starting from my breasts and back down to my sex.

The water is another sensation I can't explain. As it touches me in intimate places, I close my eyes and think of the things Brody has done to me with his mouth. I can't control the need to put my own fingers into myself and I start to energetically rub them in and out while thinking of Brody.

The harder and faster I pleasure myself, the further over the edge I go. I become frantic to release the tension, feeling as though it is Brody performing the act.

It doesn't take long for the storm to begin. I'm not concerned with anything outside the walls of the shower as my first fantasy takes me to a place I've begun to enjoy very much with Brody.

My body becomes still and then the orgasm throbs in my ears in time to the beating of my heart. A pulsating light behind my eyes matches the thrum of the blood flowing through my veins. My body quakes as though a tidal wave is forming and the waves are rolling through me—edging and quaking, edging and quaking. Then everything explodes all at once.

I hold onto the shower walls as my system goes into overload. When it's over, I feel drained and satisfied at the same time.

I can't help but wonder if Brody will have any memory of this, or if my mind has just led me to believe he's with me so I don't feel guilt for touching myself. I'm not sure that I'll be able to bring up the subject to him.

Gosh, I think, *had I known years ago this is all I needed to relieve so much stress, maybe I'd have tried it sooner. But,* I reason, *I'm sure it wouldn't have been the same without the ideas—and actions—that Brody has put into my mind and body.*

I get out of the shower wearing a huge smile. I can't wait to continue digging for info, but by the time I finish drying myself, I suddenly feel tired—like I need a nap.

I had a great night's sleep and was up early in my rush to start the day. I certainly didn't expect this. I sit down and immediately start drifting off. I feel something happening, as though I'm floating. I'm not quite asleep and not quite awake. I'm in that veiled area in between, where some believe encounters with ghostly beings can occur.

I see beautiful white wings and a bright light floating toward me. I'm so busy trying to see the face of what I think to be an angel that it takes me a while to notice the blanket-wrapped baby in the angel's arms.

The baby's face is hidden by the brightness of the light. The blanket is a soft pink and when the angel brings the baby closer, I can see its hospital bracelet. I can't quite make out the baby's name, but I can see that the bracelet reads *University of Kansas Hospital.*

That may be enough.

I sit up so fast, my head is spinning.

"Thank you, Jamie!" I cry out loud. "I know you're the one who's shown this to me."

I call Brody right away and he sounds kind of sleepy, which is odd for him—at any time, really, but in the middle of the day? *I wonder if…* No…no…I let the thought go because it just isn't possible.

"Are you okay?" I ask. "You sound kind of groggy."

"I fell asleep," he almost mumbles. "I never take naps! And something really strange happened while I was out. I'm wondering…uh, did you just get out of the shower?"

Failing again at my *almost*-never-swear policy, I scream, "Holy shit, holy shit! Yes, I did! And uh—" I feel suddenly shy. "Anyway, you need to come over here right now. I had another new dream—a vision, really—and I was shown the hospital where I think I was born! We need to go there, *now.*"

"Let me grab a quick shower of my own and I'll be right there," he tells me. "And I'm going to need some more answers on this other, uh, issue too."

"Oh yeah, you are!"

Once the words are out of my mouth, the line goes dead. But my thoughts are more alive than ever. I'm freaking out about the shower "connection" and the image from Jamie. Of the two, the vision of the baby seems more important, but being able to tap into something with Brody—or anyone, really—well, that's never happened to me before.

Maybe these two encounters can't be measured by objective importance—maybe they can only be judged by how much they'll each change my life.

CHAPTER 29

We're on our way to the mammoth main location of University of Kansas Hospital, known as KU Med. It's yet another of those two-hour-plus drives from Arrow Springs back up to KC, but I'm so anxious about this trip, I know I won't even notice. We seem so close to getting some answers, but will this trip just bring up even more questions?

My nerves are shredded. I know Jamie gave me this vision, and I'm feeling worse and worse that Brody knows nothing about her. Especially now that I've shared her with Flora. Though in my defense, Jamie and Flora had already "met." And that shows just how special our connection is concerning our gifts.

Brody accepts and believes in our gifts, as well, and I know that he'll accept and believe in Jamie, too—when the time is right.

Right now, however, the time is right to discuss something else.

"Brody, do you want to talk about this morning?" I venture gently. Since he has yet to bring up the ethereal escapade, I'm guessing he's a little flipped out by it. "I know I felt some sort of connection to you but I don't know if I was dreaming it."

Brody looks at me and swallows, as though he isn't quite sure how to navigate a conversation like this.

"Are you sure that you really want to talk about it right now?" he answers with a question of his own. "I mean, when we have all this other stuff to think about? This may take some time to explore."

"I know," I tell him. "But I've never experienced anything like that before, and it could be relevant. I'm wondering if my psychic abilities are evolving. Maybe the dreams are coming so fast, my gift is trying to catch up!" I shake my head like a wet dog drying itself off. "Actually, I have no idea what I'm talking about. Just tell me what *you* experienced."

Brody just looks at me again—like he isn't going to say a word. Then he starts talking.

"Like I told you then," he begins, "I was suddenly sleepy not long after I had gotten up. So I nodded off, and suddenly I started feeling certain…things…happening. It was like a dream, but more…" He hesitates. "Intense."

He stops talking again, and I watch his Adam's apple bob up and down erratically. He's obviously embarrassed about the whole situation.

Hell, I'm embarrassed, too! But I need answers.

"Listen, Brody," I console him. "I know this is probably as weird as it gets—" I pause. "I take that back; with me in the equation, things could get even weirder. But anyway, I really need to know."

"W-well…" he stammers. "You and I were in the shower and we were doing…things. It was as though I was teaching you ways to…pleasure yourself."

I gaze towards Brody's lap and see that he's aroused.

"So you think what happened was exciting?" I probe. "And you would like it if I—we—could do it again?"

Brody lets out a bark. "I have to admit that this conversation is making me very 'uncomfortable' right now." He reaches between his legs to "readjust." "So if you—we—don't stop talking about it, I'm going to have to pull over and take you right here in the truck."

I laugh, and then quickly cover my mouth with my hands. Brody glares at me.

"Alright," I concede. "I'll stop talking about it—for now. What *are* you going to do about that though?" I stare brazenly at his crotch and run my tongue over my lips.

Brody groans.

"Since we don't have time to do what I'd *really* like to do," says Brody, "I just need to think about something else and hope it'll go away. Which means that you need to quit licking your lips like that. But you're going to owe me big time later."

I don't answer because I realize that during our conversation, I've become quite aroused as well. Good thing I don't get an erection every time *I'm* excited; it'd be very embarrassing. We will definitely deal with this later.

Our conversation about not having this conversation keeps us so busy that the time to KC indeed flies by. As we near the hospital, I realize it has also kept my mind off the reason for our trip. But now my hands are clammy and shaking. My stomach is churning with so much anxiety, I think I might be sick.

If I'd ever felt a need to explore my genetic background, I could have jumped into the DNA info pool long ago—and maybe I still will. But for now I know Jamie wants me to be *here,* in the place where I was born. She specifically showed me that ID bracelet.

Either way, I could possibly find out who my birth parents were—or are—and I worry it may be more than I can handle.

As the GPS guides us through the final few turns, I glance at Brody. I know he hates the thing and would much rather rely on "knowing every inch of this state like a Kansas coyote knows where to find fresh rabbit holes…upwind…in a storm!" or simply his innate, manly "dead-reckoning" abilities. But for expediency's sake, he consented to being guided by the magic voice in the sky *this* time.

Brody parks and then comes around the truck and opens the door for me.

"What? No smartass remarks about being a gentleman?" he jokes.

But I don't smile. Seeing how edgy I am, he pulls me into his arms.

"Look, Mel," he consoles, "whatever we find out here, it'll be okay. You won't have to deal with it alone."

"I appreciate that," I say. "Just having you here makes me feel better."

I know Brody needs answers for legal reasons, but mostly this is for me. One day, I'll tell him just how much strength he's given me. I know I could have forced myself to do it alone, but having Brody makes it so much easier.

We hold hands as we walk into the hospital and head straight for the information desk. We explain to the pleasant elderly volunteer that we're looking for some old hospital records and she directs us to the administration desk.

The woman behind *that* desk seems rather harried. The pleasant air we first experienced is very thin here. The admin is waiting on someone in front of us and is not being very friendly. But we wait patiently for our turn. When we finally step up, she eyes us with a look that makes me want to run right out the door. Brody, however, holds me firmly in place and takes over the conversation.

"Hello, Cheryl," he says, having glanced quickly at her nametag. "My name is Brody Carter. I'm the sheriff of Arrow Springs. This is my friend Melanie Morris."

The woman looks back and forth between the two of us, not saying a word.

I presume that Brody introducing himself as a sheriff will afford us some status—but it doesn't.

"I am glad you're able to read my name tag," she finally says. "Mr.…uh…Carter—*Sheriff* Carter, I suppose. But listen, I have a lot of work to do here so if you can get to the reason you're interrupting my day, that would be fantastic."

Alrighty, then…

"Whoa, lady." Brody bristles. "Ever hear of customer service?"

"Do you want to tell me what you want?" she asks, apparently not concerned with "service" in any way. "I'm just about ready to go to lunch, so I can either help you now, or I can just go."

I have never come across anyone so rude in my life, and Brody also looks aghast. I squeeze his hand, attempting to calm him down. I guess it's my turn to try.

"We're looking for information on a birth," I explain calmly. "It would have been from twenty-five years ago. I was born in this hospital, and I'm looking for my birth mother. It's rather important, beca—"

"Listen, honey," she interrupts, "I don't really care how important it is, because it's against all HIPPA regulations to give out medical record information, as defined in Public Law 104-191, enacted in August of 1996."

I don't need a civics lesson and I really hate being called "honey"—unless, of course, it's by Brody. And so, joining the extreme company of Pete Decker and Agatha Hadley, this becomes the third time in a short span that I want to bash a complete stranger in the face. I'm trying to remain well-mannered, because I really want to get information, but it seems unlikely to happen with this guard dog on duty.

"Look," I say, my manners slipping, "I have my driver's license here that shows who I am."

She stares at the document, obviously not giving a crap what I want.

"I am *soooo* sorry, honey," she growls nastily, "legally, there is nothing I can do for you. Why don't you just pay a hundred bucks and spit in a cup? Maybe you can find out that you're really an Eskimo or something, with a father who has a string of thirty kids from Nova Scotia to Kansas."

Before I can even begin to compose a response to her diatribe, a woman in nursing scrubs emerges from a hallway and walks toward the desk. Her name tag reads *Donna*.

"Cheryl, what's going on here?" she asks.

"Nothing, Donna," Miss Rude practically hisses. "Mind your own business. I'm doing my job and these two were just leaving."

Thankfully, Donna ignores the acrimonious assault—but she isn't ignoring me. The way she's staring at me makes me uneasy.

The few seconds of stiff silence feel like an hour.

"Do you have any siblings?" Donna finally asks, still not taking her eyes off me.

"No—I mean, I don't think so," I say. "Uh…why?"

Donna glances at Cheryl and is given a look that says *Don't you dare divulge any information.*

"Oh, no reason," Donna replies. "I thought you looked familiar to me, but I must be mistaken."

I look from one woman to the other, sure that my angst shows clearly on my face. Is there something else Donna wants to tell me? If so, it's not happening now.

Turning to address Cheryl, my emotions snap. I feel even more compelled to jump over the counter and smack the smug look off her face.

"I would thank you for your assistance today," I say instead, "but, quite frankly, I've never been treated this poorly in my life. I wonder what your superiors might think about your attitude."

Brody squeezes my hand. "C'mon, Mel," he says. "She's not worth it. People like her will get the karma they deserve in the end."

I take one more look at Donna, and then Brody gently puts his arm around me and ushers me toward the exit.

When we reach the double-doors I feel the hairs on the back of my neck stand up and look back to find Donna watching me. Then she turns and says something to Miss Rude.

It's maddening that we're leaving without any answers at all. I look at Brody and see the same frustration on his face.

"I think that other woman knows something," I say.

"I agree, but there's nothing we can do about it right now."

"Maybe Flora can help us," I say. "I hate to keep bugging her, but for once we're already close to the diner. Let's drive over for lunch, and maybe we can talk to her if she's not too busy?"

"Great thinking, Mel," Brody agrees. "Let's go."

MEANWHILE, back at the hospital, Donna and Cheryl are immersed in a very different conversation.

"Donna, what the hell do you think you're trying to do? Even if you have information for or about that girl, there's nothing you can tell her."

"I know." Donna sighs. "And I also don't want to freak her out for no reason. Because I'm not even completely sure that what I think is true. But"—she looks sternly at Cheryl—"if I find out it *is,* then I'll have no other choice than to help that girl."

"You really need to be careful, Donna," Cheryl admonishes coldly. "If you overstep what's allowed by law, you could lose your job."

"I'm fully aware of what the repercussions would be, Cheryl." Donna crosses her arms. "So I suggest you mind *your* own business for a change."

CHAPTER 30

WE WALK INTO THE DINER and see Flora in the kitchen with the cook. Not wanting to interrupt, we seat ourselves in a booth and peruse the menu. With all that's going on, I'm not very hungry—which is nothing new for me.

Flora returns to the dining room and spots us right away. Looking pleased, she comes over to our table.

"Well, hello! I didn't expect to see you two again so soon. But it's definitely a nice surprise." She looks between us with a questioning look.

"What's wrong?" she asks. "You look like you've gotten bad news."

"Well, that's me!" I sort of smile. "Bad News Mel. We just came from KU Med, which I'm pretty sure is where I was born."

"Oh my gosh, Mel—that sounds like a definite step forward. But there must be more since you're so down."

I grimace. "We weren't able to get any information. The administrator there is not only a stickler for the rules, but she's probably the rudest bitch I've ever met. I can't understand how people like that even keep their jobs."

Good thing I don't have a swear jar–I've been doing a lot of it lately. Even though Miss Rude definitely deserves my insults, it doesn't make me feel great to actually say the words.

I feel Flora touch my arm and realize she's talking to me.

"Listen, Mel, you can't give up now. You have something that needs to be done and there's always a way to get the answers."

"Right," I snap. "Maybe you can go to the hospital and touch *everybody* to see what you can find out!"

I flinch as soon as the words leave my mouth. I'm being nearly as rude to Flora as that witch at the desk was to me, but I can't seem to help myself. I'm *not* myself. And I can't understand how I'm expected to be able to figure out all the factual stuff while dealing with my own personal issues as well. I've never felt like this before.

"Mel," Flora says gently, "I can't do that for you—though it would be quite a show." She smirks. "But maybe there's something I *can* do. Between all the red tape and rude administrators out there, we may need to resort to 'special' avenues."

Now I feel even worse. I should know by now to just ask Flora for something I need.

"Are you sure?" I ask.

"Of course," says Flora. "And I have an idea. Come into my office."

We follow Flora into the familiarly cramped space. Brody brings his half-full cup of coffee; I bring my overflowing dish of depression. Brody pulls the extra chair over to the desk opposite Flora and stands by the now-closed door as I sit. He reminds me of a bouncer at a bar—not that I ever go drinking or anything.

Flora starts speaking very calmly to me and takes my hand in hers.

"So here's my plan: Go back through your dreams and dig deeper than you ever have. I'll hold your hand and see if I can read something from you while you do it."

Flora's voice is so calming, it's almost hypnotic. I close my eyes and think back to the dreams. There are quite a few now. I picture the hand of the would-be murderer…and the little girl being beaten by the old woman…then the little girl playing her violin and the family helping her out…I hear the concerts… and see the maestro…and feel the happiness that collapses into horror…the violin being shattered…and the homeless woman conjuring up her scheme… *"If this bitch has to be killed to get it, well so be it!"*…and—

My visions cut off, as though a drape has been lowered over my mind's eye. I feel myself floating up and out of the diner, into another dream.

But it can't be a dream. I'm wide awake, right?

I'm no longer in the office with Brody, but I can still feel Flora. Somehow she's with me even though I can't see her as I fly several blocks and am lowered gently to the ground.

It's evening. The sky is dark and a fog surrounds everything. I walk with tentative footsteps, feeling someone or something propelling me forward. Ahead of me, the fog clears and a light shines down over a patch of flowers. No, it's not a patch; it's a single plant with many buds. They look like pods hanging down from the many branches. Nothing else is around it. The cluster of pods is interspersed with long, thin leaves with ruffled edges. Some are darker but most are light green. I don't know anything about flowers, but the tips of the leaves come to sharp, prickly points—maybe it's some kind of cactus?

The bud exteriors are encompassed by an array of pink and maroon spikes. There are so many blossoms and they're all closed tight. But then, in slow motion, they all bloom in unison. It's the most beautiful sight I've ever seen.

And their fragrance is exquisite.

The insides are white except for the centers, which have white and yellow fibers sticking up. I don't know what they're called, but I can imagine a bee pollinating the plant from that section. I'm surprised at how white the petals are; I expected them to be pink. Clustered together, the blooms look almost like a pond-lily—but I know they are much more special. I lean in for a closer look.

Just then, the sun peeks over the horizon and the blooms fold in on themselves and die. I feel a sudden loss, as if what I just witnessed was a spectacular once-in-a-lifetime experience.

I come to slowly, as if waking from sleep. I open my eyes to find myself still in the office with Flora and Brody.

"What happened?" I ask.

"Well," Brody explains, "you closed your eyes and began telling us snippets about your collective of dreams. Then all of a sudden, it was lights out for you both."

I look at Flora, taken aback that she was pulled into the vision as well.

"I really wish you'd stop doing that," Brody adds, "because I don't know how much more of it I can take." He runs his hand through his hair. "At least *this* time you were sitting down." He pauses. "Thankfully you were *both* sitting down."

"I'm sorry, Brody," I say. "But you know I don't have much choice in the matter." I glance at Flora. "I guess I should say *we* didn't have a choice? What happened, Flora?"

"That was quite a ride!" she gushes. She doesn't sound worried at all. In fact, she seems a little awestruck. "It was so exciting to see what you see!" she says. "I don't know exactly what happened, but you seemed to float away. I didn't exactly float with you, but I think because I held your hand I was able to see what you were seeing."

Brody exhales loudly. "Fabulous." He sounds more annoyed than worried, and Flora shoots him a silencing look.

"What?" he says. "Do either of you want to fill me in on the vision you obviously shared?"

I let out a heavy sigh. "It seems like the universe is playing a cruel game with me. I—" I glance at Flora. "*We*—didn't see anything helpful."

"That's not necessarily true," Brody argues. "You know as well as we do that this stuff isn't always straight-ahead and crystal clear."

"Yeah," agreed Flora. "It's more like a crinkled up treasure map than a new-age navigation system! And this clue was so interesting!"

Brody looks annoyed again. "Soooo, does one of you want to fill me in on this clue so we can see if we come up with some kind of 'X' marking some kind of spot?"

"I *swear* there's not much to tell," I mumble, still feeling down. "I was transported from the diner, but I didn't go anyplace where I saw a hand with a knife, an old lady, a crying child, a concert, or even a violin. Instead, I was shown..." I put my face in my hands. "A bunch of flowers."

Brody pulls at his hair. "A bunch of flowers?" he echoes.

"A bunch of flowers," I repeat. "Can you imagine?" Then I lose it. "I mean, what the hell does a bunch of flowers have to do with these damn dreams and finding this girl…*woman*? And what if she already murdered whoever she's going to murder and we just don't know it? Everything's taking too long. And here I am stopping to smell the roses!" I let out a hollow laugh. "This is the same as when my mother was murdered. I've waited too long to move on this, and someone is going to die because of me!"

I feel so exhausted, so confused. Nothing makes any sense. I lay my head on the desk.

"Wait a minute, Mel," says Flora. "Don't forget that I also saw what you saw." She smiles coyly. "And it just so happens I have some information for you."

Brody and I look at each other in shock.

"Wha—What do you mean?" we cry in unison.

Flora just looks at us and shakes her head.

"I'm into flowers, remember? And this one I've seen recently."

"Oh my god," I say. "Are you sure?"

"Yes, I received a flyer just a few weeks ago for what they called a 'special blooming' of the flower from your vision. It's a local florist and I was going to book tickets for my mom and me to attend. Hopefully I still have the brochure; I may have thrown it out because I have so much darn paperwork lying around and I'm a little behind on my filing."

I look around and I agree the office is a lot bigger mess than the last time we were in here.

"I'm going to need a minute," she says. "What can you do while I look for it?"

Brody and I look at each other blankly. We finally have a clue, but we have to wait. *Ugh.*

"How about you do a drawing of the flower?" suggests Flora. "Even better, go and order some lunch while you do it. I think you'll feel better if you eat something."

"Flora is right," Brody agrees. "I just realized I'm starved."

"That's nothing new," I grumble.

"You know what, Mel?" he says. "I think that on top of everything else, you're hangry. You know—hungry and angry at the same time."

I shoot him a dirty look. "I know what hangry means, Brody."

Of course, now that we've potentially caught a break, I find myself suddenly hungry, too. Or maybe the dream-flying caused it. Who knows?

"Brody, could you please grab my bag?"

He picks it up off the floor and stands there awkwardly clutching it. I smile.

"Are you seriously going to laugh that I'm holding your bag?" he asks.

I snort. "I wouldn't think of it."

I turn to Flora. "Thank you," I say genuinely. "I'm sorry for being so cranky. Take your time looking for the flyer."

"It's the least I can do," she assures me. "Sharing that vision with you was so amazing! I wish we had time to sit down and discuss the experience. But I know you need answers quickly, so just get out of here so I can find the flyer!"

We hug each other tightly and I can feel that our shared adventure has brought us even closer together.

Brody and I make our way to a booth in the back of the diner. I was happy for the privacy of Flora's office; I'm anxious about having anyone see me draw. It could still bring unwanted attention that I don't need right now.

As I take out my supplies, Brody starts peppering me with questions.

"This sure is baffling—a bunch of flowers! You think they were where this murder might happen?"

"I didn't see any landmarks or locations," I reply. "That sure would have helped! All I saw was fog."

"Fog?" He jumps on it. "Maybe they get a lot in the location?"

"I don't know, Brody," I say, my frustration mounting. "I mean, all of Kansas gets the same freezing fog, but usually not this time of year."

Finally Brody brings up something that *could* tie in to the vision.

"Do you think the name of the flower could be the name of the woman or girl in the dream? Daisy? Rose? Violet? Petunia?"

"Petunia?!" I laugh.

"Hey, I'm trying to cover all the bases here." He says the words seriously but has a big smile on his face. I guess he's trying to ease my mind by being silly.

"Thanks for trying to lighten the mood," I tell him sincerely, "but you could actually be on to something. Of course, since I've never seen this type of flower before, I have no idea the name of it. But thank goodness we have Flora! I can't believe she saw it in a brochure. I sure hope she can find it."

"Me, too. Now, let's order so you can get that drawing going."

Just as Brody says this, a waitress arrives at our table.

"I'll have a cobb salad, please," I say. "With a glass of water."

Brody places his order for a full Irish, even though it's lunchtime. I guess he must be really hungry.

"Don't worry, Mel," he says when the waitress leaves. "We'll get to the bottom of this."

His words do help me feel lighter and inspire me to sketch. Due to the flowers' exterior vibrancy, I choose my colored pencils over charcoals to create the desired effect. They'll work better on the type of paper I have with me anyway.

I conjure a vision of the whole plant and see the flowers just as clearly as the first time. I feel my hand moving faster and faster as I dive my mind further into the image. I look carefully at the make-up of the flower and the stems. I examine the roots of the plant to see how it looks from underneath.

Once I've drawn a fresh, new shoot, I fill in the leaves and then add what I call the pods. Even though they opened all at once in the dream, I keep some as pods and show others in various stages of opening. That way, a viewer can get the full effect.

I color everything in, and then, feeling a slight tingle in my fingers, I shake my hand awake. I look down at what began as a blank paper, struggling to pull myself out of the image I've created. It's beautiful—exactly how it looked in the dream. I've even captured the moonlight shining down as the flowers bloomed, and I can almost smell the fragrance that gently wafted up.

Brody shakes his head. "Damn!"

"What?" I ask.

"Your drawing! Look at that flower—*all* those flowers! I've never seen you paint or sketch, but I always wondered what it would be like. I had no idea how quick you are! Your hand just flew over the page." He pauses. "And you certainly weren't here in this booth with me. I felt the loss of you—like when you have visions. I didn't tell you, but that's the main reason I got so upset when you had the one while we were running. And then, just now with Flora." I watch his throat as he swallows. "Of course, I don't want you hurt either, but it's as if your body is here but you're not in it. It freaks me out."

I grab Brody's hand and squeeze his fingers. This is the most frightening yet beautiful thing he's ever said to me. I've always been alone during my dreams, so I have no idea what I'm like during them. And while I've had some concern about my daytime visions, understanding Brody's emotions gives me more sympathy for his sour moods.

This illumination is good for our friendship.

And in the same breath, it's romantic. I feel it moves us forward in our relationship. We still haven't broached the L-word. I'll probably be the one to say it first. I don't really expect him to tell me that—yet.

Given how I feel, I *must* figure out how to tell Brody about Jamie—but without damaging everything we are to each other when he finds out how long I've kept it from him. Which is forever.

Flora's voice breaks into my thoughts.

"I'm so sorry, guys. I must have tried to quickly clean my desk, and it didn't seem important at the time, so I must have thrown it out."

At our fallen expressions, Flora produces a slip of paper with flourish. "The good news is that, though I don't remember the exact name, I kinda remember where the flower shop is." She points to the paper. "So I drew a rough map for you. I thought you could go see if you can get any information, or a new brochure. It's right here in Kansas City, about thirty minutes away."

As we examine her map, Brody pulls out his phone and searches on flower shops in Kansas City honing in on the streets Flora has listed.

"I found three viable options," he tells me. "Let's head out as soon as we're done eating—we should have time to stop by all of them, if necessary."

Our lunch arrives and I can't believe how much food is on Brody's plate. His eyes may have been bigger than his stomach.

"I need to contact Daly on the way," he says, grabbing his fork. "Today's her first day back, so I want to make sure everything is alright."

"Sounds good," I say. "I'd like to talk to her, too."

We both dig into our food. Although I only got a salad, it's large, and I eat the majority of it. Guess I was hungry!

Guess I was wrong about Brody's stomach too, I muse, watching him take his last bite.

"What'd you think of the full Irish?" I ask.

He rubs his bloated belly. "I *think* I may not need to eat again for a couple of days!" We both laugh. "It was delicious," he adds.

After Brody pays the bill and I gather my things, Flora follows us out.

"Listen, both of you—please call me and let me know if there's anything else I can do. I really hope the flower shop helps you find the answers you seek."

I hug her and thank her yet again for her help. When we release our embrace, Flora moves in toward Brody, but he not-so-subtly moves away. She chuckles and then chases after him as he runs around the truck and climbs back in.

I suddenly recall Brody complaining about Flora's hugs. Even though they seem to be joking around now, I don't think he *really* finds it funny.

CHAPTER 31

Brody starts the car and enters the address to the closest of three flower shops into the GPS.

I try to get settled, but this whole hug hang-up is really weighing on me. Not in a jealous way—I'm just super-curious.

"Brody?"

Lost in thought, he doesn't seem to hear me. My, how the tables have turned. He finally looks over and smiles as if he has no idea I said anything. I take his hand.

"Where did you go?" I ask—a question *I* have heard so many times.

"Huh? Nowhere. What are you talking about?"

"You seem to be off somewhere in your mind."

He runs his hands around the steering wheel. "This case just seems to get more convoluted with every clue. I'm praying we can figure out *something* concrete soon."

"I want that, too. But there's something else I'd like to figure out first." I try not to sound too heavy. "How come you're avoiding Flora's hugs?"

His look says he doesn't want to tell me.

"Come on," I push. "It's not like she's some evil creature come to steal your soul."

Brody checks his mirrors and pulls out of the diner parking lot.

"I really don't want to get into this," he says, rubbing his hand through his hair, "but I get the feeling you're not going to stop bugging me unless I do. So I'll give you this: When you were kidnapped, she hugged me to find out something about me. We were in crisis, so I understand, but it bothers me because my thoughts and feelings should be my own."

He places his earpiece in his ear and uses voice command to dial the station, effectively ending all conversation about hugging.

I'm totally shocked. I can't help but wonder what Flora found out.

Brody gets on his call, and as he talks to Daly, I can tell he's still carrying a lot of guilt about her attack. But I think his blame is misplaced—none of this would have happened without my dreams.

After she updates him on work, he transfers the call to the truck's speakers so I can join the conversation.

"Hi, Daly," I say. "Are you sure you're okay to be back at work so soon?"

"Yes," she asserts. "It's been quiet today, anyway."

"I told her she should have taken more time," Brody interjects. "Molly was doing just fine filling in for her."

I'm surprised to hear him direct such vehemence towards Daly, but she gives it right back and I get the feeling they've had this conversation before.

"Listen, boss," she says, "I don't like what went down any more than you do. But it happened and now it's done. I won't have you coddling me, as if you need to ease your conscience. You may run the show around here, but you don't know everything. You don't know what I went through and I don't want you to, but if I hadn't known I could depend on you to always come in right on time, I wouldn't have been able to hold on for as long as I did. So, in a way, you saved my life."

I hear tears in her voice and then it's as if she's wiped them away and her words are strong again. "I don't want you to think anything else about it. The doctors cleared me to come back and I'm here to stay for as long as you'll have me."

I see Brody wrestling inside himself and put my hand on his thigh. Everyone who knows Brody knows how much his employees mean to him. I don't know whose idea it was for everyone to call him boss, but it works. They're a family and he is the leader and protector.

"If you have any headaches or any problems at all, you better let me know right away!" he barks, conceding. "I don't want you to overdo it. We need you, and I'd rather have you at the top of your game."

"You got it, boss. Now if you're all done lecturing me, do you want to tell me what's going on? You haven't been in all day."

I remove my hand from Brody's leg as he snaps back into work mode.

"We're working on another dream-slash-nightmare of Mel's," he explains, "and we just caught a break and are going to check out a possible clue."

"Oooh…can you tell me anything about it? It's kind of dead around here. Please give me something to do."

I nod at Brody and he quickly fills her in on what's happening.

"This sounds really exciting!" says Daly. "If anyone can figure this out, you can, boss."

Brody and I both smile at her enthusiasm.

Daly falls silent for a moment, and we don't realize she's looking up information on the computer until she starts speaking again.

"Hmmmm…I searched on the info you gave me and, sure enough, I found a flower shop hosting an annual 'special blooming' event, so people can come view the one-time opening of a special flower. It's apparently called a 'Kadupul,' which is native to Sri Lanka and said to be the most expensive flower in the world. And, geez, this gets more exciting by the second—and a little more cosmic, too—because the blooming is tonight!"

"Daly!" Brody shouts at the phone. "What's the name of the shop and where and when is the event scheduled for?"

"The florist is called From Bud to Bloom. They're hosting an in-house afternoon-evening event, which starts at 2:00 p.m. with wine and hors d'oeuvres and runs until midnight or so," she tells us.

We look at each other. This just feels so right.

Daly obviously agrees. "I don't believe it, boss," she says. "It's like someone or something is putting all these pieces together like a big supernatural puzzle—I've got goose bumps! The website says the blooming could happen 'any time after sundown' and that 'on this special day we celebrate and stay open as long as the Kadupul blooms and its fantasy fragrance fills the room.'"

Brody takes my hand, the excitement growing between us that we may finally be getting somewhere.

"Thanks for all your help, Daly!" he says. "I'll check back in with you soon."

After we hang up, I start thinking about Jamie again. If we're nearing the end of this journey, I don't want Brody to find out about her before I have a chance to tell him the way I want to. The GPS says we have about twenty minutes until we arrive at the shop; it'll have to be enough time.

"I need to talk to you about something," I say.

Brody's expression falters.

"This isn't about the hugging again, is it?" he asks.

"No," I assure him. "It's something else." I struggle to find the words to say what needs to be said. "We've been spending a lot of time together recently," I start, "and it seems like a good portion of it in this truck."

He raises his eyebrows.

"Don't tell me sex in this truck is on your bucket list, too!" I say.

He raises his eyebrow at me, but says nothing.

"Forget it, Brody," I say. "I have to draw the line somewhere."

We both laugh, but I'm actually thinking it would be a great idea. One that'll have to wait, though.

"Does this have something to do with your weird behavior lately?" he asks.

I tilt my head wondering which weird behavior he's referring to. I seem to have several lately.

"Maybe," I say. "It's a specific behavior that you may or may not have noticed."

I wring my hands as nerves take over. This is stranger than the usual strange for me. I'm afraid he'll look at me differently after he knows—or be angry I never told him. Probably both. But there's no way around it. I have to be brave.

"I need to tell you about someone who's been in my life for a very long time," I start.

Brody looks perplexed. "You have no family left, Melanie," he says. "Who is this person?"

"It's not really a person," I try to explain. "Mostly, it's…a presence."

I try to read his expression. As Flora said, he's good at hiding his emotions. But his eyebrows are drawn together, and I feel the urge to put my finger on the big wrinkle that shouldn't be there.

"I'm not sure what you mean, Mel," he says. "Is this like a vision?"

Right now, I wish Brody could read minds. It would make this so much easier.

"Actually," I say, "I think she's a ghost. And she's been with me since I was a small child. Sometimes when I'm alone and sad, she comforts me."

He turns slowly, with a look that says *Duh, Mel.*

"It sounds to me like you have a guardian angel," he says aloud.

I'm amazed at how well he's taking this. "Do you believe in such things, Brody?" I ask. If he does, this'll be so much easier.

"I didn't use to believe in anything like that, Mel," he says. "But since I met you, my mind has opened more than I could have ever imagined."

As tears roll freely down my face, I fall even more in love with him. I wonder how I could have been nervous to tell him anything.

"There's more," I go on. "Sometimes when I have a vision, I can feel her, and I know she's behind it. Many visions over the last few weeks have come from her, and this flower-blooming is one of them. That's why I'm so confident in what I said to you: I know she would never let me be harmed. Maybe that will take away some of your worry."

Brody takes my hand. "So you're telling me she guides you in doing what you were put on this earth to do?" He squeezes gently. "You were put here to save people, Melanie, so she must be your guardian angel."

I look up at him. "I know you're right. But I think there's more to it—I'm just not sure what." I pull my hand from his and rub my sweaty palm on my jeans. "I can't believe I was so worried about telling you this! I could kick myself for not trusting you to understand!"

Brody gives me a gentle smile. "I think you should know by now that you can share anything and everything, and that any and all secrets are safe with me."

I look down at my lap. "I do know that now. And I won't be forgetting it anytime soon. I'm so sorry for thinking you would be anything other than what you are."

I move over to the center of the truck so I can snuggle up to Brody as we drive the rest of the way to the florist.

CHAPTER 32

WE PULL UP IN FRONT of From Bud to Bloom and gasp at the number of people at the shop. It must be almost a hundred. A large white tent has been set up in the parking lot, where patrons are standing at little round bar tables enjoying wine and finger food, celebrating as they wait for the "grand opening" of the Kadupul.

This looks like so much fun.

We get out of the truck and make our way toward them, but I suddenly stop.

"You okay, Mel?" Brody turns to me.

"I hear a strange violin playing," I say. "Is it coming from the event?"

Brody's quizzical expression tells me it's not.

I sense this is some sort of "auditory vision" I'm supposed to follow. Was this rare flower—this *Queen of the Night*—sent to lure us here simply so I could discover something else?

I don't have time to ponder the convoluted conundrum. I grab Brody's arm as my sight disappears and my hearing intensifies.

"Brody, I can't see!" I take a deep breath—I can't panic now. I need to lean on Brody. "Help me back to the truck."

Brody leads me carefully, helps me inside, and shuts the door.

This is the oddest sensation. I would not want to be blind.

"What do you want me to do, Mel?"

Brody's voice startles me. I hadn't realized he'd joined me in the truck.

"Start driving," I tell him. "We'll adjust toward the sound."

Brody pulls out of the parking lot. As he progresses down the street, the violin music fades. I grab his arm in panic.

"We need to go back the other way!" I shout.

I feel we're on the cusp of answers, but if we go the wrong way, we'll completely miss out.

Without hesitation, Brody immediately flips a U-turn. But then I feel him pull over.

"What are you doing, Brody? We don't have time to stop!"

"I'm attaching the portable lights, Mel. I want to be able to go fast without getting pulled over. I'd use the sirens, too, but I don't want to drown out what you're hearing."

We're back on the road in seconds.

The violin's volume increases, and I tap my foot, giddy with the excitement. This is finally it! I just know it.

Of course, I also feel trepidation—especially when the violin grows faint again.

"Have we passed any side streets since you turned around?" I ask.

"Yes, just a minute ago," he says, already flipping another U-ey. "Shall I go down it?"

"Yes!" I say. "And please hurry!"

We complete our turnaround and soon after, I feel us make a left.

"The music is piercing now!" I cry. "I know we're on the right track!"

"My god, Mel!" Brody shouts. "I know we are, too! There's a house on fire!"

At his words, my sight returns and my eyes take in the flames before us. I feel unsteady, but I don't have time to be weak. We're finally here!

"Brody!" I screech, unable to control my voice. "This is the house from my dream—the one about the woman with the violin! I recognize the old architecture and the small broken window up in the gable." As I look more closely, a frenzy of questions pour out of me: "Oh my god, what is that guy doing in the front yard? Is he bleeding, Brody? Where's the woman?"

"I don't know," he says, "but I'm pulling over—*now*!" Brody wrenches the steering wheel and hits the brakes hard. Suddenly his arm shoots across my torso. "Mel, he's got a knife! Call 9-1-1 and stay in the truck!"

I grasp for my phone, my gaze still fixed on the house.

"Do you hear me?!" he repeats. "You need to stay in the damn truck!"

Brody takes a moment to retrieve his gun from the safety box under his seat. When he opens the driver door, I hear the man shouting. He sounds completely out of his mind.

"Someone help me!" he shouts. "Something happened to my wife! She went crazy and tried to kill me! She set the house on fire and stabbed me! With *this* knife!"

As he jumps around screaming, I can see that his shirt is torn open and his midsection is covered in cuts and blood. He looks like he's been wrestling an alligator.

Brody runs toward the man, drawing his gun along the way. He extends his hand forward and seems to be talking to the man.

I ease my window down a few inches.

"Take it easy, pal," I hear Brody say. "Let's put the knife down and sit on the ground, okay? Where *is* your wife?"

The man drops the knife.

Slowly and easily, Brody picks it up by the handle and puts it in an evidence bag he pulls from his pocket. He carries them with him all the time.

The man suddenly erupts again. "That's what she tried to kill me with!" he repeats. "She's in the house somewhere, the crazy bitch! Frankly, I don't know where and I don't care. I just know that she went insane and stabbed me! More than once! I can't believe this shit. Look what she did to me!"

The man is now in full agitation mode.

Brody is now in full cop-mode.

He finally gets the man to ease up on the hysterics and lie down on the grass, far from the burning house. They appear to be talking, but I can't hear the conversation.

Meanwhile, the entire front of the place is engulfed in flames. If the woman really is inside, I need to get in that house!

I quickly call 9-1-1 and give them the info; then I slip quietly out of the cab. Brody is so busy, I'm hoping he won't notice.

Make your way to the back.

The words come from nowhere and I realize it's Jamie. Hearing her voice comforts me. But I'm still afraid of what I'll find.

A row of bushes borders the home from its neighbor, and I run alongside it, keeping as low as possible to avoid detection. I make my way on to the back porch. The smoke isn't as bad here and I don't see any flames. I open the door and step inside.

I was so right about being afraid. A woman is lying on the floor of a small kitchen, and I don't know if she's dead or alive.

Are we too late?

Her hand is tightly clasping a knife, and she's surrounded by a pool of blood. Does it belong to her or the man in the front yard? Or maybe both?

I can't see the woman's face; she has long hair wrapped around it in a sopping, tangled mess. I crouch next to her, keeping one eye fixed on the knife.

She's breathing! She's alive! But all the more reason to be wary of that blade. I gently pull her hair back from her face.

I gasp. It's like looking in a mirror! We could be twins.

The biggest difference is that her right eye is bruised and swollen.

I'm in total shock. My hands shaking, I sit down next to her on the floor, weeping at the damage that has been done to her face and body.

There's so much blood, I can't tell if it's flowing from wounds or if it's just spatter. I'm so deathly afraid that this woman won't make it.

I lift my hand to her face—maybe to make sure it's real. This woman who could be my twin sister!

Suddenly, the non-swollen eye pops open. It widens when she sees me.

"Who are you?" she asks, her voice a whisper. "Are you a ghost?"

"I'm Melanie," I tell her through tears. "Help is on the way."

It dawns on me that I haven't heard any sirens yet. Where is the fire department? The paramedics? Shouldn't they have answered my call by now? Maybe or maybe not. I've lost all sense of time.

"Who are you?" I ask, a flood of questions deluging my mind. How can we look identical? If she *is* my twin, where has she been all this time? Is this why Jamie brought me here?

But I don't get any answers. Silently, the woman releases the knife and tries to lift her hand to my face as I did to hers. She screams out in pain. That's when I notice the odd angle at which her left arm is bent. It's obviously broken. I urge her to lie still. Thankfully, the flames and smoke are still in the front of the house. Hopefully the cavalry will arrive before she needs to be moved.

Tears flow down both our cheeks as we look at each other. It's so odd. I've had many strange experiences in my life, but none of them compares to this. Am I really looking at a possible twin I didn't know existed? And if not, then who the heck is this person?

I'm jolted by a loud snapping sound.

A few more minutes have gone quickly up in smoke.

The second floor above us is now fully aflame, and the wooden beams supporting it are crumbling. One crashes in front of the back door and my body jumps at the loud thud.

Smoke pours into the kitchen. I can barely breathe! My eyes water and I can't see now, either. Coughing and sputtering, I grip on to this woman with all I have in me.

I have to get her out, now!

I place her good arm around my shoulders and start to help her up. But a large beam from the upper floor collapses on top of us.

I hear a scream and then realize it's coming from me. I pray it will be heard over the roar of flames.

The last thought that runs through my mind is that I may not make it out of this one, and that Brody is going to be really pissed I didn't listen to him.

CHAPTER 33

*J*AMIE IS USING ALL HER STRENGTH *to hold the fire away from the kitchen. She's controlling the wind with a power she didn't know she had.*

Seeing the beam crash on top of the girls, she loses control—but only for a moment. She immediately fights back.

She knows it's her responsibility to protect the two women on the floor. Without her help, they'll never survive—especially with the entrapment they now face.

She MUST gain control. Even if what she's about to do is against all the "rules." Because in the monstrous middle of this cataclysm, rules matter very little.

Jamie has always recognized the power of love—a force that can provide strength beyond anything imaginable. But right now her "control" is fueled by an even greater, opposing force: a deep, intense anger. Its origin is her miserable childhood and all the losses she endured in her lifetime. Letting her emotions rage is like nothing she's ever experienced, or allowed herself to experience.

Rarely in her life did Jamie speak an angry word, or even raise her voice. That's the reason she's where she is now. Her kindness and generosity gave her a special position in the hereafter. But she did suffer greatly in life. And what she's doing now, in this moment, is for all the women who have suffered as she did.

She MUST save them.

She draws upon every ounce of anger from every moment of her past to drive her forward, letting the feeling grow and allowing it to flow into her heart.

Her strength increases.

She can feel the frenzy pulsing around her spirit form. She can hear the beating of drums in her head and throbbing all around her. It's as though her own heartbeat is pounding in her ears even though her heart ceased to function a very long time ago.

Every memory she has increases her rage. A torrential storm thrums inside her. Feeling strange, she glances around and sees her own unearthly form. She's somehow become a visible apparition. But she has no time to ponder it. She is floating on a field of fury.

She decides to see if she can channel her wrath to push against the fire. She summons her resentment for losing her life so young, for not being able to care for the family she left behind, for atrocities committed against her in life, and against her family after her death. She unleashes her outrage at the drunk driver who took her husband's life, and her bitterness for all the abuse she endured at the hands of her mother.

A gale of bitterness flows through her—resentment she thought she had long ago released. She sets it free, aiming every bit of the force toward the flames and heat.

She knows this is her last hope of saving the two earthly souls whom she loves above all others.

Breaking the chains of her spiritual form makes her feel so commanding. Never in her short life did she experience this. If she'd allowed herself to acknowledge her inner rage back then, maybe things would've turned out different.

Looking down at the two girls unconscious on the floor, she creates a wind so mighty, it lifts one end of the fallen beam off their bodies.

She's created a hurricane in the house with the girls in the calm eye, protected. She'll continue to control it for as long as possible, but it won't be forever. She prays fervently that someone will come save these two women who represent the love, the anger, and the position that has enabled her to do what she has done for so many ethereal years.

I FEEL MYSELF COMING OUT of a dream. A wind tunnel screams around me, tossing debris from the fire around the house like paper in a tornado. Above me, I see an outline of…*something*.

I try to pull myself to my feet but I'm trapped.

I feel an angry vibration surround me. I hear and feel turbulent thoughts. I'm not sure how, but I recognize they're coming from Jamie.

I look up and realize that the outline I saw is *her*. The voice that's been with me since I was a girl. But the soothing presence is somehow now visible. And *terribly* enraged.

Her emotions pulsate around us so strongly, it's indescribable. She's in the center of a roaring rage—no, she *is* the rage. It emanates from inside her and she's *become* this storm. A storm that's protecting us from the fire.

I can't keep my eyes off her. Seeing her is something I've longed for my whole life. And she's beautiful beyond anything on this earth.

Then—the large beam trapping my body rises into the air. I see her form float around and around with outstretched arms, protecting us, saving us.

Jamie looks at me. Her smile is the most gorgeous and peaceful thing I have ever seen.

But her expression turns to worry. Can she hold the fire back long enough to save us? I grab my companion's hand, consumed by the depth of my fear. All goes dark as I drift back into oblivion.

CHAPTER 34

Brody is standing in the front yard waiting for the locals to arrive. This chaotic drama seems to have gone on for hours, but he knows in reality it's been only a manic matter of minutes. Brody's "full cop-mode" expands as he tries to keep a frenzied man sedate and alive while trying to make sense of what is *really* going on. He'd rather not leave the bleeding man until the paramedics, or at least until the police and firefighters, arrive.

The front of the house is burning hotter and faster by the second, so Brody pulls the man further from it. Brody continues to try to talk him, but he can't even get a first name. The guy just keeps repeating that this is his house and that it was his wife who stabbed him.

Ripping fabric from the man's shirt to create makeshift bandages, Brody is amazed this guy is still alive with all the knife wounds inflicted to his chest. Somehow, most don't seem to be deep. Inspecting them more closely, Brody sees that some slices run in the opposite direction from the others. *Hmmm…*

His police postulations are interrupted by a loud scream that chills him to the bone.

Melanie!

He knows before he even looks at his truck that she's not in it. His blood starts to boil, but not with anger—with fear. He looks back toward the house and sees what looks like a tornado inside. His mind races.

The high-pitched whine of sirens fills the air as fire trucks and ambulances finally converge on the scene. *Thank god.* Brody needs to get into that house *now!*

Brody quickly brings the EMTs up to speed and cautions the new arrivals to keep a close eye on the stabbed man. "There's definitely something not right with his story."

As the firefighters hook up their hoses, everyone appears awestruck by the scene. Surely none has ever witnessed—or felt—the kind of crazed cyclone that is all but blowing the entire house apart from the inside out.

While everyone is mesmerized by the bursting blaze, Brody slips his way to the back.

He knows Mel is in there.

One of the firefighters spots him and follows. He tries to grab Brody's arm, but he'd be better off trying to lasso a bus. Brody will not be stopped.

Over the roar of fire and wind, Brody quickly explains that possibly two women are inside, one for sure. He also explains that he's going in there whether the firefighter likes it or not.

"I'm glad you're here, though," Brody shouts. "Because if there *are* two women, it'll take both of us to get 'em out! And their time is pretty much up!"

The firefighter nods his agreement. The two men jump onto the back porch. All the windows are blown out and thick black smoke is streaming out of them. The backdoor is jammed shut, they discover, probably pushed outward by the squall from the inside storm. The firefighter holds up his ax to assure Brody that one way or another they *will* get inside to the women.

Brody rips off a piece of his shirt and fixes it over his face. He tears another piece to cover his hands. Then he tries again to muscle his way through the back door. There's no way he can or will live without Melanie, and he won't let her go without fighting for her life with his.

The firefighter motions Brody aside and starts pounding the door with an ax. His efforts create deep holes in the wood, but something's still blocking the door.

Brody decides to go in through a window. He uses part of the shirt covering his hand to remove what's left of the glass. He doesn't think about his actions before diving through the window frame into hell.

Amazingly, there still isn't much fire in the kitchen, but there's plenty of smoke and debris. A big part of the ceiling has collapsed.

He still can't figure out the brutal wind blowing all around them—especially since the air outside is calm.

And where the hell is Melanie in all this?

He lifts his eyes upward, about to pull at his hair, and that's when he sees it. At first he assumes it's a figment of his imagination, but since knowing Mel, he's learned that a spectral being floating in the middle of an inferno might just be more fact than figment.

With wind whirling all around it, the being looks directly at Brody. Her face is so familiar, he thinks at first maybe it's Melanie—now a ghost somehow taming this fire. The thought that she's gone feels like the firefighter's ax striking him straight through the heart. When he looks again, the ghost gestures her head toward the center of floor.

Through the thick smoke, Brody finally spots two women. They're lying side by side, holding hands. A ceiling beam appears to be suspended above them, floating midair.

He signals the firefighter—now also inside—and points to the ceiling beam and the women beneath it.

"Please tell me what the hell *that* is!" the firefighter yells. "How is that damn thing just hanging in space?!"

"I don't know!" Brody shouts. "But I think that's a ghost or an angel of some type." Realizing how that must sound, he adds, "And bud, if you don't believe in that kind of shit right now, you will when this is over!"

Both men grab the beam to swing it away from the women. It's glowing hot, but Brody doesn't care.

Meanwhile, the firefighter keeps staring at the apparition, his eyes wide even amidst the heavy smoke.

"I know that's something you'll probably never see again," Brody interrupts, "but we need to get these two out of here."

Brody rushes over to the pair and quickly assesses them.

"I think the one with long hair has a broken arm," he tells the firefighter, "and probably additional injuries. So I'll let you handle her. Besides, the other one's with me."

The firefighter nods. As he proceeds to carefully gather up the wounded woman, Brody knows this guy's going to be talking about this rescue for a long, long time.

Brody gently lifts Mel in his arms. She blinks a few times before becoming immediately frantic, trying to tell him something. But he can't hear her over the ceaseless roar of fire and wind.

"Brody, did you see her?!" Melanie shouts even louder. "She has to be my twin, right? There's no other explanation for her to look just like me. I never knew I had a sister! This must all be part of—"

"Mel, let's just worry about getting the hell out of here!" Brody yells, carrying her toward the door. "We can talk when we're safe."

"No, no, you can't just leave her!" Mel cries hysterically. "She'll die."

"It's okay, Mel," Brody soothes directly into her ear to make sure she hears him. "We've got her. Stop fighting me now. Everything will be okay."

Brody risks one more "Lot's wife" look back over his shoulder, and he can't believe how much the ghostly figure looks like Mel. But there's no time for more contemplation. The house is rapidly collapsing in on itself. It feels to him like a closing scene from a movie, when everyone rushes out the back door to the final grinding gasp of the home's last breath, narrowly escaping certain doom.

And that seems a fitting climax to this mysterious journey— with all the truths coming together in the most real of trials by fierce fire.

Brody carries Mel out the back of the house and heads around to the front. When they reach the street, the scene is completely chaotic. The firefighters are diligently working to put out the fire, but it appears to be a lost cause.

Brody and his companion gently lay the women on the grass near the ambulances so they can be tended to by paramedics.

Brody finally gets a look at the second woman and stifles a gasp. He remembers Mel's words. *"She must be my twin, right?"* Boy, she wasn't kidding!

The woman is unconscious but breathing. Brody contemplates that there's nothing left of what was once her existence in this house.

Mel is now on a gurney ready to be placed in the ambulance. She's already hooked to oxygen and is being bandaged along her arms.

"What are those for?" Brody asks.

"Just a couple of small burns," the young EMT tells him. "She was very lucky—they both are. Most people don't get out of situations like this."

Brody can't think about what might have been. There's still too much to do.

"You'd better have your hands and arms looked at too, sir."

Brody looks down at smattering of blood and burn marks.

"I don't think the blood is mine," he assures the EMT, "and the burns aren't that bad. I'll get them checked out later."

He looks out at the smoldering pile of rubble that used to be a house, scanning the scene intently.

"What is it, Brody?" Mel asks.

"It's the husband," he says. "The crazy guy. I need to know where they took him. Hopefully, everyone's going to the same hospital." He looks around. "I'll go talk to the officer in charge and contact Barney to come up to give me a hand." He looks at her. "You know, we need to get to the point where I'm not always sending you off to some hospital while I run off chasing potential perpetrators." He eyes her sternly. "And by the way, if I remember correctly, you promised you would stay in the truck."

"I'm sorry." She sighs. "But I *had* to."

"I know." He half-smiles. Then he kisses her.

"I don't know what happened here today, Mel," he tells her, "but I *do* know the local police will want to talk to your…uh, *sister*…? *And* her husband."

Brody jogs toward the group of cops. He finds the captain and introduces himself, only vaguely explaining how he ended up in another jurisdiction. He hands over the evidence bag containing the knife and says they saw the fire as they were driving around the area. No reason to provide more info than necessary right now.

He recounts how when they pulled up, the man holding the knife—presumably a resident, along with one of the women found in the house—was stabbed and bloody and ranting about *something*.

"Where was that guy taken?" Brody asks. "What hospital?"

"The only people going to the hospital are the two women," the captain tells Brody. "We're not aware of anyone else involved. It'll be up to the fire investigators to tell us if any more bodies turn up."

"Captain." Brody gets in the officer's face. "When I happened upon this scene, the guy running around with the knife looked like an extra from a bad slasher movie. I asked the first responders to keep an eye on him because we *need* to talk to him. He may or may not have been stabbed by his wife, but I'm damn sure he's up to his gory eyeballs in whatever really happened here today. So, if he did slip away, we need to find him *now*!"

CHAPTER 35

I'M IN THE AMBULANCE, on a jump seat, looking over at "my sister"—the only thing I can think to call her—who's on a gurney. A single paramedic tends to both of us.

Staring at the woman, I identify tiny differences in our looks; but essentially we're identical. Her hair is longer than mine. I think that's good, so the responders can tell us apart. As I continue to stare, she opens her good eye and stares back.

This is our first moment together, free of fire and fear.

"I'm Melanie," I say. "Who are you?"

"My name is Sabrina," she whispers. "I can't believe that you're real." She hesitates. "*Are* you real?"

I take her hand in mine. As I do, I look down and examine it. I know this hand. It's long and lovely, just like the hand in my painting. And also just like mine.

"I'm as real as you are," I reply. "And I…I guess I'm your sister. Your *twin* sister." I look into her eyes. "I feel a connection to you—one I think I've felt all along. Long before this moment."

She looks so confused. Of course she is. How could she have any idea what I'm talking about?

"Am I going to be arrested?" she asks, obviously deciding to deal with practical matters first.

I squeeze her hand. "I'll explain everything later, but for now, we'll both talk to the police and tell them what happened. I'm hoping both our stories combined will be enough to convince them of your innocence. I'm so happy I finally found you."

Though she's obviously still confused, she grips my hand back and nods.

We continued holding hands until the ambulance pulls in to the hospital bay. But now I detect a new fear in her eyes.

"Don't worry," I assure her, "I won't let them take you after I've just found you. Please trust me. You must be strong, though, because the next few hours are going to be difficult. You need to tell them everything. The truth is what they want to hear."

"Okay," she says, "but please stay with me. I know I'll be stronger if you're with me!"

Tears run down my face. "You couldn't get rid of me if you tried."

BRODY WATCHES THE AMBULANCE drive away with Mel and her twin. It's an odd thing to contemplate, considering that most of the time he's known Mel, she's had no family around—no one to love or care for.

Despite his shock, Brody is forced to turn his focus on finding the husband who somehow disappeared from the scene. The sheriff explains to his subordinates that Brody will lead the investigation, for which Brody is extremely grateful. He's promised to explain everything to the sheriff later.

One thing Brody isn't willing to reveal until necessary is Melanie's gift. He knows no one's buying that he and Mel just "happened" to see the fire from a distance—especially after seeing the two identical women pulled from the house. Brody urges them that finding the missing husband is top priority and that further "details" will have to wait until they do.

He tells them about the husband's claims, but asserts that he doesn't believe the scenario. He describes the inconsistent wound marks on the man's torso and also that, given the man's size and strength, he should have more easily taken control of the knife, or at least had more defensive wounds on his hands and arms.

As soon as the explanations conclude, the manhunt begins. The streets have already been blocked off and a perimeter established, so now all garages and enclosures in the neighborhood will be searched. Thankfully, thinks Brody, it won't be too easy for the man to hide; a trail of blood is a pretty good giveaway.

Essentially all they need to do is follow it from this yard to the next and the next.

And that's exactly what they do.

In short order, the husband is found hiding in a garage only three houses down. Sitting in the corner trying to staunch some of the wounds, he looks up in apparent shock to find them standing in the doorway. Brody asks the other officers to step out and request another ambulance; that will give him a minute to ask a few questions.

"Why did you run from the scene?"

Brody waits for an answer, but nothing.

"If what you said about your wife attacking you is true, you should've stayed and gone to the hospital. Those wounds need to be treated. The only thing you've achieved by running is bringing suspicion upon yourself."

"I was—" the man stammers. "I mean, I *am* confused. I've lost a lot of blood. Besides, you could be in cahoots with her. She's crazy! If given the chance, she'll kill me. Keep her away from me!"

Brody knows something is seriously wrong. Clearly the husband is the crazy one—or at the very least, the true abuser in this relationship. Because Brody certainly believes Mel's dreams over this guy's rambling.

After the man is taken away via ambulance—and also solidly in police custody—Brody goes back to his truck. He's told all the injured were taken to KU Med.

The University of Kansas Hospital.

The birthplace of Melanie.

And the workplace of the "rule-abiding" Cheryl and the mysterious Donna.

Could this day pile on any more layers of intrigue?

By now it's quite late. Brody knows he's not going to get any real sleep tonight as he heads for his truck to speed his way back to KC and the hospital. He takes one last look at the burnt shell of what was once someone's home and registers sadness for the loss. Then he thinks about that flower—that Kadupul. That beautiful flower's short life comes and goes in a heartbeat, something he will *not* let happen to Mel and the new life that is blossoming for her. And for them.

He rushes north on the Interstate, now with just three objectives. Number one is seeing Mel. But he also needs to question her "twin" and the husband, doing what he can within the legal system. Which one first? He wants to clear Mel's sister ASAP, but he also needs to tie up her husband quickly so he can't do any more damage.

He remembers what Daly said about the name of the perfume made from the Kadupul: *Midnight Miracle*. He looks at his watch and manages a smile.

"I could use one of those right about now," he says out loud.

CHAPTER 36

I REFUSE TO LEAVE HER, even for a minute. I've promised myself that the only way they'll get me away from my newfound sister is kicking and screaming. Thankfully, they agree to keep us together in the ER.

We let the staff do all the talking. At least for now.

After setting her broken arm, they ascertain she also has a concussion. Both will heal, but they express concern beyond her physical injuries. Looking at Sabrina pointedly, the doctor says her swollen eye appears to be from a punch to the face. Sabrina looks down at her lap but doesn't respond. The doctor doesn't press it. I guess that's the cops' job.

I suppose if she *had* been trying to kill her husband, he could've hit her while fighting back, but I don't believe a word of it. I'm the one having dreams, and I know what's been going on behind closed doors.

I also know that until Sabrina's ready to tell her story, I'm not going to interfere. As an abuse victim, she's going to need to learn to stand up for herself. If she can't, her healing process will take a long time—if ever.

But at least she has me now.

They finally move us to a room—again, thankfully, together. I've turned into sort of a defender, holding fast to my insistence that they don't separate us. I'm not sure which of us is technically the "big sister," but since she's the most vulnerable right now, I'm taking the reins.

Once we're in the room alone, she finally speaks. "You said in the ambulance that you thought we were sisters…twins?" she murmurs. "How is that possible? I was never told I had a sister—or anyone."

"I was adopted as a baby," I explain, "so I never knew my biological mother or father—much less about you. If I had, you can believe I would've done everything in my power to find you. And now—"

We're interrupted by Brody entering the room. He leans over me, and we hug and we kiss and cry.

"We can't keep meeting like this." He grins through watery eyes. "We need to start keeping you away from sadistic kidnappers and three-alarm fires."

Sabrina has the look of someone who's just walked into a very complex movie.

And she has.

Introducing her to Brody, I'm now in full sobbing mode: the man I love meeting what I think is my long-lost sister. We inform Brody the doctors are keeping us both overnight, maybe longer. But the good news is we'll both make a full recovery.

Brody pulls up the guest chair. "Well, I guess I'd better get comfortable!"

Sabrina and I look at each other.

"What do you mean?" I say. "Aren't the cops coming to question us?"

"I stalled them off 'til morning," he tells us. "I figured you could both use a minute to regroup. Especially given"—he waves his hand between us—"uh, this."

We both giggle. It's the first time I've laughed since…I can't remember. And it feels good.

He tells us he'll stay overnight in the chair.

"Actually…" I say, "I wouldn't mind some alone time with"—I look at Sabrina—"uh, this."

We all smile.

Brody and I share a look of understanding, and he stands up. "Okay, I get it." He heads for the door. "But I'll be close by if you need anything. I'm going to get a cheap motel room and convene with local police in the morning. And, by the way, Sabrina, your husband has been taken to a different hospital, far from here near Lawrence. Distance and a deputy outside his door will keep you more than safe." He gives us a mock salute. "Get a good night's sleep, ladies. Tomorrow will definitely be a day of questions—and hopefully, a lot of answers."

"But one more thing, Sheriff…" Sabrina hesitates.

"Brody."

"Uh, Brody, you said I'd be safe here, but doesn't my husband actually think I'm dead? Does he have any clue that I was…*saved*?"

Brody looks uncomfortable. "I haven't talked to the investigators or Sheriff Williams down in Lawrence yet, but I'm sure your husband will ask. What the investigators tell him is up to them and how they choose to handle things. But frankly, from the strange nature of this case and early signs of domestic abuse, I would think he'll be quite distressed when he eventually learns of your survival." Brody nods at her reassuringly. "But I promise you this: Both his distress *and* your survival will continue."

After Brody leaves, Sabrina and I look at each other. We know we need to sleep but there are so many things I want to talk about. I'm afraid she's too tired, though, and I'm not even sure where to start. I don't want to frighten her by going directly back to yesterday and all the mysteries that were stampeding around the giant fiery elephant in *that* room but…

I don't have to worry about it long. She has some ideas of her own.

"I'm tired," she begins, "but I'm dying to know: How on earth did you end up at that fire? And finding me?! That can't be a coincidence."

I smile as I find myself doing the "Brody thing" of tugging at my hair, looking slightly down while gathering my thoughts.

Finally, I look up at her.

"Well, it's pretty hard to explain, but I'll try my best." I take a deep, fortifying breath. "Since I was a young girl, I've dreamed about murders."

Sabrina looks stunned. She doesn't speak.

"I didn't know they were anything but nightmares until my adoptive mother was murdered. And I had dreamt the whole thing beforehand."

Now she's not silent. "You saw your adoptive mother being murdered in a *dream*?!" she gasps, sitting straight up in her bed. "And then she *was* murdered?!"

I look down again, figuring out how to explain. "I didn't see it all at one time," I say. "I see pieces of what the fates—or whoever or wherever else dreams come from—decide at the time. Usually I create paintings as I go, so I can keep track of the reality I'm dealing with. Then the cops use my artwork to solve cases." I look at her wryly. "I'm sure they'll have a field day with the ones I painted about you."

She leans back in the bed, and I see her wince, trying to make her casted arm more comfortable.

"Do you want me to put a pillow under your arm?" I ask.

"No, but thank you," she says quietly. "Please tell me more."

"When I first dreamt of my mother's murder, I started drawing everything I saw. But by the time I went to the police, it was too late. They found her body the next day; she was already dead."

Sabrina winces again, but clearly not because of her arm this time.

"I'm so sorry!" she says, slowly shaking her head. "I can't imagine the pain you must've felt."

"You're right. I felt a lot of pain. *And* guilt. I'd waited too long and it was too late for anyone to save her."

I don't smile this time as I lower my head and brush a few stray strands of hair back from my face.

"Anyway," I say, raising my eyes to look into hers, "I still have dreams of impending murders and that's what brought me to you."

I can see she's the most shocked by *this* revelation. But I continue on before she can comment.

"I...I dreamt that you thought about killing your husband," I confess. "I dreamt what you felt. That's what started this search for you: to stop you from committing murder. I knew from the beginning that you weren't anything like the horrible man who killed my mom—or like any of the other murderers I've had dreams about. Because I wasn't afraid when I dreamt about you. Instead, I felt pity. But I had no idea until I saw you that you could be my twin sister."

We are both now soaked in quiet tears.

Sabrina finally breaks the silence, "You have to understand, that although you couldn't save your mother, you did save me. By finding me in the fire. But I'll admit that if I hadn't been knocked unconscious, I might have killed Robert to protect myself. I knew in my heart that he'd never let me leave him. He had control of everything, and he wanted me to bow down to him as if he were a king. I couldn't do it anymore."

She looks down at her arm and then back to me, wiping away tears with her free hand. "Robert—uh, my husband—has been physically abusing me for years. The hospital can verify that when they perform X-rays, or whatever tests they do. I'm sure they already noticed my arm's been broken before. The damage he's done to my body is mostly hidden—scars, breaks. He hits me everywhere but the face." She touches her eye in sad amusement. "Usually, that is."

I lean toward her and gently brush my hand along her cheek beneath her swollen eye.

"And then came today," she says, taking a deep breath. "*Today* is when I told my husband I wanted a divorce. That I was done being abused by him and was ready to get away. He came at me immediately and I knew that he'd kill me if I didn't protect myself. I grabbed a kitchen knife. But all I managed to do was to make a tiny cut on his arm—certainly not enough to stop him. He overpowered me quickly and I knew I was in trouble."

I want to say something comforting, but I fear interrupting her rumination, so I just nod mutely.

"He started yelling and calling me names and that's when he punched me. He must've knocked me out. We were in the kitchen and I think I must've hit my head on the counter when I went down.

"I woke for a few minutes," she goes on, "and I saw him pouring gasoline in the living room. It was probably the smell that woke me. I've never been so afraid. I think he wanted to let the fire burn enough to make sure I was dead and destroy the evidence of what happened. Then he would have called 911 and told them his fabricated story." She looks up at me. "I don't know how long I was out, but thank god you and Brody showed up quickly enough to foil his plan."

"Sabrina," I tell her, "when we pulled up to the house, Robert was out front. He had a knife in his hand, his shirt was ripped open, and he had numerous slash marks across his body."

Sabrina manages a twisted smile.

"If he has more than one stab wound, he inflicted it—or them—himself. That's the exact kind of thing he'd do: implicate me to exert his power and control. Very little is beneath him. He's a narcissist and no way would he ever allow me to leave him. I know my...*husband*."

She practically spits the vile-tasting word out of her mouth.

"I didn't wake up until I saw you and that other woman," she continues. "But then again," she suggests, "I may have been hallucinating...or seeing something in the smoke that wasn't there. It was frightening and chaotic in that fire."

I sigh. So she did see Jamie.

"You weren't hallucinating, Sabrina," I tell her. "But you could save yourself a lot of trouble by not mentioning that to the cops right now."

"What do you mean?" Sabrina asks.

I try to find the right words. "It took me a lot of energy and explaining and *proving* to get law enforcement to understand that there are other forces out there that can't be questioned and fingerprinted and confined within walls of natural law. Explaining the *super*natural takes time and work, and it gets really complex."

"Like that other woman?" Sabrina asks.

"Like that other woman."

I smile.

"You look tired," I offer. "Maybe we should get some rest? Like Brody said, tomorrow is a big day."

Sabrina nods as she leans further back and readjusts her arm again. She seems comfortable as she drifts off to sleep. I feel comfortable too, and it's a comfort I'm guessing neither of us has experienced in a long, long time. Maybe ever.

CHAPTER 37

WE AWAKE AT ALMOST the exact same time. I wonder if that's typical of twins. But before I can ponder the question, or can even utter a "good morning," a nurse comes in to check on us. *And* to tell us that as soon as we've cleaned up and eaten breakfast, the police will be here to ask some questions.

Fine.

But questions are one thing; interrogations are another. And if they want to separate me from Sabrina for any length of time, I won't let it happen. I'll fight with every last breath in my body. I'm sure Brody has been talking with the locals since he woke up, and I hope he's set them straight that Sabrina is the victim here. Otherwise he might have to use his power to get *me* out of the KC jail!

Two officers enter. They lay things out quickly and to the point: Yesterday's *event* and its aftermath has left them with a full file of felonies—from *possible* attempted murder to arson to domestic abuse to evading police, coupled with a few assorted misdemeanors along the way.

And Sabrina and her husband are in the middle of it all. Until it's all sorted out, the couple will each be considered *suspects*. I am also a "person of interest."

I feel a rush of anger.

"Wait just a minute. Do you think maybe you could talk to her before calling her a suspect? And me, as well? Maybe you should not take the word of one person over another."

The one I presume is the lead officer looks down at his notes. "Excuse me, miss, can you confirm your name for me?"

"I'm...I'm Melanie Morris. If you look at us, you'll see that we're twins. We just found each other yesterday in the middle of that hell her husband created. We never knew the other sister existed and—"

"I've heard of you," he interrupts, pointing his pen at me. "I remember reading in the paper that you're a 'psychic to cops' or something to that effect. And you work with the sheriff's department over in Arrow Springs, right? We'll need to question *you* after we're done questioning Mrs. Cellini."

I'm a little shocked to hear that I'm more well-known than I'm aware of. And I'm *really* shocked to hear Sabrina called by her married name for the first time. It just makes this whole scene cold and dehumanizing.

"Well, good, great," I say. "I'm glad you're aware of what I've done for law enforcement, and I'm happy to answer any questions. But you do know I'm staying in this room while you question my sister."

"Well, good, great," the officer retorts right back. "Thank you for your service and we'll extend to you any *professional courtesy* possible. But you do know you *won't* be here while we question your sister."

I'm shocked, excited, enraged, and embarrassed, all at the same time. But I do really like the sound of that: "your sister." And I plan on protecting her, starting right now. And if that entails avoiding getting dragged off by an angry officer, well, so be it.

"Alright," I relent. "If you could call a nurse to show me where to go, I'll go. But one question: I'm sure Sheriff Carter has been in touch with you; could you tell me where he is?"

"Sheriff Carter has indeed been in touch with us, and he's helping us by detailing what he encountered at the fire before we arrived. We've extended all professional courtesy to him as well. I understand that early this morning, he accompanied another of our officers down to Lawrence to question Mr. Cellini."

With that, he opens the door and calls for a nurse.

As I'm getting up, I'm relieved to see that Sabrina is somehow not exhibiting fear. She looks strong and ready to tell her story. She looks up at me and holds out her uncasted hand. I give her mine and she squeezes it, as if drawing strength from me. It makes me happy she feels some sort of trust or bond with me, even though we don't really know each other yet.

As the nurse escorts me out, I hear *my sister* begin talking with the officers.

"I'll tell you everything. But please don't call me Mrs. Cellini—I don't want to be known by that name any longer. I just want to get back to being me. Sabrina."

The nurse gets me situated in an empty room.

"I'll come back and get you just as soon as the officers tell me it's okay," she assures me.

"Thank you."

I'm guessing I'll be here awhile. In fact, the police will probably come in *here* to question me. But I know Sabrina has quite the story to tell first.

FINALLY, IT'S MY TURN.

"Ms. Morris, are you feeling well enough to answer a few questions?"

"I'm well enough to answer whatever you'd like, officer. I'm also well enough to go home," I add, "and I'm hoping that will happen soon!"

"We hope so, too. But for now, please tell us about the events of yesterday's fire and how you perceived it from the unique perspective many believe you have."

Here we go…

I tell them about my dreams. How I saw the abuse and how Sabrina's husband screamed that he would kill her. I tell them about my paintings. I show them photos on my phone of everything I created. They seem amazed by the detail— and accuracy—to actual events. I see their surprise when they diligently check the date of each photo and confirm they all were taken well before yesterday.

I'm so relieved that one investigating officer has heard of my past contributions, because it makes things so much less *complex* that he's willing to listen. And after he's listened, he tells me they have all the information they need. At least for now. The county prosecutor will make the final determinations.

"But if I were you," he adds, "I'd take my sister home and help her relax while we deal with Mr. Cellini. Contact the insurance company about the house, breathe deeply, regroup, and be ecstatic you both came out of this alive—*and* with each other."

I'm wheeled back into the room with Sabrina.

Together again.

Sabrina recaps all she told the police, including being raised by her grandmother, the rise and fall of her marriage to Robert, and the abuse she suffered from both.

"Fame and fortune is all he ever wanted," she laments. "It's ironic that the violin is what finally gave me freedom from her—and in turn imprisoned me to him."

I grab her hand. "There's another huge part of all this, Sabrina," I reveal. "A vital, important part." I pause. Best to start at the beginning. "Obviously *your* grandmother is *my* grandmother," I start. "Tell me about her. I know *some* of it, from dreaming your life, but I know there's more."

Tears well in Sabrina's eyes. "She never told me about you or any other family," Sabrina recalls. "She told me my mother, *our* mother, left because she didn't want anything to do with me. She told me my mother said I was too much to handle. My—*our*—grandmother was the same as Robert. She wanted a slave—not a granddaughter. She was, and I suspect *is,* if she's somehow still alive, a drug addict and an alcoholic."

So much of what she's telling me was a part of my dream, but I let her continue uninterrupted. It's cathartic for us both— for her as she exorcises it and for me to hear her own voice telling it.

Though it's also hard to hear. It must be so much worse for her.

"You don't have to tell me all of this right now, Sabrina. I mean, if—"

"No, I need to get it out of me once and for all."

And she does—from the violin to the violence and everything in between. All the details of the stories I've witnessed, and more.

"I enjoyed my reprieve with that 'surrogate family' after I left my/our grandmother," she says. "The ones who helped me get into the music school where I met Robert. But he wouldn't let me contact them once we married. He wanted all control to be his. I *did* want to kill him," she admits. "And Grandma, too. To stop their abuse of me, but mainly so they couldn't hurt anyone else. I didn't care if I went to jail. As long as I saved someone else from being treated in the same way they treated me for so long."

I squeeze her hand, which I realize I'm still holding.

"You don't have to kill anyone," I assure her. "The police will see the truth of what happened, and your husband will be prosecuted. Then we'll do everything we can to find your—*our*—grandmother and make sure she, too, is prosecuted. I'll have Brody check the laws pertaining to child abuse; there must be some recourse that isn't beyond statutes of limitation."

As I say all this, I have a terrifying idea. I feel sick.

Sabrina senses it and sits straight up.

"What is our grandmother's name?" I demand.

"I— I'm not sure what she'd be using now—like I said, *if* she's alive. In fact, I've spent most of my life trying to forget her name, but of course I never could." She sighs. "Her real name is Agatha Hadley."

I feel like I've been gored in the stomach by a bull. Sabrina can feel my reaction. It's time for me to spill *my* guts with more "gory" truth.

Here we go…

If she thought the murder of my adoptive mother was bad, I now must tell her about Pete Decker and Stan Harris and my kidnapping and torture and the serial murders.

Sabrina's hand flies to her mouth; she can't even try to hide her horror.

I explain how we tracked down phone numbers from the killer's records, including one belonging to an old woman, whom we visited in jail.

"She told me she knew me," I explain. "As well as my mother. She said my mother was a prostitute who basically *sold* me."

Sabrina appears to be holding her breath. I wait for her to exhale before *I* inhale deeply. It's almost like our breathing is in sync.

"And this woman's name…"—I have to choke out the words—"is Agatha Hadley."

Sabrina looks thunderstruck. But I can't stop now.

"And this woman—my, our, grandmother—well, Brody and I determined that *she* is the one who contracted Stan Harris to murder my adoptive mother."

Sabrina's body falls back on the bed. Her good hand grips the bedrail.

"I should've killed her a long time ago!" she wails. "I could've stopped all of this if only I'd followed through."

I shake my head vehemently. "No, Sabrina, you would've gone to prison. And this is beyond both of us now. We need to let the Law take care of her, as well as your husband. When their time comes, I know they'll have to face their own retribution upon their deaths. We both know you don't need their blood on your hands."

"You and I have been through so much in our lives." Sabrina is now sobbing. "And it's far from over for me. Even if I'm not arrested, I'll have no home, no money, no anything. He's left me with nothing."

"That's not true!" I retort. "You have a twin sister who isn't going to let you out of her life. Do you think I'll just let you go?" I take her hand and look into her eyes. She needs to know what I'm saying is the truth. "We'll sort out the details of your husband's fate and any insurance that may come from the fire. And regardless, you can come live with me!"

I try to smile.

"I would presume we're the same size, and I have plenty of clothes."

Sabrina hangs her head low. "I…I don't know what to say…I…"

"Look at me, Sabrina," I urge gently. "I know we don't know each other yet, but at one time we shared a space much smaller than my house. I already know we're going to be very close. I won't have it any other way. We've found something most people don't get a second chance or even a first chance to have. We have each other and I wouldn't want you anywhere but with me."

We hug each other for a while and cry together for all the years that we've missed. I lie on the bed with her as if we're little girls, with no more words needed for now. I wish we'd been together our whole lives, but it's too late for that. We *will* be together for the rest of our lives, and I'm determined to make the most of them.

Just as the tears are beginning to dry, the police come back in to tell us Sabrina's husband has been officially arrested and charged with a litany of crimes.

The day of answers continues…

"He admitted to everything and should be spending a long time behind bars," they inform us. "We expect there to be no bail, so I don't think you have to worry, but I can post an officer at the door if it'll make you feel better."

Sabrina shakes her head. "No, but thank you very much." She smiles at me. "I think I'll be okay from here on out."

"You may have to testify at trial," the officer continues, "but until then, I suggest you focus on your own healing. A good counselor wouldn't be a bad idea."

I appreciate the officer's extra words of kindness and nod at him in thanks.

As the officers head out the door, Sabrina looks at me again, and I know in my heart we'll get through anything together. And I *will* find her a counselor. For the rest of her life, she'll feel safe and happy. I'll make sure of it.

CHAPTER 38

SABRINA IS UNDERSTANDABLY EXHAUSTED, so I return to bed and watch her sleep. I can't believe I have a twin sister. I think about all the things we'll do together.

I'm almost asleep when my phone beeps. It's a text from Brody telling me he's on his way to the hospital. Then a nurse and doctor step into the room. No nap for me, I guess.

I look over and Sabrina is awake now. I wish she'd been allowed to rest a bit longer. The doctor explains that due to the extent of Sabrina's injuries and her concussion, they want to observe her for one more night. I, however, have been cleared for release.

"No, I don't think I'm ready to go," I say. "I can't just leave my sister here alone."

The doctor tries to placate me, saying she'll be closely monitored, but I'm not having it.

I'm about to launch into my argument when Sabrina speaks up. "Can I please have a few minutes alone with…my sister?"

The doctor nods and exits.

Sabrina grabs my hand. "Melanie, so much has happened and I'm so excited to have found you…or, actually, for you to have found me. But I just want some time tonight to take it all in. And I think you should go home and do the same." She smiles playfully. "Besides, I don't have anything to wear home, so you'll have to bring back some of those clothes you promised." She looks at her feet and then up at me sweetly. "Shoes, too. I don't suppose you have anything in a size seven?"

I suppress a smile. "You know I do, and that's a dirty trick!"

She looks just a little guilty. I'm crying again and we're hugging each other when Brody walks in the door. We turn in unison to face him, and I see his face light in shock.

"What's wrong?" I ask, panicked.

Brody shakes his head. "Well, Mel, maybe you two should look in the mirror."

Sabrina and I make our way to the room's little sink and stand gazing at our reflection. Viewed side-by-side, our resemblance is eerie. We're the exact same height, with identical skin tone, hair color, and features. I suppose this is true of all identical twins, but having grown up an only child, it feels especially…strange.

"If it weren't for your haircuts," Brody interrupts. "I wouldn't be able to tell you two apart."

Hmmmm! I'd like to think he, of all people, would be able to. I glance back at him, and he winks. *I knew it!*

"They're letting me go," I announce. "Sabrina has to stay, but she tricked me into leaving to bring her back some clothes."

"Good one, Sabrina!" says Brody. "I couldn't have dragged her away otherwise. You'll soon learn that Mel is very stubborn."

Sabrina smiles, but it doesn't quite meet her eyes. My guess is she has some fear of men. She'll learn quickly that Brody's nothing like the man she was married to.

Brody hugs me and asks if I'm ready to go.

I nod, although I'm still loath to leave Sabrina. I've just found her and my fear is that somehow during the night I'll lose her. I know that sounds crazy, but I can't help how I feel.

I give her my number telling her she can call me any time, day or night, making sure she understands it'll be no bother at all.

Finally, having done all I can, I leave my sister at the hospital.

THE DRIVE BACK to Arrow Springs is fairly quiet, and I cuddle as close to Brody as I can.

"She'll be okay, Mel," he assures me.

"I know. It just feels like I left a piece of myself back there," I explain. "One I never knew was missing."

Brody squeezes my hand and then lifts it to his lips for a soft kiss.

"I mean, she's my other half," I go on. "How could I not have known she existed?"

"Maybe if we'd met Flora sooner, she could have told you," he says wryly.

I see his point. Aside from psychic powers, there's no way I could have known. And at the end of the day, that *is* the only way I found her. A small smile tugs at my lips.

"But all you can do is move forward from here," he continues. "Let go of second-guessing. Is that the reason you're so down?"

"Partly," I admit. "I have so much more to tell you. There are so many more layers to this than we could have imagined— including more police work for you."

Brody nods. "Speaking of that," he says, "do you want to hear about my questioning of Sabrina's husband?"

I hesitate. "I do," I say, "but not right now. Let's just get home."

"I couldn't agree more," Brody says.

Driving in reflective silence, we arrive at my house in what feels like record time. I'm surprised to see all the lights on.

"What's going on, Brody?" I ask. "You plan a surprise homecoming for me or something?" I joke.

Brody looks at the house and then into my eyes. "No, Mel," he says seriously. "Tonight is just for you and me. You scared me back there, and I haven't had time alone with you since the fire."

I gaze back at him. "I'm sorry, I—"

He cuts me off by opening the truck door and exiting. Then he comes around and helps me out of the truck.

"Come on," he says, pulling me toward the house. "You look beat. And I have dinner waiting."

I follow him in confusion.

"How did you manage *that*?"

I hand him my keys and he unlocks the front door.

"I called Daly," he explains, "and told her where to find your spare key. And now…" He opens the door with a flourish. "We shall enjoy a nice, hot meal, picked up from that great new Italian place near the station. Daly was happy to do it."

Stepping into the entryway, I look at Brody wryly. "You really love that place, don't you?"

He shrugs. "Oregano's? Yeah. I mean, I know it's nothing fancy, but I do."

With that, Brody grabs my hand and leads me to the dining table, which is set with candles and flowers. The plates are empty, because I assume the food has been stored elsewhere to keep it fresh. The tears start again.

"Come on, Mel, it's just a couple of flowers. It's nothing to cry about."

I sniffle. "You know it's not that. I love the flowers, of course. *And* the fact you would do all of this." I wave my hand at the table. "But I want more than food."

I give his body the once-over.

"Take me to bed, Brody," I plead. "And make love to me until all of this is cleared from my mind. I want you so much right now."

He doesn't require any more convincing. I'm guessing he needs this, too, if just to ease the fear he felt for me. He scoops me up and carries me up the stairs toward my room. He murmurs softly in my ear, and though I can't understand his words, just the husk in his voice starts the drums pounding.

He sets me gently on the bed and begins removing my clothes. First my shoes, then socks, and then my jeans and panties. He pulls me back to my feet to remove my shirt and turns me to unclasp my bra. As he does so, he kisses the length of my neck. It feels like he has plugged into every nerve in my body and sent an electrical current straight down my core.

I perch myself on the edge of the bed to watch him remove his clothes. It feels like I'm in a fog…like my brain is dissolving as I watch every part of his body become visible to my roving eyes. I can't get enough of looking at him.

But then he lays me on the bed and trails kisses from my mouth to my neck, and then to my breasts. Shooting stars streak behind my eyes and I feel like I'm ready to implode. He's so gentle with me, like I'm a fragile piece of glass. At the first stroke of his tongue to my center, I have a delicious orgasm that flows through my body like a lazy river on a sunny day.

Words aren't necessary. His emotional exploration tells me everything he feels. He won't allow me to get my hands on *him* yet, and although I yearn to reach for him, I don't think I can lift my arms anyway. A million tiny pin pricks light my skin as he slowly makes his way up my body.

As he rises over me, bracing himself at my entrance, I look into his eyes and I know. I'll never be able to be without him—without this amazing, loving, strong man in my life. A tear slips from my eye at the thought, and he kisses it tenderly away.

"No, Mel. No tears now. Let me love you. Sometimes I want to carry you away from all your dreams and visions. And this is how I want to do it. I love you so much. Look into my eyes and see everything I feel for you."

I cry fully then with the joy I feel. He's said the one thing I've wanted to hear from him for so long. But he doesn't give me time to say it back; he seems to already know. He plunges deep inside me and the tears dry quickly as pleasure takes over and the pressure builds again.

Our lovemaking turns from a gentle river to a raging flood that batters my senses as he plunges in and out of me with fierce determination, taking us both to the edge. It's as if he's claiming me as his own. But he doesn't need to—I already belong to him in every way. He will be the only man I'll ever know this way, and I don't and never will regret one minute of it.

We shatter in each other's arms and then lie panting for what seems like forever. My eyes are closed, but I feel Brody looking at me so I open them. I see in his gaze the words he murmured as his body made love to mine.

"I love you, Mel," he repeats. "I think I've loved you from the first moment I saw you in the police station. I loved that fifteen-year-old girl who was brave enough to bring something to the police she knew would make her look crazy. And...

maybe this is an odd time, but…ever since then, I've wanted to say something." He looks even more intensely into my eyes. "I know you carry guilt for not coming to us earlier. But your mother loved you and I'm sure she wouldn't want you to hold onto that anymore. So please, Mel, forgive yourself and let it go. Love yourself as much as I love you."

I'm too stunned to speak.

He turns away, as if to get out of bed.

"Wait, no—" My hand stops him. "Please don't leave. The words I want to say aren't coming because I've waited so long to hear them from you—not *really* believing I ever would. I'm in shock and overwhelmed."

Brody turns back toward me and pulls me into an embrace.

"That first meeting is also the first time I knew I loved you," I admit. "Every time I saw you after that, it was as if my heart was a ticking time bomb and I was just waiting for the explosion to go off—for you to find someone else to love and forget all about me." I look up at Brody through my lashes—as if I still need to be shy around him. "I've loved you since that exact day, and I can't believe it's taken us both this long to tell one another. I love you more than I could ever love anything or anyone in my life."

I put my hands on both sides of his face and run my fingers gingerly over his lips. I ache to kiss them, so as I think it, I place my lips gently against his and let them linger.

"Of course, you're going to have to share my love with Sabrina now," I add, "as she also holds a part of my heart. But what I feel for you is so much more than anything I've ever felt. I think I've been afraid to love you, because I've lost so much in my life, I was worried that if I loved you, I'd lose you, too."

Unshed tears fill Brody's eyes now and I try not to make a big deal about it. I wipe my own away so he can see everything I've ever felt for him since that very first moment. We kiss each other passionately as we bask in our newly spoken love.

My stomach rumbles, and we laugh, ending the moment.

"Let's go and eat before you melt away to nothing," he suggests.

"Yes, let's!" I agree. "Suddenly I'm starving."

Brody winks at me. "Don't you remember me telling you how much energy lovemaking burns?"

"I do remember," I say, smiling, "and every time we do it, I feel famished."

We both dress quickly but stop several times for passionate kisses en route to the kitchen. I'm so happy, but I still have things to reveal to Brody—things I know will try to diminish our joy. I promise myself I won't let it. Our newfound love is strong, and we'll get through anything together from here on out.

We work together to prepare the dinner. I fill two plates with Oregano's signature spaghetti and meatballs from a warming tray atop the stove, while Brody puts their "world famous" garlic bread in the oven. As we wait for both items to reheat, we dish up antipasto salad from the fridge and Brody lights the candles.

Though I hate to ruin the romantic mood, I launch into filling Brody in on Sabrina's and my conversations—starting with her childhood.

"Man, I know you told me about this 'grandmother' in the dreams," Brody responds, "but now she sounds even *more* like a wicked bitch who deserves to be punished."

He gets up to grab our plates of spaghetti from the microwave and then goes back to retrieve the bread.

"That's one of the things I want you to look into," I say. "The statute of limitations on child abuse. Because I *would* like to see her punished...even though she's my grandmother, too."

Brody drops his fork. "Oh my gosh, Mel. I'm so sorry!" Absorbing my words, he smacks his head at his own obtuseness. "I wasn't even thinking about that!"

"I know," I say. "And this is one of the last pieces of the puzzle, Brody." I set down my utensils as well. "Because my grandmother is someone you and I have both met..." I pause so he can brace himself. "It's Agatha Hadley."

Thunderstruck, Brody leaps from his seat and starts pacing.

"Well, it all makes sense now! That old lady at the prison saying she knew your mother and telling you she—"

He stops himself from finishing *that* sentence, for which I'm grateful.

"And that also means…" He looks even more dumbstruck as the full implications of this revelation hit him.

"That my bio-grandma is the one who had my adoptive mom killed," I finish for him.

Brody sits back down with a thud. "Oh, Mel. I can't even imagine what you're going through right now."

"I know," I agree. "I mean, why would she do such a thing? Was it just to hurt me? Could somebody be that cruel?"

Brody goes back to pacing. "She would also be the one who separated you and Sabrina. As the conniving sort, she would have had a compelling reason for both actions. What could it be?"

"Sabrina told me that all Agatha cared about was drugs," I share. "And, of course, money to buy them with. So her actions would have been greed-based."

"But did she profit in some way from the murder?" Brody asks.

"Not that I know of! So I simply don't get it."

Brody comes around the table. "This will definitely require further investigation." He takes my hand. "There's no way we can solve it tonight."

"I agree," I say. "But I know she needs to be punished for everything she's done. I don't want her to come back here in five, ten, or even twenty years and spoil our happiness. And definitely not Sabrina's. We have to make sure she can't interfere in our lives again."

Brody is quiet for a few minutes. "There *are* laws to protect children, and if we can pin her for the murder, she'll go away for a long, long time. Probably forever. You know I'll do everything I can to protect you and Sabrina."

"I know you will," I say softly. "I know you will."

We clear the dishes from the table, and as we place them in the sink, I turn to Brody. "I love you, Brody. And I want to enjoy being with you. So let's forget about all of this for tonight, and go back to bed so you can show me how much you love me again."

Brody smirks. "Wait, I just showed you how much I love you. I think this time it's *your* turn to show me how much you love me."

We both laugh and race each other up the stairs. And I show him how much I love him in ways that, before Brody, I had no idea existed.

CHAPTER 39

The next morning, Brody and I wake up and just lie in bed gazing at each other, basking in the bliss of being in love.

Then I remember what happened the day before. It seems like such a far-off nightmare—though not all of it.

"I need to go pick up my sister at the hospital," I say.

"Sister…" Brody replies. "That's a word I'll have to get used to hearing."

"You're telling me!" I snort. "And there are still a few things she and I need to figure out. Like our parentage."

Brody looks thoughtful. "Maybe we can ask Flora to meet us and help pick up any clues. We need to fill her in anyway."

"Good idea," I say. "You know, I really like being in love with you. You're so smart!"

Brody gazes at me tenderly. "I feel the same, Mel. But people are going to get sick of us really fast if you keep saying things like that to me."

I lift my chin. "Too bad for them, then—they don't have to hang out with us!"

Brody grabs me and tickles until I give in.

"Okay, okay! I'll stop."

It's going to be amazing being in love with Brody—*and* for him to know it. But I guess being a dork about it is going a little far. I've never been in love or in a relationship before, so it's going to take some getting used to.

We talk and laugh all the way to the hospital. But when we arrive, it's time to get serious. I don't want to act too crazy and scare Sabrina off from living with me. The irony is that this is the first time in my life I *don't* feel crazy.

We meet Flora outside the hospital and tell her everything that's happened since we left the diner two days ago.

Was it only two days? I marvel. It seems much longer.

As we talk, Flora keeps looking at us strangely. Finally, her face lights in a wicked smile, and she comes over and hugs me.

"Congratulations!" she says. "I wondered when the hell you two were going to figure out you were in love." She winks. "*And* do something about it."

I crack up. Brody, on the other hand, raises both arms in the air to keep her from hugging him. So instead, she kisses him gently on the cheek.

He eyes her suspiciously. "What'd you see this time?" he demands.

"Nothing!" She spreads her hands in innocence. "I'm just so happy you've acknowledged and shared your feelings with Mel. I wish you both much love and happiness for a very long time."

I hug her again and, frankly, I don't care if she sees everything I feel right now. I'm happier than I've ever been and if what everyone says about my facial expressions is true, well, then the whole world is going to know it anyway.

When we make it to Sabrina's room, I introduce her to Flora, who appears stunned for obvious reasons.

Sabrina's ready to go except for clothes, and as promised I've brought a few outfits for her to try. She emerges from the bathroom dressed in jeans and a t-shirt, which of course fit perfectly.

Our resemblance is kind of scary! Wouldn't it be a hoot to do our hair the same and trick a few people? I keep the thought to myself because I think it'll be a while before Sabrina's up for any tricks. She's still fairly skittish. And *that's* a difference between us I hope to permanently change.

Sabrina looks between Brody and me. "You two look happy today!"

I smile. "Well, sister, we *are* happy…to have found you! But also each other. I'll tell you all about it when we get home."

We walk into the hallway, talking and laughing as I push Sabrina in the hospital-mandated wheelchair. And there, across the hall, mouth gaping wide, is Donna—the staff member we saw when we tried to get information about my birth.

It suddenly hits me that she asked if I had a sibling.

My good mood goes right out the door, and I march over to her.

"So, Donna, it looks like I *do* have a sibling," I start in. "She's still alive—apparently, no thanks to you—after her husband burned down her house, trying to scorch her along with it. So *now*, do you want to fill us in?"

Donna looks between me and Sabrina…and bursts into tears.

Crap! Was I *too* cruel? Before I can contemplate further, she comes over and hugs me fiercely. She does the same to Sabrina. It seems as though she actually does care about us. Just what the heck is going on here?

"Is there somewhere we can talk privately?" Brody murmurs.

Donna nods and escorts us to a private room off the hallway. Brody immediately grabs the tissue box and offers it first to Donna and then to me and Sabrina. I reach for it, shaking uncontrollably. I know this is going to change everything.

Meanwhile Brody is back in "cop-mode."

"Why don't we all just a take a breath," he suggests. "I'll go get some coffee. Who'd like some?" He waves his hands. "Never mind—everyone's getting a cup. Please don't start until I'm back," he admonishes.

I watch as the man I love leaves the room. He obviously agrees this is going to be big and wants us all to settle in and brace ourselves. I also think a room full of crying women might be hard for any man.

I pull a chair next to Sabrina's wheelchair so we're across from Donna, who's still hiccupping from her crying jag. When Brody returns, she gratefully accepts the coffee and takes a few deep, restorative breaths.

Brody and Flora move off to the side so the three of us can speak more intimately.

"Way back, when I first started working here in labor and delivery," Donna begins, "a young woman came in. She was heavily pregnant and in labor."

She takes three more unsteady breaths.

"She was all alone, and she told me her husband had been killed in a motorcycle accident. Not long after, she found out she was pregnant. She was traumatized by the loss, but at least she had the babies, whom she already loved with all her heart."

"Babies?" I interrupt. Sabrina and I look at each other.

"Yes," Donna replies calmly. "She was having twins. Although she was almost fully dilated, she had to be rushed in for a C-section, since the first baby was breech."

I grab Sabrina's hand and we both squeeze tight as I try to surmise which of us was born first.

"There were complications." Donna's voice shakes. "The woman was able to look at each of her daughters, but that was all. She passed away soon after they were born."

Sabrina and I let out the breaths we've been holding and tears flow freely down our faces.

"The twins were kept in the NICU as we searched for family to take them in. They were a bit premature anyway, so some time there was necessary. The mother had a fairly common last name so trying to find close relatives was like searching for a needle in a haystack, especially since she came into the hospital by herself. She seemed to literally have no one, which is quite unusual for a mother giving birth."

Donna is effectively shredding the tissue she's holding in her shaking hand. She looks down in realization and balls it into her fist.

"Meanwhile, my husband would come pick me up at the hospital each day, and we'd always check in on the girls. We fell in love with them. We began navigating the necessary channels to adopt them." Donna looks down at her hands. "We had a daughter who died, and we wanted to fill the void. To give a new child—children—our love." She looks back up at me.

"Then one day I came into work, and the babies were gone. The doctors said Child Protective Services had tracked down their maternal grandmother. She'd presented proof of who she was, so they had to let her take them."

Sabrina squeezes my hand harder. I can't imagine what she's feeling. Or maybe I can.

"We were devastated and tried to find her," Donna went on. "It would be difficult for anyone to handle two babies, so we at least wanted to offer our help. But the address she'd provided was a boarded-up empty house."

Everyone in the room gasps.

"I became terrified for the babies. I hired a PI, but even he couldn't find them. We kept running into dead ends."

"My grandma changed her name a lot," Sabrina breaks in, the truth obvious. "She was good at hiding from drug dealers, so she would've been hard to find if she didn't want to be."

Donna nods. "So just to be sure…" She looks at Sabrina and then back to me. "What is your birthday?"

We both utter the same date at the same time. Then we laugh through our tears.

"So, Donna," Brody interjects for the first time since the discussion began. "Do you remember the name of the woman, the mother? That *common* last name and…uh…her *first* name?"

"Of course," Donna says. "I was the nurse who held her hand in death and then investigated her life. Your mother was so special; I could see it in her eyes. Her name was Jamie…Jamie Hathaway."

I can't hear or see anything. My ears ring loudly as if a shrill alarm is going off in my brain. Everything goes black and I think I'm going to faint.

I don't realize I'm crying until I hear Sabrina sobbing and whispering that everything will be okay now. But I still feel the darkness taking over.

When I finally open my eyes, Brody's in front of me. "Melanie, look at me. Right now." He almost sounds angry. "Don't you pass out on me," he warns, gripping onto my shoulders. "She needs some water. Someone bring me water. Now!"

Donna runs from the room, and Brody gently turns my face back toward him. The more I concentrate on him, the less I feel the blackness overtaking me.

"Think about it," he says. "Your mother did all she could to protect you—no matter that it was from a place not many would understand. From what you told me yesterday, she's been with you your whole life."

I look at Sabrina. And though I shouldn't be shocked by what she tells us, somehow I am. "When I was younger and Agatha used to lock me in the closet," she says, "I would always hear a voice. She was so kind and so gentle. I thought somehow she was an angel and that I was going to die. She never told me who she was, but now I'm sure it was our mother—so I guess she *was* an angel."

Just then, Donna rushes back in with the water. But we both look past her. Because there, floating next to the wall, is an apparition of a young woman. I don't know if angels can cry, but ethereal tears run down her face as she glides toward us.

Donna looks up and moves quickly out of the way. Her face doesn't register fear, though. All I see is concern and caring—like she must have had on *that* day, twenty-five years ago.

Jamie addresses Donna first. "I know you did everything in your power for me and for my babies. I thank you for that and please don't ever feel guilty." She reaches for Donna's cheek, and Donna closes her eyes as if she can feel her touch.

Next, Jamie turns to me and Sabrina, love shining from her eyes. "I'm sorry for all the unhappiness you've both endured. If I could have done more to prevent it, I would have. I have broken so many rules to be with you over the years, and I'm afraid my actions these past few days have angered many. I'll have to go away soon, but I take solace in seeing you both together. I have more love for you than I've ever felt for anyone, and I loved your father with all my heart. Please don't ever believe anything different. Be strong, my girls. I will miss you."

And with that, she's gone.

I look around. The whole room is either frozen in shock, or crying their eyes out. Looking at all these people who have become my family—or who I know *will* become my new family—I realize Sabrina and I have been lucky. Our mom loved us so much that she protected us from beyond the grave. She apparently gave up moving on and seeing her husband again, which was a huge sacrifice. She did everything she could to make our lives less miserable. I can't imagine what life would have been like if she'd never died—and it's probably better if I don't. It's too sad.

Of course, I loved my adoptive parents. I don't want to lose those memories, either. Jamie is a huge part of that life as well, and I hope and pray she isn't gone for good. Whoever makes the "rules" where she is, should understand a mother's love and the rage a mother would feel at her children being hurt.

Time for some more of those deep breaths.

We finally leave the hospital: me, my new twin sister, my new friend Flora, and the love of my life. We hug Donna and exchange phone numbers with her. I promise we'll stay in touch, and I know it will make her happy.

But right now I want to go home.

I feel a strong need to paint. I have no idea what the image will be, but I'm sure it will be the most special painting I've ever done.

CHAPTER 40

Six MONTHS LATER

I gaze out over my yard, reflecting on how peaceful it is. It was not so long ago I was drenched in sweat, awakening from nightmares that echoed with the *"thrumming of a heart that had been broken into a million pieces."* As I sip my coffee, I marvel at how the pieces of such a crazy puzzle have fallen together into something I could never have imagined.

Today won't be just a party. Today's celebration will commemorate the reclaiming of lives. The piecing together of friends and family and futures that have been torn apart, tortured, and twisted. Most in attendance have traveled through planes of existence that few will ever experience.

I actually haven't had a dream since finding Sabrina. But I don't believe the visions are gone forever. I don't think they were brought to me only by Jamie. Though she orchestrated the most recent series to help me find Sabrina, I feel the other murder dreams are my gift. Of course, I haven't always felt this way! But I've come to understand there's more for me to uncover in the world. More lives that will need saving. So I want to try to help people for as long as I'm allowed. Hopefully, my newly created family and I will never have to face such grave danger again, but when you dream murders, you must be prepared for anything.

I go inside to shower and dress for the day. When I finish, I walk by Sabrina's room—a room she and I had so much fun decorating together. It's funny, because I've always called it the guest room, but until now, I've never had a guest! And she's so much more than that.

I head downstairs and pause to look at my "most special painting," a canvas work I've hung over the fireplace. It's three loving female faces—two exactly the same, and the third, in the center, a close likeness. That's Jamie, of course. *Our mother.* She looks so beautiful with a bright light behind her depicting exactly the angel she is. Sabrina cried when she saw it.

The good news is that Sabrina and I barely cry anymore unless they're happy tears. As we were adding finishing touches to Sabrina's room, she asked if she could hang a few art pieces in there. I took her to the painting room and showed her the dream sequence that led me to her. She asked to keep the one from her concert, as well as the sketch of the Kadupul, since in the end that's what led us to her. We got it framed and it looks lovely hanging on her wall.

Sabrina is doing wonderfully considering everything she's gone through. She's been in counseling and continues to heal with each appointment.

I've had my share of healing "appointments," too—when I head regularly over to Brody's for a little "overnight therapy"! Brody and I haven't had any more "psychic connections," but we're willing to give it a try should the opportunity present itself again.

Each day is proving to be better and better for all of us.

Especially today.

The weather is warm and beautiful—perfect for the tables with market umbrellas we've set up in the back yard.

Flora and Alene will be here soon; the diner is catering the food and Flora made centerpieces. Donna and her husband, Tom, will be right behind them, all coming down I-49 from KC.

And of course, Daly will be here with Barney and Molly. I invited Stella too, but someone had to stay and work the station, so she volunteered. Over and over she has shown how sorry she is for what happened with Pete. Every time she looks at me, I can see how much she wishes she could go back and stop what occurred. And over and over, I've assured her it wasn't her fault. Stella is just another of us whose life was "torn apart, tortured, and twisted"—and who also survived.

And that's exactly what today is about.

Sabrina sneaks up behind me as I'm surveying the yard.

"Flora is here with Alene," she whispers. "Do you want me to tell her not to hug you?"

"That's okay." I smile. "I'll do some dodging!"

We walk around to greet daughter and mother as the approach along the side of the house. I meet Flora's eyes, but as she comes in for an embrace, I walk straight to Alene and hug her first. Brody is behind me, and I see Flora go in for the tackle. He sidesteps as always and we all laugh. Our hellos have become like a football scrimmage! As he stands beside me and puts his arm around my shoulders, Flora looks a bit forlorn, and I feel bad about having to avoid her.

When I asked Flora to cater the party, I told her it was to commemorate Sabrina and my finding each other after all our years apart—a "Celebration of Sisters," if you will. And it is… partially. But knowing Flora, she may suspect my ulterior motive, so there's no way I'm letting her get an "early read."

Brody helps Flora and Alene carry the bounty into the kitchen, and as everything gets situated, he and I stand with our backs to the door, prepared for a quick "embrace escape" if necessary. My need for this is temporary, but I muse whether Brody will always have to strategize!

Flora and Alene decline our help with the food, so Brody, Sabrina, and I head outside to set up the centerpieces they brought. They are gorgeous! As I marvel at the white ceramic vases—all different shapes and sizes—filled with purple irises, white roses, and greenery, I realize I wouldn't even know an iris from a rose if it weren't for Flora! And it's amazing how she created just the perfect bouquet for each vase.

Oh my! I notice a glass-blown fairy rising out of the center of each. It reminds me of Sabrina and Jamie and myself, and how we've risen above the dreams of rage to find each other and contentment. I wonder if Flora planned that, or if it's just my impression. I'll definitely have to ask her.

As I continue my perusal of the fairies, I see each has been inserted with a long glass stem hidden among the flowers. I can't imagine how Flora had time to make them on such short notice—especially while planning and preparing all the food. I really do owe her for this!

Brody comes up behind me as I place the last masterpiece on a table. "You okay, Mel?"

I lean back into him, just to take a moment.

"I'm great. And just thinking about how lucky we all are."

He squeezes his arms around me as he's done so many times lately, and as always, I find peace there.

Brody kisses my hand. I grab his hand and then Sabrina's as we make our way back into the kitchen.

Flora has outdone herself here, too. The counter is overflowing with salads: green salad, pasta salad, potato salad, fruit salad…you name it. I also spot mini-meatballs and roast beef rolls, which I can't wait to dig into. Plus, some standard snacks like chips and dip, and cheese and crackers. Mixed in among these American classics is an Irish stew Flora has just started offering at the diner, served with thick slices of soda bread. It smells heavenly and will be one of the first things I dive into. She plugs in the large slow-cooker to keep it warm.

The food is finally set up just in time for us to welcome our remaining guests. Donna and Tom arrive from KC at the exact same time as Daly, Barney, and Molly. Everyone is here! Well, almost…

We ask them all to assemble in the yard. I watch Daly make her way out, thankful she's doing so much better and seems back to herself. She never complains, but I've noticed that Brody still fawns over her, especially as he takes her arm to help her outside.

We invite everyone to please prepare themselves a drink of choice and then take a seat. We've also placed ice buckets of wine and champagne on the tables, along with water and soft drinks. Once everyone is comfortable, Brody comes up behind me and we're ready to start our "welcome speech."

"We want to thank everyone for coming today," Brody begins. "We think of all of you as family and hope that you feel the same."

I look out across the yard at all who have come together at our request. I can't believe that when this whole chain of events started, I had almost no one in my life. Now everyone here truly is family, and I hope for it to grow even more in the future.

Everyone smiles and nods.

"Mel and I have something we want to tell everyone."

It's my turn and I'm suddenly nervous. Brody takes my hand and places a gentle kiss on it. A couple of "happy tears" run down my cheek and the encouraging smiles and nods become even warmer as the group senses I'm about to make an *announcement*.

They're right.

"We wanted to let everyone know," I say, brushing away the tears, "since you are so important to our future, that Brody has… has asked me to marry him."

Suddenly everyone is talking at once and they're looking at my hand, which currently has no ring on it, in order for us to keep the secret we were holding.

"And what was your answer?!" shouts Barney, his smile as big as he is.

Everyone explodes into laughter.

"Well, thank you, Barney," I say. "You've provided the perfect segue for me to share our story."

Brody squeezes my hand.

"Pour a little more wine and let's get to it!" I urge.

Drinks replenished, I launch into the tale of our engagement. "Not too long ago, *this* guy over here"—I point at Brody who's smiling but also doing his hair-pulling thing, apparently nervous for all to hear about his "moves"—"picks me up for an early dinner date. My first tip-off that something was amiss is that we didn't head for his favorite 'pasta palace' like usual."

"Hey, they serve damn fine Italian food!" Brody defends.

Everybody laughs.

Brody takes my hand in his. "I decided what I was about to do required someplace a bit more upscale. So I found one near Grand Lake." Everyone nods knowingly, apparently agreeing this was a suitable idea.

"Brody insisted that I get gussied up," I moan. "And you know how I hate dresses and makeup."

The girls laugh at this, while the guys just shake their heads.

"We pulled up to the restaurant," I go on, "and I was, for once, happy that I'd listened to him."

This is met with minor chuckles.

"Our table was overlooking the lake, and when we were shown to it, a bucket of champagne was already chilling! Brody even pulled out my chair."

I hear a gasp, followed by a lot of laughter. Brody just shakes his head.

"We had the most amazing prime rib dinner ever." I sigh, just remembering it.

"And for dessert?" prods Daly.

"Just the best crème brûlée on the planet!" I say.

Daly throws back her head. "This story is getting better by the minute!"

Everyone giggles.

"After dinner, Brody suggested we walk along the shore near the restaurant. We took off our shoes and strolled along the sand, holding hands. It was a little chilly so he gave me his jacket."

"*Aww's*" by all the women fill the yard.

"Well, when we arrived back in front of the restaurant, the wait staff had set out a blanket with a picnic of champagne and strawberries."

More "*Aww's*" echo through the crowd.

Molly slaps Barney's arm playfully. "You know, I hope you're taking notes about all this! You could really learn a thing or two from this guy."

Barney snorts as everyone else tries in vain to stifle their outbursts.

"My first thought was to wonder if he'd been taken over by aliens," I admit. "But then if he was trying to get me drunk."

"Maybe both!" Barney shouts to another round of laughter.

"I sat down on the blanket," I go on, "and he started kissing me until I felt like I was floating. And by that point I really was."

I notice Tom flush a bit and shoot him an apologetic look.

"Then he gently pulled me to my feet and knelt down in front of me as he reached into his pocket and brought out a small ring box." A hush falls over the group. "I put my hands to my face as I could see what was coming. He said he wanted to do this the right way."

"I'm only doing this once," Brody interrupts, "so, yep, it was gonna be perfect!"

I see tears rolling down Donna's cheeks. "Tears were rolling down *my* cheeks, too," I confide, "as Brody looked up at me with such incredible love and told me everything I mean to him."

I am barely able to speak as I finish my story. "Then, finally, he asked, 'Will you marry me, Melanie Morris?'"

Saying nothing more, I grin down at Barney.

"I'm *pretty* sure I know what the answer was now," he says softly, standing up to hug me.

Everyone else claps and jumps up for *their* share of hugs and congratulations.

Flora makes her way over and grabs my left hand. "So, where *is* the ring?"

"I took it off so we could keep our engagement a surprise," I explain. "But it's beautiful." I look at Brody knowingly.

"Where did you find it, Brody?" Flora asks.

"Well, now we have *you* to thank for a perfect segue," I say. "Because that's another special story."

I motion Brody to take the lead.

"With Mel's dreams coming fast and furious," he says, "I didn't have much time to think about the ring—let alone go get the one I wanted."

"Wait!" Alene interjects. "I think we should start at the *very* beginning."

Brody nods.

"The first time I met Mel was when she came into my shop," says Alene. "I had a beautiful antique ring she was just mesmerized by. But when Brody walked in, Mel tried to play it off—she clearly didn't want him to see her eyeing it."

"But I did," says Brody. "So on my next trip to KC I went back to look at it, and Alene offered to set it aside for me." He looks at her gratefully.

"Are you kidding? It was a relief!" Alene sighs. "For years, potential buyers kept backing out, and Mel seemed like the perfect owner."

Brody nods in agreement. "I didn't know when and I didn't know how, but I knew Mel had to have it. But under *no* circumstances could Alene let Flora know I wanted it." Brody glances at Flora. "I'm sorry, but I wanted to see where my relationship with Mel went without that pressure on me. When she and Sabrina were trapped in that fire, though…I *knew* that if she got out safely, I would never let her go again. So, when she was in the hospital, I finally called Alene and picked up the ring. And now that I finally feel like these two"—he looks between Sabrina and me—"have settled into *their* new life together, I thought it was time for Mel and me to begin *ours*. And I was able to give her the surprise I imagined right from the start." Brody smiles widely as he concludes his story.

"It sure was," I chime in. "The best surprise ever!"

Brody takes my hand and, reenacting the scene, gets down on one knee and pulls the ring out of his pocket.

"The first day I saw you looking at this ring, your eyes were sparkling, and I knew you were destined to have it. Melanie Morris, will you marry me and love me for as long as we may have in this world and on into the next?"

And even though we've already done this, I start crying again. That was my favorite phrase of his proposal because we both know that there *is* a next life.

"Yes, I will, Brody James Carter. I love you so much."

Brody slides the ring back on my finger, and then stands and kisses me. Everyone cheers and claps.

The next thing we know, we're surrounded by loved ones.

"I have to admit that when he opened that box on the beach, I was shocked," I say, taking his hand. "In fact, I'd forgotten about the ring. It was such a fleeting moment in my ever-crazy life. And back then, I didn't see any need for it."

"But now the ring is yours," Brody says. "And I'm yours, too."

Everyone in the crowd "Awwww's" again loudly—except for Barney, who shouts "Whether you want him or not!"

Brody and I laugh.

I gaze into Brody's eyes. "I want him, no matter what."

Everyone applauds.

"We'll be married in spring," I tell them. I look over at my sister. "Which leads me to another special question. Sabrina would you come up here, please?"

Sabrina is the one person (besides Brody and me) who knew before the party that we were engaged—there was no *way* for us to keep it from her!—but she looks surprised. She moves warily to where we stand.

I take her hand. "Sabrina, my sister, my other half—literally—it would make my wedding day perfect if you would be so gracious as to stand up with me as my maid of honor."

Crying more of those "happy tears" we just can't seem to get away from, Sabrina says yes, of course. Everyone gathers around for more hugs.

It's been an affectionate afternoon!

I turn to Flora. "I'd also like you to stand with me. You've become a great friend and sister, in more ways than just our gifts."

"I would be honored to stand with you, Melanie," she replies through tears. "And I feel the same." Flora and I hug for a few minutes—and yes, *more* happy tears.

Of course, when Flora turns to Brody, he moves away.

"You *have* to get over your fear of Flora's hugs!" I urge.

"Never in this lifetime," he vows, extending his right arm. "She's needs to stay at least this far from me forever."

We all laugh, knowing that forever we'll also joke about this issue.

Everyone here realizes that many of us have traveled through "planes of existence few will ever experience." Even without details, they understand how deeply that power has affected us all.

I turn to hug Daly. "How are *you* really feeling?" I ask.

"You know I love you two like my own kids, but you need to stop worrying so much. I'm back to my old self and I couldn't be happier for the two of you."

I hug her again and then watch as she embraces Brody. Another link in the family chain has been set.

It will be complete when Brody's parents come meet our new family at the wedding. We called them with our engagement news, of course, but since traveling over here twice wasn't really feasible, it makes more sense for them to come out for the actual wedding.

Molly and Barney are next and I look at them quizzically. "What do you two have up your sleeves? You look like cats that swallowed the canary."

"Well—" Barney starts, but Molly thrusts her hand over his mouth. She can barely reach, being so much shorter!

"We don't want to take away from their day, Barney!" she says.

I can see that he's about to burst.

"Don't be silly!" I say. "I insist that you tell me what has you so excited."

Molly beams and I figure it out without being told. But I let them do the telling anyway.

"We're going to have a baby!"

Brody pats Barney on the back and I hug them both as everyone congratulates them. Just thinking about the continuation of their family makes me even happier.

Could this day get any better?

Flora and Alene come over, and as I at long last wrap my arms around Flora, I apologize for evading her.

"I trust you," I clarify, "but we *so* wanted this to be a surprise, and that's a little tough in this crowd!"

Flora laughs. "I get it! But now, back to that ring."

"Of course!"

I lift my hand and she takes it in hers.

"Yup, it's definitely the one from my mother's shop."

Suddenly, she squeezes my fingers tightly and I know something is happening. She's getting a reading or a feeling or something.

A crowd gathers round us in anticipation.

After holding my hand for a few minutes, Flora finally speaks. "Melanie, this ring is even more special than we realized. There's a reason others who sought to purchase it were led to something else. This ring was meant for *you*, because…because…it was Jamie's wedding ring."

"Well, I'll be damned!" says Daly, grasping at Molly's hand, her eyes wide.

"What?!" I'm flabbergasted. "What did you see?!"

Sabrina comes over, and we cling to each other as we and our guests—our family—listen, enraptured. If there were any doubts about our unique "planes of existence," they are long gone now.

"I'm seeing your father propose with the ring," Flora says, her eyes shut tight. "Jamie murmurs his name as she kisses him and tells him she'll marry him."

"His name?" I plead. "What is it?"

"'Conrad,'" Flora says.

Donna sighs loudly and appears near collapse. Tom holds on to her tightly.

"That's it!" Donna cries. "Conrad Hathaway. She told me his name amidst all the chaos but with everything that happened afterwards, I completely forgot." She dabs her eyes. "We were losing her, but she wasn't losing herself. She was telling us things, trying so hard not to drift away. Trying so hard not to leave her babies. I remember now."

All eyes and ears are now on Donna. Flora is still in a trance state.

"Your mother was a fighter," Donna goes on. "She kept reliving the life she wanted so desperately not to leave. She told me her husband was a tough guy on his motorcycle, but he so loved playing his violin and—"

"His violin?!" Sabrina gasps.

"Yes," Donna affirms, her eyes also closed as she digs into her memories. "She said he could roar off burning rubber, one minute, and then play such soft and sweet music the next."

By now we're all sobbing.

Brody puts his arms around Sabrina and me.

"This seems like the right time for Sabrina's gift," he whispers. "I think we need to come full circle to piece this all together."

"You're right," I tell him, nodding to Alene.

She disappears and while we wait for her return, Flora and Donna both come back to the here and now.

As Alene rounds the corner, she's followed by a family of four.

Sabrina's mouth gapes. It has been seven long years since she's seen the Andersons, the family that took her in, but she obviously recognizes them. Brody had asked her permission to locate them, but she had no idea he'd succeeded.

The kids—Evan, now seventeen, and Ava, eighteen—must have especially changed a lot. But for them, Sabrina probably has too.

Tears streak down her cheeks and she holds her hands over her mouth to suppress the sobs. Then she rushes over and they all hug and cry together.

"When, how did you get here?" she asks.

"We just arrived. We're sorry we couldn't get here sooner."

Sabrina tries to explain how sorry she is for not being in touch, but they assure her it's okay; Brody explained everything she's been through.

When Sabrina introduces them to me, they seem taken aback. Although they've been told we're identical, I'm sure it's still a shock. They meet the rest of our group and are welcomed with open arms. We all have a lot in common and I hope they'll be in our life for years to come.

Alene steps forward and hands Brody a large rectangular box with a bow around it.

Everyone assembles around us: Tom, Donna, Flora, Alene, Molly, Barney, and Daly—and now Carolyn and David with Evan and Ava.

"In addition to this being our surprise engagement party," I say, shooting Flora a sidelong glance, "this event *is* also a 'Sister Celebration.' So in addition to the *biggest* surprise,"—I smile at the Andersons—"Brody and I have another gift for you." Brody hands the package to Sabrina.

She unwraps it and falls to her knees.

"Alene picked it out," I tell her.

Alene smiles. "Flora and I were drawn to an old pawn shop in, well, let's just say not the best part of KC. But this violin is vintage, maybe even…as we've just found out…maybe even something like your father would have played?"

Alene looks at Flora.

Flora closes her eyes again and wiggles her fingers. "I have a pretty good source that says it *was* his."

Everybody gasps.

I'm in awe of her at this moment.

Sabrina grabs the frayed bow that came with it and looks lovingly at the Andersons. "Without your love and support, I never would have gotten as far as I did. And though my path has taken a different direction, the gift you gave to me is priceless."

She tunes the violin and readies herself to play. I wonder if she still plays with such strong emotion as that first concert I dreamt about. Her eyes close as she lays the bow across strings that certainly haven't been changed in years and swipes the first note, and I have my answer. A hush falls over our group.

I recognize the song instantly as the one from my dream— the solo that made her famous. I feel the same passion I did then—and maybe even something more, as she plays for the family that gave her a chance to become something she never thought possible. The family that wasn't able to attend that first of many concerts.

Sabrina's performance is followed by what feels like minutes of silence, and a few not-so-quiet tears.

Then everyone leaps up to give her an uproarious standing ovation, just as they did at her concert long ago.

As the clapping finally dies down, Brody says, "Well, how about a little…uh…more wine…and something to eat?"

We were all in agreement, but no one can even think about food until we have one more long group hug.

THREE MONTHS LATER

Sabrina, Brody, and I are sitting at the graves of Conrad and Jamie Hathaway, reflecting on all that's happened.

The warmth of our party's group hug eventually gave way to some cold, hard legal realities we had to face. I didn't think I would *ever* go back to that horrible prison, but I did—with backup. Sabrina and I confronted our grandmother, Agatha, together. We laid out the impossible-to-know details of all her crimes, assuring her that between child abuse and hiring a hit man, she'd spend the rest of her life there—or someplace worse. Somewhere amongst a Guinness Book of Records "most four-letter words in two minutes" tirade, she threw up her hands and actually legally confessed; screaming in front of the guards, God, and everybody that she should have sold us both to human traffickers in KC and that she paid way too much to that "idiot Stan or whatever the hell his name was!" to murder my adoptive mother in hopes that she could swoop in and claim whatever estate was left to me, since I was underage and she was my only living relative. Thankfully that part of her freakish plan never quite clicked in.

Also not getting out of prison anytime soon—or hopefully in their lifetimes—are Robert Cellini and, especially, Pete

Decker. Stan Harris isn't any threat, either, of course, given that he's six feet under.

On the investigative front, it didn't take long for Sheriff Brody Carter of Iroquois County, Kansas, to dig into law enforcement databases and gather facts about a Conrad "C.H." Hathaway, motorcycle accident victim. Those facts included his burial site, a little over halfway between here and the outskirts of KC.

As for Jamie, after Agatha snatched-and-ran with the babies, Donna had made some inquiries as to what happened to Jamie's body. It turned out that, as next of kin, Agatha had made arrangements for her daughter's burial—but had paid with a fraudulent check. With Agatha no longer reachable, Jamie's body was considered unclaimed and had been scheduled for cremation. Donna and Tom generously stepped in to pay the owed balance before that could happen and Jamie's body was interred as originally planned.

Now, we decided to have Jamie and Conrad buried together for all eternity in a place close to home. We organized an airy headstone with an angel engraved next to ethereal text, wonderful words that we're seeing for the first time today:

> *Conrad and Jamie Hathaway*
> *Separated in life too soon,*
> *reunited to rest peacefully together.*
> *Their love in life continues into the next.*

"I know how powerful Flora's visions are," I say, staring into the gleam of the new white marble, "but how can we be *sure* that this ring was really my mother's?"

"I'm sure that when Agatha came to 'claim' the two of you," Brody replies, "the hospital had collected all that Jamie had in this world and put it in a nice, neat little plastic bag that they gave to your legal grandmother. That would have included Jamie's ring, which I'm even more sure Agatha immediately pawned and put the few bucks she got for it up her nose or in her veins.

And somehow—and we all know by now that 'somehow's' are a big part of our lives—it wound up in Alene's shop, just waiting for me to buy it for you!"

I nod.

"It's most certainly hers," Sabrina agrees.

"Do you think the same about the violin?" I ask. "That our grandmother pawned it?"

"No doubt the authorities directed Agatha to wherever Jamie was living so she could 'tie up loose ends,'" says Brody. "And grab anything else your mother may have owned."

"I know Grandma wouldn't have kept anything someone else cared about," Sabrina chimes in. "It would have been gone in a heartbeat."

I take her hand in mine, two hands that are exactly the same, and nod in agreement.

"Besides hearing Jamie, have you ever felt you had any 'powers,' Sabrina?" I ask.

"The only 'gift' I know of is playing the violin," she tells us. "I guess that's my 'superpower' because I'm pretty good at it."

"Pretty good?!" I say, giving her *a look*. "You're a master. And now you have this vintage, near-magical instrument to rekindle your spark! There must be plenty of orchestras from here to KC to Joplin to Wichita and beyond that would love to have you."

"Actually, I don't want to go back down that road. What I'd really love to do is teach, to bring up the next generation of virtuosos.

"Ohhh…that's a beautiful idea! And you should do it at the house! I'd love to hear the kids go from squeaky to smooth!"

"Music is so therapeutic." Sabrina sighs. "And I so look forward to returning to its power. But…"

"But what?" I ask. "What is it?"

Sabrina looks shy.

"You know you can tell us anything," I urge.

"Okay," she agrees. "But promise you won't think I'm being silly?"

I use my finger to make a cross over my heart. I know it's a bit childish, but since we never had a childhood together, it feels more than right.

"Cross my heart," I say.

"It's just that I see how happy you and Brody are and I wonder if I'll ever have that. I'm not one bit envious, mind you, it's just that sometimes—well, pretty much all the time—I miss having someone to hold me."

I look at Brody, and yes, he's back to his awkward hair-pulling.

She rests her head on my shoulder. I think of the process she went through to get her divorce; even though it cut and burned deep, it was worth it. She's free now.

"Someday you're gonna meet a man who sees and appreciates everything you are, and he's going to grab you and kiss you breathless. You won't be able to get rid of him because he'll love you like I love you."

"Like a sister?" She laughs.

And in this moment, I know she's going to be okay. Maybe not today or tomorrow, but one day she'll overcome everything that has tried to break her spirit. She will soar with happiness.

I understand that rage can serve a purpose. Our family's suffering was the origin of Jamie's rage that saved us from the fire. Sabrina's rage gave her the courage to leave her husband. But rage is no longer needed. So it will end here, with us.

I know this.

So does Brody.

And so does someone else.

As we get up to leave the graves of Conrad and Jamie Hathaway, I hear the soft whisper of wind in my ears, and know Sabrina does too.

"I love you, my daughters."

THANK YOU FOR READING!

I sincerely hope you enjoyed reading
Origins of Rage as much as I enjoyed writing it!
It's been a labor of love for many years
and having it finally in the hands of readers
like you is a dream come true.

To encourage more people to enjoy the book,
it would mean so much if you would **post a review**
on your favorite book platform.

Please visit my **website**
and follow me on **social media**
to learn interesting facts about me
and my upcoming projects.
You'll also be alerted about book signings,
contests, drawings, and much, much more!

Thank you again for spending
your valuable time with *Origins of Rage*.

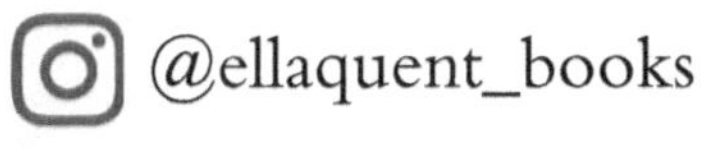 @ellaquent_books

 groups/ellaquentbooks

www.EllaGraff.com

ACKNOWLEDGMENTS

A HUGE THANK YOU to Beyond Words Editing's Jennifer Thomas-Hayes and her husband, William Hayes, for their hard work and dedication to the editing process, helping me not only add more than forty thousand words to transform a novella into a novel, but also reshape the entire manuscript into what it is today. They helped make a dream a reality and bring to life something that seemed impossible.

A big thank you to OriginalSyn for what is possibly the most amazing cover. Something I never could have imagined. And for creating the perfect logo for my publishing company, Ellaquent Books.

Another thank you to Kevin W W Blackley Books who, after reading my original manuscript, afforded me the opportunity to meet Jennifer Thomas-Hayes. He was the first to see the dream and understand my vision for a wonderful writing journey.

And to my test readers, who unknowingly made all my dreams come true with their rave reviews.

ABOUT THE AUTHOR

ᴇʟʟᴀ Gʀᴀꜰꜰ ɪꜱ ᴀ ꜱɪɴɢʟᴇ ᴍᴏᴛʜᴇʀ of three wonderful children and a grandmother of four. She has lived in Buffalo, New York, since 1988, having been born and raised in Jamestown, a small town south of Buffalo.

A part-time accountant for a local financial advisor, Ella loves numbers almost as much as writing. Almost... In her spare time Ella enjoys gardening in the summer and hand-crafting jewelry.

But her biggest passion is writing.

It has been her lifelong dream to publish a book and that dream has finally come to fruition.

With *Origins of Rage* completed, Ella has many more books already in the works.